BONE
DUST
WHITE

BONE WITHDRAWN
DUST
WHITE

Karin Salvalaggio

MINOTAUR BOOKS
NEW YORK

BONE DUST WHITE. Copyright © 2014 by Karin Salvalaggio Ltd. All rights reserved. Printed in the United States of America. For information, address St. Martin's Press, 175 Fifth Avenue, New York, N.Y. 10010.

www.minotaurbooks.com

LIBRARY OF CONGRESS CATALOGING-IN-PUBLICATION DATA

Salvalaggio, Karin.
 Bone Dust White / Karin Salvalaggio.
     pages   cm
 ISBN 978-1-250-04618-5 (hardcover)
 ISBN 978-1-4668-4632-6 (e-book)
 1. Women detectives—Fiction.   2. Murder—Investigation—Fiction.
 3. Missing persons—Fiction.   4. Mystery fiction.   I. Title.
 PR6119.A436B66 2014
 823'.6—dc23

                                                    2013050958

Minotaur books may be purchased for educational, business, or promotional use. For information on bulk purchases, please contact Macmillan Corporate and Premium Sales Department at 1-800-221-7945, extension 5442, or write specialmarkets@macmillan.com.

First Edition: May 2014

10 9 8 7 6 5 4 3 2 1

For my children,
Daniela and Matteo

Acknowledgments

Thank you to my agent, Felicity Blunt, whose belief never wavered; my friends Simon Curtis and Elizabeth McGovern for a key introduction—clearly it was fate; my editor, Matt Martz, and everyone at Minotaur Books, for saying yes and then bringing out my best; Curtis Brown UK—amazing, amazing, amazing; my dear readers Karen Drake, Nella McNabb, Paul McNabb, Atussa Dorudi Cross, Julia Bell, and Fiona Melrose, for reviewing those early drafts and then telling me in the nicest possible way to get back to work; my children, Daniela and Matteo, whose patience and encouragement saw us through all those evenings when I was writing and dinner arrived by motorbike; my parents, Karin and Graham Breck, who always knew I had it in me even if I couldn't see it myself; my extended and loving family in California, Alaska, Montana, North Carolina, the UK, and Germany; my road and everyone who lives on it—I can't name names but it is the best street in the world; my fellow scribes at Friday Night Writes, Tanya Datta, Terry Eeles, Tray Butler, Fiona Melrose, Timothy Graves, and Marissa Chen, whose guidance was key when things in Collier started to kick off; my patient friends Carolyn Morgan, Alison Lee, Diane Oakley, Nicolette

ACKNOWLEDGMENTS

Krajewski, Lynn Noyce, Genni Combes, Sue Smith, Monique Roffey, David Sinden, James Kennedy, and everyone else who let me go on and on about the bloody book I was writing—I consider myself fortunate that you're all still speaking to me.

A final comfort that is small, but not cold:
The heart is the only broken instrument that works.

—T. E. KALEM

BONE
DUST
WHITE

1

"He's hurt her, she's bleeding."

With the phone to her ear, Grace slips away from the soft spill of light coming through the kitchen windows and leans heavily on a refrigerator crowded with family photos. The upturned corners snap back against her spine.

"Grace Adams," she says into the crackling void, twisting the phone cord in her fingers, "153 Summit Road."

Grace waits, her fingertips darkening in the twist, a pulse forming inside the small purple blooms. Slim and fragile, she drowns amongst silk waves of carp swimming across a kimono three sizes too big for her. Her round face is as pale as a serving plate and a single strip of white cuts through her straight black hair. Between shallow breaths, she steals glances out the windows, turning this way and that, tangling her feet in the kimono's hem. She bites hard into her fingernails, shredding one with her small white teeth. A thin line of blood follows a trail of dried cuticle. She presses her thumb to it, trying to stop the flow.

"Yes, on the trails behind my house." It's as if she's being smothered. With every word she gulps for air. "I saw him," she says, "I saw him do it."

"Just try to stay calm," says the voice on the phone. "You're safe as long as you stay inside your house."

Grace retreats to the shadows thrown down by a wall separating the kitchen from the hall and gazes into the darkened entryway toward the front door. The security chain isn't attached.

Grace speaks in a whisper. "I don't feel safe."

"It's important that you remain calm. Help is on the way."

Straining against the phone cord, Grace upsets a glass shelf of porcelain figurines, and her skittish hands fail to catch them as they fall into a clattering heap. She tries to set them upright but knocks several more over and one drops to the floor. She picks up the small ballerina and stares at it. Its pearly white shoulders are coated in dust.

The voice on the phone asks her a question and Grace peers out the kitchen windows as directed. "I don't know. I think so. I can't see him anymore."

Grace had been up in her bedroom when she saw something move through the trees. She squeezed between her cluttered desk and the window to get a closer look. A woman walked slowly along the trails snaking through the woods behind the house. Grace watched her progress. Even from a distance it was clear she was unwell. She'd almost reached the gate at the end of the garden when the man appeared. Not more than ten feet apart, she greeted him like an old friend. Her unfamiliar face changed though. Words were spoken. Her mouth gaped wide in silent surprise, her eyes pleading. As she backed away, she called out Grace's name. Unsure what to do, Grace ducked down low so she couldn't be seen. Her hurried breaths misted over the glass. It wasn't until she wiped away the fog with the long sleeve of her kimono that she saw the man's knife. He lunged at the woman and she staggered away, clutching her side. Farther up the slope, they disappeared in the deep bracken and seconds later he stood alone. Never altering his stride, he vanished over the ridgeline, his receding silhouette outlined by pale light. Fingertips pressed to glass, Grace waited but he did not return.

A swell rises up in Grace's throat and the phone slips through her fingers. It hits the floor and as the cord retracts it skips on the carpet like a flat stone across water, eventually coming to rest under the breakfast bar. Grace hurries to the bathroom, her kimono falling from her white shoulders, revealing the red nightgown underneath. Unable to keep her balance, she grips the toilet with both hands. The pressure in her chest could rip her in two perfect halves. Bile comes up until her throat is scraped raw and her stomach is a hollowed-out bowl. The mirror isn't kind. Her eyes are nests of broken blood vessels shadowed by a sickly blue. She runs the water until it's warm and presses a cloth to her face. Sobbing, she sinks to the bathroom floor but from the kitchen the phone calls out her name. Faint at first, it grows in volume as Grace focuses in on the sound.

"Hello? Grace," it says. "Are you okay?"

Stretching her arms and pulling her body along, she climbs a horizontal wall of carpeting. Her hands shake and the phone jumps from her fingertips. "Please hurry," she says, hanging tight to the back of the sofa and drawing herself upward to her feet. She sways, emptied out and half crazed. For a few seconds she can't remember why she called.

"Yes, I'll stay in the house." Her white-knuckle grip on the handset is unyielding.

The hilltop community, where she lives with her aunt Elizabeth, is all but abandoned. Long before most of the homes were finished the developers went bust. Concrete foundations are disappearing under creeping vines and wooden frames stand like exposed rib cages. Every winter more roofs cave in under heavy snow and arsonists burn the rest. Sometimes groups of homeless move in but they never stay long. It's too far from Collier, the nearest town. So out here in her faux Tudor castle, there are no neighbors to call on.

Leaning against a counter crowded with clipped coupons and medical insurance forms, Grace glances out the kitchen windows again. Beyond the locked wrought-iron gate and high garden wall the wooded hillside looks flat under a thickening sky and colorless trees stand like sentinels, leafless and silent on the still winter morning.

On the other side of the garden wall the forest stretches for miles before hitting the boundary between her country and the next. Grace went there once with her uncle Arnold when he was still alive. While walking an isolated trail, he'd stopped quite suddenly, telling Grace to stay where she was. "Go ahead," he said after turning toward her. "Step over the line." Fearing it was some sort of trick, she hesitated. But he insisted and she was young and did as she was told, even lifting a leg high when he indicated the exact spot. He grinned and welcomed her to Canada. She wonders what her uncle would do now that she has a new heart and could run all the way to that invisible border if she chose to. It is only a month since the transplant operation and she already feels stronger, but after years of uncertainty she doesn't trust it will last.

Grace walks to the back doors and presses her forehead against the glass.

The woman in the woods knew her name.

All the while the phone is calling her back to the kitchen and the early winter morning. "Grace, are you still there?"

She says a quiet yes and listens.

"There's going to be a delay. A truck's jackknifed on Route 93. They'll get to you as soon as they can."

Grace runs her hand across her kimono and pauses when she feels a ring of keys through the thin fabric lining the pocket. Very gently she rests the phone on the kitchen counter. A rush of cold air comes into the house as she opens the French doors. The paving stones on the back porch are like ice against her bare feet. Her eyes go wide from the shock.

Imagining unseen things pinching at her toes, she steps out onto the untended lawn, the long hem of the kimono trailing behind her like a slug. Halfway across she steps on a stone and winces. Bending over to pick it up, she folds her fingers around it. It's as flat as the palm of her hand.

Grace peers through the gate and takes her time to scan the wooded hillside. Other than her breathing, there is no sound. No wind, no birds. Nothing.

Hand to chest, her fingers tremble, tiny movements that mimic the frantic pounding of her heart. As her fingers increase their pace, she arches her white neck back, revealing a latticework of tendons stretched to the breaking point. Grace recalls the woman's screams and shrinks back toward the house. As she's turning to leave she hears something soft and primal coming from the woodland.

Moaning.

Her eyes follow the sound. Upward toward the ridge, the woman is lying somewhere amongst the undergrowth. Grace wants to forget, but in her head she can still hear the muffled echo of the woman's voice. She has to know why this woman knows her name. She takes the key from her pocket and slides it into the lock in the gate, wincing when the ungreased cylinders roll and grind against one another plaintively. Her heart is already pounding hard when she takes off in a run, but her legs are awkward and buckle beneath her. She has to stop a few feet up the slope and rest her palm against a tree.

Grace listens. She wants to be sure he hasn't returned.

She starts moving again and the cold air burns her throat. She barely has time to fill her lungs before coming up for air again. Her heart pumps hard. She keeps putting her hand to her chest, a look of surprise on her face. She's not used to this. The hill rises steeply, but she follows the scent, low branches snapping at her like wolves.

Grace finds the woman in a small clearing. She is twisted on the ground, one of her legs bent behind her unnaturally and the other stretched out and barefoot. Grace focuses on the cast-off shoe and the pine needles that sit thick on the forest floor, looking everywhere the woman is not. But the woman's hands reach out slippery and dark like eels, grasping at her before sliding away.

"Grace," the woman says. "Help me."

Dizziness blurs Grace's vision. She's faint from running. She can't think along straight lines. Looking hard into the woman's eyes she is trying to find someone she's seen before. The woman's hat has fallen away and her gray hair is lying in a tangled web, catching late autumn leaves and pine needles in its strands. She is far too thin. Her skin wraps

5

underlying bones like melted candle wax and her pale lips are framed by deep grooves. Wisps of white hair sprout from her pointed chin. The eyes dance though. They dart around Grace's face like a hummingbird collecting nectar.

"Please, Grace," the woman says.

Grace hesitates. She's not thought to bring anything. She thinks of her kimono and looks up at the sky, knowing it will snow. It's so cold. Her feet are bare and her small hands are trembling. Her eyes follow the ridgeline searching for the man with the knife. She thinks of dragging the woman back to the house but knows it's too far. They'd never make it. Grace unknots the kimono's belt, and a sea of cherry-colored carp slips away. She presses the silk to the woman's chest and feels the blood seep through the thin fabric. The dark tide swallows the carp in seconds.

The woman's words are so soft they're weightless, floating through the air like gray-winged moths. Grace collects them all. The woman shapes her story into something Grace can almost forgive. She tells Grace she's sorry for having stayed away so long. She drifts off and Grace shakes her awake.

Her startled eyes look up at Grace in surprise. "You're all grown up." She touches Grace's cheek.

Grace presses the kimono harder against the wounds. Her efforts have exhausted her. There are too many ways her mother can bleed.

"Shush, Momma." Grace turns toward the house and strains her ears for the sounds of sirens, but there's nothing. "You rest now. Help is on its way."

Her mother tilts her chin upward toward the darkening sky. "You know why I left. You know why I couldn't come back."

"I never understood."

Something that sounds like laughter escapes her mother's throat. "I just wanted to see you one last time."

Grace leans in close and raises her voice. "Tell me who my father is."

Her mother's eyes close. "You'll have to be careful. They're still look-ing for the money."

Grace grabs her mother by the shoulders and speaks as loud as she dares. "I don't understand."

Her mother's voice fades and Grace catches only whispers.

Her mother's voice sputters and Grace loses hope.

Her mother's voice goes out and Grace is alone.

The cold settles into Grace's chest like a stone. She kneels, clasping her mother's hands together with her own like they're in common prayer. The woods are closing in, and above her the sky sits heavily, draping the morning in a blue-hued cloak. From their woodland nest Grace watches the first snowflakes drift down, lazy and slow. They melt against her bare skin but all around her the moldering leaves turn white. Grace cradles her mother in her arms, feeling the sharp bones where there were once fulsome curves. The mother she remembers had a red-painted mouth and kohl-rimmed eyes set into a face framed by dark waves of hair. A haze of cigarette smoke. The clink of whiskey on ice. Laughter that continued long after a room fell silent.

Grace's lips are as cold as her fingertips and her bare limbs taper out like wires from her thin red nightgown but she doesn't shiver. Aside from her frantic eyes, she lies perfectly still, curling up for warmth where there's none to be found.

At the base of the hill, the back of her house rests in winter's palm. Fat snowflakes fall like bits of white plastic in a globe, but beyond her damp lashes she can see right into the kitchen and dining room. All the lights are on. It's a stage. Her eyes shift upward, and she looks straight across into her bedroom window. From where she lies, Grace can't escape its outward gaze. The ceiling light blinks at her erratically before going out. She stares hard into the dim interior, struggling to pick out familiar shapes from beneath her sleepy lids. Beside her, her mother gives way to the cold, cold ground. Everything around Grace slows to the same pace of her mother's failing heart.

An ambulance screams up the last bit of her road and slows to an off-key halt. Its unseen doors slam shut, and behind Grace a startled bird takes flight. The shadow of the crow passes over, solid and black, its wings fluttering faster than her heart. From the highest branches it calls out to others of its kind, the falling snow muffling the sound.

Grace imagines she's so small she disappears. She's drifting into this new reality when she finally hears help coming up the hill to claim her. Through her half-closed lids she can see them move through the trees. In her head she'd assembled an army but there's only two men struggling up the slope. They wade through knee-deep leaves and newly fallen snow. They look small and vulnerable with their heavy cases. She wants to call out to them but her voice sits frozen in her throat. Only their belted radios crackle with life. The sound sends more crows flying up to the barren trees that tower above them like scaffolding.

A dispatcher's disembodied voice asks if they've found anything yet and the two men stop moving. Their eyes sweep a wide arc across the snowy woodland. They see nothing. Grace wants to move but she's frozen by more than just cold. Fear now sticks to her skin like snow. Her pale throat feels severed. She wants to reach up and touch the invisible wound, but her hand stays where it is. Her silence is killing her. More birds call out. The moody blue light of winter shows off their black silhouettes. Caw, caw, caw echoes between the tall trees. The radio crackles once more and when at last they find Grace and her mother, the men come to a halt. The older paramedic is standing the closest, a few more steps and he would have trod on their bodies.

"Damn," he says in a low rolling voice that hints at thunder. He moves forward as he speaks. "That ain't right."

Behind him, his partner scratches around his belt trying to grab his radio, but he keeps missing because he can't tear his eyes away from what he's seeing. When he does find it, his hands shake so much he can hardly push the buttons.

"Where in the hell are the cops?" he yells into his microphone. His eyes dart around the wintry scene. "We've got two bodies out here . . . They're covered in snow, for God's sake . . . No, me and Jared . . . Where you said, but you've got to go through the side yard."

Jared pulls off his gloves and plucks Grace's wrist from the tangle of bodies. "Carson, take a second to calm down. I'm going to see if anyone's still breathing."

Grace feels her eyelids flutter; her curiosity wants to gaze straight into that voice. She feels the familiar prodding of her wrist. It is limp in his bare hands. His knees creak, and there is a smell of coffee, cigarettes, and booze on his breath.

He slaps her lightly on the cheek and the shock opens her eyes. His face hovers too close to hers. She panics. His lips form words she can't hear because her mouth is wide from screaming. Her body arches upward and thrashes from side to side, following the will of her new heart, which pumps like a foreign beast in her chest. All that untried blood racing through her veins is more than she can handle. She wants to run again, see her feet move like wings, but he straddles her, grasping both her wiry wrists in one of his hands and holding her head down with the other. She can hear him now.

"I've got you," Jared repeats over and over again, and then finally, "You're safe."

Everything that holds Grace together unwinds like a spool and her body goes limp under Jared's weight.

His partner, Carson, kneels next to her mother. His first-aid case is open, lying askew in the snow with its contents spilling out. He slaps on surgical gloves and rips away the plastic wrapping on a syringe with his teeth.

All Grace can remember is blood. Pressing against the flow was like trying to stop the coming of winter. She speaks in a whisper, her teeth chattering together so hard she can't keep her face still. "Is she going to be okay?"

Jared sits in the snow beside her, catching his breath, as if fighting ninety-eight pounds of flesh and newly fused bone could ever trouble a man of his size. "We're doing what we can." His expression is anxious when he turns to her again.

Grace's nightgown has slipped away, but when her fingers pull at the lace straps, Jared's hands are once again on hers, stopping her and her dignity from going any further. His curiosity almost reaches out and runs its fingers across the broken skin, but he pulls his hand back just in time.

Embarrassed, Jared shrugs off his heavy winter coat and wraps it around her. He can no longer look her in the eye. "You need to stay calm now."

Grace knows what Jared saw, what he almost reached out and touched. The long angry scar cuts a jagged line down her sternum. Like fresh meat, it's still raw. "I'm so cold," she says, noticing her bloody hands for the first time. They're sticky. She holds her splayed fingers out in front of her and stares at them.

His voice is all business again. "We best get you warm then."

Grace is so tiny his coat goes down to her knees. Opening a case, Jared unrolls a silver blanket. He lifts her up and sits her down a little ways off before wrapping her legs up in foil. As an afterthought, he pulls off his knitted cap and pushes it down around her ears.

He looks her in the eyes. "You'll be okay. Just try to stay calm. I need to look after your friend."

Grace sobs, taking big gulps of air but never getting enough. "She's not my friend. She's my mother."

His expression is different when he glances back over his shoulder. He looks confused. He digs his fingers into his dark hair. "Your mother?"

Grace burrows deeper into the coat, averting her eyes. She laughs because she's nervous. "She's been gone so long I didn't know her. I didn't know my own mother."

Her wet cheeks are pink with shame. He reaches out, placing his hand on her forehead, perhaps thinking she's feverish. She leans into it, curving her neck like she's a kitten.

"We're going to do all we can," he promises. "You just stay quiet now."

From where Grace sits shivering among the frosted bracken, she watches them work. Their voices are frantic, their actions desperate. She sees her kimono, thrown clear and half buried in fresh snow. She concentrates on it. It's ruined now, reduced to a wad of damp blood and silk. Pressing it to the knife wounds did nothing to stop the bleeding. Farther up the hill, the ridgeline has disappeared beyond a thick veil of snow. She concentrates on the dark trunks of trees and tries to pick out shapes.

More voices. Shouting. There are stretchers and the whir of helicopter blades. It sounds as if the army she'd imagined is finally moving through the trees. She looks at her mother again and knows they're too late. She curls up, falling asleep too easily and vanishing into dreams once more.

2

Detective Macy Greeley steps away from the counter at the ice rink and spreads her arms wide. "Seriously? Do I look like I want to rent a pair of ice skates?" The heavy winter coat she's wearing is unbuttoned, revealing a stomach well into the third trimester of pregnancy. She places her hands on the little shelf that's formed below her rib cage and frowns. There's something about the young man in front of her that she finds especially irritating. She decides it's his youth, which he's clearly wasting.

Perhaps thinking she's skated in from the parking lot the young man parts his long drape of hair and leans forward to inspect her feet. "Well, if you want to skate it's kind of mandatory?"

"That goes without saying."

"So, do you want to skate?"

"Nooooooo," she says, removing her purple knitted cap. Bright red hair frames an angular face and other than a matching shade of lipstick she wears no makeup. She lifts a finely plucked eyebrow and flashes her state police badge. "Like I said before, I'm meeting a colleague. I don't want to skate."

"Oh yeah, you did say that." He casts around for the buzzer to open the barrier.

But Macy doesn't move. She keeps her badge raised up in his face, and her eyes dart about as they try to make contact with his. She leans forward when she has him in her sights. "Are you stoned or are you always this stupid?"

He stands slack-mouthed and still, only breaking into a smile when he sees her wink. "Stupid, I guess." He laughs, finally noticing her condition. "You're pregnant. You shouldn't skate."

"Congratulations," she says, dropping the badge and walking through the open barrier. "Go to the head of the class."

Her boss, Ray Davidson, spends his lunch hours playing ice hockey. The time is sacred, and no one, not even his wife, dares disturb him. Cap in hand, Macy walks along the high Plexiglas wall separating the rink from the spectators, making her way to the café where he'd said they could have a quiet word. Back at the office they'd already been having a quiet word next to the coffee machine when he'd told her to meet him here. Why he couldn't just string together a few more quiet words then and there is a mystery. Macy puts her cap back on. Inside the skating rink it's as cold as it is outside. The city of Helena rests under a fresh coat of white snow. There's a crisp quality to the air that never fails to lift her mood.

A group of hockey players crash into the wall next to her, and there's Ray's face pressed against the partition. His nose is squashed with his nostrils flared outward like a pig's snout. He grins like an idiot, revealing his red gum shield.

Macy continues walking, and Ray follows along, skating in a slow lumbering glide. Well over six and a half feet in skates and padded out in hockey gear he dwarfs Macy. At the gate, he removes his gloves and helmet. His dark hair is damp and plastered to his forehead. He brushes it away with his fingers and casts around for his sports bag. "Thanks again for coming to meet me here," he says, bending low to put on his blade covers.

Macy gestures to the empty tables at the quiet end of the café. "Order something for us to eat. I've got to find a bathroom."

Macy joins Ray at the table and there's a green salad sitting at her place. She glances over at Ray's burger and fries and narrows her eyes. Ray knows better than to mess with her when she's hungry. "What's this?" she says, plucking a fry from his plate and ladling it into the ketchup.

"It's a salad. It's healthy."

"I can see that." She shifts their plates. "Now it's your healthy salad."

Ray laughs it off and orders another burger from the girl behind the counter, picking at Macy's fries until it arrives. They both ignore the salad.

"So what's this all about, Ray?" Macy looks out at the rink where his team continues to practice.

Ray wipes his full mouth with the corner of his napkin and reaches around behind him to rifle through his gym bag. Without saying a word he places a file between them and slides his index finger along the name.

Macy shrugs. "Arnold Lamm is dead."

"And as of this morning so is his sister-in-law Leanne Adams." He picks up the file and thumbs through it, handing Macy a preliminary report from Collier's sheriff's department.

Her eyes skim through the information. "Leanne Adams finally resurfaced."

"And she was murdered on the same day."

Macy holds a fist to her mouth to stifle a yawn. "It says here that her daughter might have seen the killer."

"It also mentions a baby-doll nightie, a bouquet of roses found in a garbage can, and hints at a compromised crime scene. The paramedics arrived too late to save Leanne, but they still got there before the cops. I want you to interview the medics and Grace Adams before Collier's sheriff's department steps in and fucks it all up."

"Ray, I'm three weeks from going on maternity leave."

"Actually, it's four weeks. I checked."

"I'm in no condition to go gallivanting across the state."

"It's a two-hour drive. That's hardly gallivanting. Besides, aside from me you're the only one left that worked on the original case."

"It's been eleven years. Anyone can read the file." She summarizes the case between bites, stabbing her French fry in the air when she makes a point. "The bodies of four Eastern European girls are dumped in a roadside picnic area. Our informant fingers Arnold Lamm's trucking company. We investigate. A mysterious fire wipes out the driver manifests. A mysterious brake failure wipes out our informant. Shortly after, Leanne Adams is pulled over for speeding, heading north to the Canadian border. According to the trooper, she had four female passengers. No one sees Leanne for eleven years and upon return, she's duly murdered." She finishes off her French fry and picks up another. "It's not rocket science, Ray."

He taps the file. "Leanne knew something."

Macy pushes her plate aside and picks up the police report again. "Of course she knew something. That's why she's dead."

"But if the daughter can identify the killer our case against Cross Border Trucking isn't dead." He raises his voice. "They might still be in business, Macy." He holds up a picture of the youngest girl they found in the roadside picnic area. "Katya was only fifteen and had been sexually assaulted and left to die. Can you imagine how scared she was?"

Macy leans back in her chair. A couple of mothers have shown up with a group of young girls. They're all dressed like ballerinas but wear ice skates instead of slippers. The youngest one smiles at Macy. Macy gives her a little wave before turning to Ray.

"As I recall, there was something wrong with Leanne's daughter," she says, remembering a young girl with an unfortunate haircut.

"Grace Adams had a lot of health problems. Her aunt and uncle adopted her after Leanne left town."

Macy pictures the squalid little trailer behind the truck stop where Leanne and Grace once lived. The police didn't realize Grace had been abandoned until they broke in three days after Leanne vanished from Collier. There'd been an anonymous phone call, otherwise they might never have gone looking for her.

Macy flips through the report. "How old is Grace now?"

"Almost eighteen."

"The girl must be traumatized."

"I imagine so."

"Remind me what our informant said about Arnold's wife, Elizabeth. Did she know what her husband was getting up to?"

"He wasn't sure, but my gut instinct tells me she must have known something."

Macy sips her drink through a straw. "More likely she pretended it wasn't happening."

"The informant told us it was a ring of four or five guys who were very close to Arnold Lamm."

"Didn't we make up a short list at some point?"

"Yeah, we came up with a couple dozen names, but for one reason or another, we eliminated most of them."

Macy taps the edge of the table with her fingertips. "There are two more that we can strike off. Scott Pearce is serving an eight-year sentence for armed robbery, and Walter Nielson was murdered four years ago in Boise."

"I'll check on Scott Pearce's status. He may have gotten early release." Ray hesitates. "I need you to go to Collier and lead the investigation into Leanne's murder. Initially I'd rather they didn't know you're working the old case as well. It may make things easier."

Macy sits quietly for a few seconds. During the original investigation she and Ray had come up against a great deal of resistance in Collier. It was nearly impossible to get anyone to cooperate, including the police. She stares hard at Ray. "Collier is a shithole. I don't want to go."

"Sorry," he says, staring right back. "I'm going to pull rank on this one. You know I'd go if I could."

Macy crosses her arms over her belly. "What's in it for me?"

"Isn't my undying gratitude enough?" Ray gets up to order coffee but comes back with two slices of pecan pie piled with whipped cream. "This should cheer you up."

Macy picks up a fork. "You sure know how to make a girl happy."

"If only that were really the case."

Macy runs her fork across the whipped cream, making parallel tracks. "Why didn't you just tell me all this an hour ago back at the office?"

Ray waits for the waitress to finish serving their coffee before answering. Under the table Macy feels his well-padded knee bump against her leg. "I thought it would be nice for us to touch base," he says.

"Is that so?" She skewers her pecan pie with her fork. "I guess it's too bad that I have to get going if I want to reach Collier before dark."

Macy parks her patrol car in the long circular driveway of her childhood home. She'd driven across the capital at high speeds with the sirens on, but switched them off when she passed into the gated neighborhood. In the seven months since she totaled her car in an accident she's been driving state-issue vehicles. She thought her mother, Ellen, would balk at having a patrol car parked outside the house, but she and all the neighbors love having it there. Apparently it makes them feel safer at night. There is virtually no crime in this end of town, so Macy isn't sure what they have been worried about. She waddles up the snow-covered walkway, waving to Ellen, who's come to the door to meet her. On the drive across town Macy kept her instructions brief. *Mom, please pack a bag for me. Don't be silly, you know what I like to wear. No, I don't know how long I will be gone. Yes, I'll be careful.*

Ellen insists on carrying the suitcase out to Macy's car. "Are you sure you don't want something to eat? I could whip you up some lunch. There are some leftovers from the dinner we made last night."

"Thanks, Mom, but I've already had something."

Ellen slips the suitcase into the back end of the car and takes a deep breath. "Your brother called this morning. I'm afraid it's just him coming this Christmas. Charlotte is going to her parents' house with the kids."

Macy takes hold of her mother's hands and squeezes them. "It's not been a good year for the Greeleys."

"I don't know how I would have coped without you staying here with me."

Macy manages a smile. "You know I feel the same way."

Ellen looks back at the house. "After your father died I felt lost in my own home. It was too quiet."

Macy places a hand on her belly. "It won't be quiet for long."

"Have you decided whether you'll stay on after Christmas?"

"I'd be crazy to leave." Macy reaches for the car door. "I don't know the first thing about babies."

"Well, between the two of us I'm sure we'll manage."

Heading north on Route 93, the Flathead Valley spreads out on all sides. It's stopped snowing, but the winter sky sits low, its thick mist clinging to the trees and hillsides like foam. The cell phone rings, and she takes a quick glance at the screen, ignoring it when she sees it's Ray. It's the second time he's called since she left him sitting at the table back at the ice rink. By the time she'd finished her dessert she'd had enough of his company. Without saying much more than good-bye she grabbed the files he'd brought along and hurried out the door.

Macy passes through the town of Walleye Junction, stopping briefly at the diner for coffee. From her table, she can hear the other patrons gossip about the murder. She's relieved that no one mentions Leanne Adams by name. Collier's sheriff's department doesn't have a reputation for keeping information to themselves, but so far they've managed to avoid leaking the victim's name to the press.

Despite Macy's protests, the waitress pours more coffee. "Sorry, honey," she says, gesturing toward Macy's patrol car. "You look like you should be at home with your feet up."

Macy smiles over her cup. "For all I know they might be up right now. I haven't seen them in weeks."

High-pitched and unrestrained, the waitress's laughter comes out in short uneven blasts, making her sound as if she might have more than one personality tucked up inside her head. Macy shifts away a fraction and asks for the check.

There are only three towns in the upper reaches of the Flathead Valley. Collier is the farthest north, Wilmington Creek is more central but a bit to the west, and Walleye Junction lies in the south where the valley begins to widen. To the east the remote peaks of the Whitefish Range run all the way to the Canadian border.

Back at the ice rink Ray briefed her on the situation in Collier now that their sheriff's office is under investigation. There'd been a scandal involving the outgoing sheriff. Ray didn't have to go into details. Macy had read the stories in the papers about the fancy cars, the unnecessary travel expenses, and the three-story addition slapped onto the back of the sheriff's otherwise modest home.

"The acting sheriff, Warren Mayfield, is a good guy," he said between bites of pecan pie. "He's just in over his head."

Macy is nine miles out of Collier when she puts in her first call to Mayfield. He's eager for her to get settled into her hotel room before they start working.

"That's very kind of you, Sheriff Mayfield," she says, popping a piece of chewing gum into her mouth. "But I think the Collier Motor Lodge will hold my reservation. I'd like to get started immediately if you don't mind."

She listens to Warren's disjointed voice rise up from the speakerphone, her mouth settling into a weary scowl. He suggests they meet at the morgue, and she balks. As far as she's concerned the morgue is the medical examiner's domain. She prefers seeing coroner's reports in black-and-white with photos attached only where necessary. Even then she'd rather not look.

"No," she says, tapping on the steering wheel impatiently. "It's only just after three. I want to visit the crime scene before dark." She reaches over and grabs the initial report. "I'd also like to interview the witness and the two medics."

The line goes quiet and for a few seconds Macy thinks Warren might have got cut off. She's about to redial when he speaks again.

"Given her recent heart transplant her doctors are reluctant to let us interview Grace Adams until she's had a few days to recuperate."

Macy tries to keep one eye on the road as she sifts through the paperwork. "When in the hell did she have a heart transplant?"

"Recently. She's only been out of the hospital a couple of weeks."

Macy drums her fingers on the steering wheel. "I'm just coming to Collier. I'll meet you at the house on Summit Road in twenty minutes."

The Flathead River loops around Collier like a distended belly. Churned up by heavy snowfall in the higher elevations, the water is milky gray. Macy crosses it on a wide, brutal-looking bridge before passing through the industrial end of the town. The factories and lumber mills are picked-over carcasses. Scarred by weather, graffiti, and arson, they serve as a constant reminder of what Collier once was. Save debris, the parking lots are empty. It's become a junkyard of sorts. The entire contents of foreclosed homes have been left to the mercy of scavengers and windswept decay. Stripped of anything of value, the odd little groupings of old sofas, beds, and rubbish sit around fire pits. Junked cars complete the disturbing tableaus.

Macy follows the directions she's been given, taking the business loop to avoid traffic on the southern end of town. Halfway round, the unfinished road is blocked off with orange and white barricades and she's redirected back to Main Street, where she comes across a long line of traffic. She flicks on the siren and pulls into the suicide lane, pushing aside the cars and trucks that get in her way. There's a roadblock set up in front of another bridge spanning the northern bend of the Flathead River. Instead of letting her patrol car pass, the officer on duty pulls her over to the side.

He's someone she's come across before, but she can't remember the name. "Detective Greeley," he says, the corners of his mouth curling upward. "You late for your birthing class?"

Macy shows him her badge so he remembers his manners. "That's right, sweetheart. My boyfriend loaned me *his* patrol car so I'd make it on time."

He looks over his shoulder toward the other officer on duty. "What do you think, Gareth? Should we let her through?"

Instead of answering, Gareth turns his back to them and continues speaking with the motorist he's pulled over.

"I'm looking for the Lamm residence." She picks up a sheet of paper and reads the address again. "It's out on the northern edge of town."

"Not really much of Collier left once you get that far north. Just follow Route 93. You'll hit a series of switchbacks. The exit for the Northridge development is on the third one. You can't miss it."

Macy doesn't want to but she thanks him, rolling up the window and cursing under her breath when he feels obliged to direct her out into the flow of traffic. She waves and tells him to *fuck off* with a cheerful expression he doesn't notice. It's only half past three and she's losing daylight.

Outside 153 Summit Road, Sheriff Mayfield leans against his patrol car waiting for her. His is the only car she's seen since she turned into the neighborhood. He wears a heavy coat and hat and carries a flashlight. It's impossible to read his expression but Macy can tell he's older, perhaps just shy of mandatory retirement. Macy grabs a flashlight from the glove compartment and gets out. She gestures toward the house, not bothering to disguise her astonishment. The building wouldn't be out of place in a theme park. There are iron grilles on the lower windows and it has a double front door made from thick beams of oak. It's built like a fortress. It even has turrets.

"I didn't know they had castles in Collier."

The sheriff reaches out and shakes her extended hand warmly. "Just the one." He introduces himself and gives her a brief summary of what they've learned so far. They make their way around the side of the garage, taking the same route as the police and paramedics. "We found a car with Canadian plates parked up the road a bit. It's not registered to Leanne but we know she was driving it. We'll need to track down the owner."

Macy glances up at the house again. She wants an excuse to have a look at Arnold Lamm's office. "No one has been in the house?"

"Elizabeth wouldn't allow it."

"That's not very cooperative."

"All the action took place in the woods behind the house. She doesn't see any reason for us to go traipsing through her living room."

Macy spots the unfinished frame of another large house some two hundred feet away. "What kind of a neighborhood is this anyway?"

"A failed one. Some nutcase had the grand idea that Collier needed a golfing community. The developers lost their shirts when the economy collapsed."

Macy hadn't seen a single finished home on the drive up from the neighborhood's entrance. "So how many people live up here?"

"Two."

She stops and rests her palm on the trunk of a tree. The land rises up ahead of them. They're following a well-trodden path through the snow but footfalls fan out in all directions. There isn't a breath of wind and it's completely silent. "Two households or two people?"

"Two people. Grace Adams lives here with her aunt Elizabeth Lamm. There used to be three, but Arnold Lamm died of a heart attack last winter."

Beside them a high stone wall rises upward more than ten feet. Above it Macy can just about make out the darkened windows of the upper floors. In the shadow of the hillside the light is dim enough to use a flashlight. She directs her beam to an upper window.

"The witness, Grace Adams, stood up there?"

"Yes, ma'am," he says, guiding her farther up the hill, offering his arm when she steps off the path and sinks into the snow and bracken. "Grace has the bedroom up there in the eaves. From there she had a clear view of the murder scene."

They dip under yellow crime-scene tape and continue up the hill. "And she'd no idea it was her mother."

"I'm only going by what the paramedic told me. Grace only knew it was her mother once she'd come outside to help."

Macy looks down the slope toward the wrought-iron gate built into the garden wall. It's an isolated location and Grace was vulnerable once she left the safety of the house. "Her coming up here. Kind of a crazy thing to do."

Warren Mayfield takes off his hat and scratches his head. He's almost hairless and his skin is heavily freckled. "That's what I thought."

"So she must have spoken to her mother."

"Got no idea about that."

"When do you think we can interview her?"

"We're hoping for tomorrow, but given her condition it might be a few days. The girl nearly died of exposure."

"She was only wearing pajamas. A red baby-doll nightie?"

Warren says he's not seen the nightie. "Like you said it seems like a pretty crazy thing to do."

They come to a small clearing where the slope flattens out before rising up steeply toward the ridgeline. Crime-scene tape weaves among the tree trunks like string art. An area of snow the size of a double bed has been scraped away, revealing bare, damp earth. There's no sign of blood but there are plenty of footprints. It's impossible to tell which ones might be the killer's.

"Pity about the snow," he says, looking around at the heavily trampled ground. "Kind of made a mess of the evidence."

"When the body was moved, did you take everything you could from the immediate area?"

"We've got a few garbage bags of stuff in the freezer in town."

Macy kneels down to take a closer look. "The medics said the bodies were covered in snow?"

"Yes, ma'am. It was coming down heavily. A bit more time and they'd have been covered completely."

"The site isn't secure." From where they stand she can see directly into Grace's window. She walks the perimeter of the crime scene, her flashlight picking up a confusion of footprints. "When did your guys leave?"

"About an hour ago."

Macy frowns, but the fact is she's not sure there's much of a crime scene to protect. She shifts her gaze toward the darkening woods, positioning her beam to what appears to be an opening in the trees. "Is that a road?"

"It's a fire trail."

"Where does it lead?"

"There's a whole network of trails out here. Some snake in a loop around the neighborhood while others, like this one, end somewhere along Dray Creek Lane."

Macy looks up at the sky. It's nearly dark. "What's the forecast?"

"More snow in the morning."

"We'd best head out to Dray Creek Lane then."

At the curb in front of the house, Macy pauses at the garbage cans. "This is where you found the roses?"

"Yep, there was a price sticker from Olsen's Landing on them."

"What's Olsen's Landing?"

"It's a fishing camp on the northern end of town. There's a gas station and mini-market out front. We spoke to the owner this afternoon. There's no record of sale. The flowers are in buckets near the front door. They may have been stolen."

"Any chance they have security cameras?"

"It's not that kind of place."

Macy looks down the road. There are no streetlights. "Did the city collect the trash this morning? Someone may have seen something."

"Pickup must have been today. Otherwise the cans would still be in the garage."

"We need to find out what time they came."

"I'll make the call when we're heading over to Dray Creek Lane."

"You said you found the car Leanne drove nearby?"

"We found it parked in the driveway a couple houses along. Grace's address was scribbled on a piece of paper sitting on the passenger seat. Leanne had the car keys in her coat pocket."

Macy debates walking up to see where they found the car but decides against it. "If Leanne drove down from Canada, she wouldn't have gone into town to get flowers for Grace. It's a good half hour out of the way."

"It also would have been odd to bring her daughter roses. That seems a bit of a romantic gesture if you ask me."

"Fair enough, but it's not your typical mother-daughter relationship, so we can't rule it out."

They leave their vehicles parked at the turnout for Dray Creek Lane and continue up the road on foot using their flashlights.

"The garbage pickup was around half past nine this morning," says Warren.

"That was well before Grace Adams called nine-one-one."

"Yeah, it's a bit early for them to have seen anything, but I'll interview the crew tomorrow."

Macy points out the parallel grooves that run five feet apart through the snow. Unfortunately the tread marks are lost under a fresh layer of snow. Macy and the sheriff walk to the side of them, swinging their beams to the right and left. They've gone about a half mile when Warren gestures toward a bend in the road.

"The trailhead should be just up there."

"What's out here anyway?"

Warren doesn't hide his frustration. "These days not much other than meth labs. During hunting season it gets busier but aside from that there's no reason to come up here. The road dead-ends another mile or so further on."

Macy tells him to stop when she finds what she's been looking for. "You see that?" She traces the outline of a rectangle where the snow isn't as deep with the beam of her flashlight. It's roughly the size of a car. "At some point today there was a car parked here."

The sheriff leads her to a rusted length of metal chain strung between two posts. "I'll have my boys check in the morning, but if memory serves that's the trailhead you're looking for."

By the time Macy and Warren have walked back down the length of

Dray Creek Lane, Macy's legs ache. She leans against her car to catch her breath and Warren notices.

He opens her door and gives her a hand getting in. "Look, I know the paramedic Jared Peterson well. He's a good guy."

Macy purses her lips and gazes out over the steering wheel into the darkness. It's starting to snow again. "Jared Peterson," she says before turning to face Warren.

"Why don't you head on to the Motor Lodge, and I'll send him over to talk to you. You can interview his partner, Carson, tomorrow. Near as I can tell it's really Jared that you want to speak to anyway."

At the Collier Motor Lodge, there's a pile of messages waiting for her. She looks beyond the reception desk past the big stone fireplace and settles her eyes on the bar. She'd know that profile anywhere. Jared Peterson sits alone nursing what she's sure is whiskey. His head is tilted upward, and his eyes never leave the flat-screen television. Macy can hear what sounds like the running commentary of a basketball game. She's trying to think when she last saw him and realizes it's been at least four years. For a long time she missed his company. They'd been so close and then nothing. He faded away like the rest of them. The receptionist gestures toward the bar and adjacent dining room.

"Detective Greeley, I forgot to mention. Jared Peterson has come by to see you."

Macy asks the receptionist to take her bags up to her room and goes over to meet Jared, tucking her hair behind her ears and straightening her shirt as she makes her way.

The first thing he does is laugh at the size of her. "Jesus, Macy, how did that happen?"

"The usual way."

He lifts his arms. "A hug for old times' sake."

Macy braces herself. "If you insist."

Jared drops his arms. "Sorry, I forgot that you weren't much of a hugger." He waves the bartender over. "How about I buy you a drink instead?"

"In my dreams," she laughs, ordering orange juice and a plate of na-chos. She points out a table in the corner. "Do you mind? I don't really do barstools much these days. It's not a good look."

He walks ahead, deftly pulling out the chair that faces away from the basketball game so she can sit down.

"Gosh," she says, settling in. "This is just like our last date. You watch the game and I do all the talking."

Jared raises an eyebrow. "How long has it been?"

Before answering Macy searches her bag and places her phone on the table in front of her. "Long enough for it not to bother me anymore. Four years, I think."

Jared holds up his glass in mock salute. "Here's to your lucky escape."

"You're still quick. I like that."

"Most people don't," he says, ordering another drink when the wait-ress comes by their table.

Jared pulls his hair away from his face. There is a small scar above his lip where the doctors stitched up his mouth after a meth addict he was treating hit him with a broken bottle. The closed-over holes of sev-eral piercings are visible along the length of one of his earlobes. Macy remembers how he used to wear earrings when he was off duty. When they'd met in a bar down in Helena he'd looked very different from how he does now. Collier's only punk. She relaxes in her chair and observes him as they settle into a conversation. Even though he'd actively avoided meeting her parents he asks after them and is sorry to hear that her fa-ther has passed away. They talk about work and winter, carefully avoid-ing questions about their present circumstances. She sees that some things never change. He still has an irritating habit of flicking his eyes up at the television screen each time he thinks her attention is directed elsewhere. She takes a sip of her orange juice and focuses on work.

Macy opens her notebook and takes up a pen. "So tell me about this morning."

"Bit of a mess, really." He twirls the ice in his glass and checks the game again, wincing when he doesn't like what he sees. "Route 93 was all but blocked. Multiple pileup. We had to edge our way through. They were none too pleased when we drove past the worst of it."

"And when you arrived at the house?"

"The house was locked up so we had to go around the side. It was snowing pretty hard by then. Several inches had built up in the time it took us to drive out there."

"What did you see?"

"Nothing at first. It was too damn quiet. For a few minutes Carson and I thought it was some kind of prank call. Dispatch told us to look higher up the slope." Jared closes his eyes. "That's when I saw them lying there together."

"Describe it for me."

Jared opens his eyes a fraction wider and takes a sip of his drink, looking everywhere but directly at Macy. "At first all I saw was a red stain in the snow. It took me a few seconds to realize what I was seeing. I could see the outline of the two women lying together. Grace had her arms around her mother. Both of them looked dead."

"It sounds as if their bodies were staged."

Jared leans back in his chair and folds his arms. "You know the girl was nearly naked. It's amazing she didn't die from exposure. She completely freaked out when I took her pulse."

"What do you mean?"

"She started screaming and thrashing around." He reaches up and touches his cheek. "She clipped me at least once. She's surprisingly strong considering her size."

"Adrenaline will do that."

"Yeah, I've seen it happen before."

"Did you speak to her?"

"A bit. She said she was cold. After she calmed down she went quite limp, almost like she was about to pass out. She was covered in blood and near freezing." Jared holds up his hands, showing Macy how Grace had stared at the blood. "Truthfully, she seemed really out of it. I wrapped her up as best I could and told her I was going to help her friend."

"At that point you still didn't know it was Leanne Adams?"

Jared takes his drink from the waitress and makes room on the table for Macy's order of nachos. "I'd never have guessed it was Leanne Adams. The woman was legendary around Collier. I'd seen her a few times from a distance. She was big." He swirls the ice in his whiskey. "The lady that died was nothing but skin and bones. I thought maybe she was a meth addict."

"We'll have to wait for the autopsy report to find out."

"Anyway, I told Grace I needed to help her friend and she started crying. That's when she told me it was her mother. She seemed embarrassed. She said she'd not seen her mother in so long she hadn't recognized her."

"Did she say anything else?"

Jared keeps his gaze on the table for some time. "No, I think that was all. I sat her down a few yards away and went to help Carson with Leanne but we both knew it was too late. It may have always been too late. I reckon she'd been stabbed at least a half-dozen times."

"So you were out there on your own all that time?"

His gaze settles on hers and it's like looking in the mirror. Macy can tell that Jared doesn't sleep much either. When he speaks again his hooded eyes drift downward like they're about to shut.

"It wasn't ideal." He glances up at the television. "I can't shake the feeling we were being watched."

"I doubt the killer stuck around. It would have been too risky."

"Yeah, you're probably right."

Macy yawns into her clenched fist. "I'm sorry. It's been a long day."

Jared jiggles the ice in his drink and raises the glass to his lips. "It's really good to see you again."

Macy waves at the waiter to come to their table and reaches for her wallet. "Likewise. It's just a shame it wasn't under better circumstances."

Macy pays the bill and leaves Jared alone with the sports channel. Inside her hotel room it's stuffy and smells faintly of urine. She turns down the thermostat and cracks open a window before leaving a message on Ray's voicemail.

"Hey, it's me," she says, feeling stupid. "I just wanted to check in."

Spread out like a starfish on the bed, Macy stares up at the ceiling lamp. It's shaped like a wagon wheel and hangs from a heavy length of chain. Trying to find something of the man she once knew, she listens again to the messages Ray left on her phone earlier in the day. Every word is closely guarded. Never going off script, he says the same thing in three separate messages. *Give me a call when you get a chance.*

Macy checks the clock on the bedside table. It's late. Ray will be at home with his wife, Jessica, and their three children. Seven months have gone by since they renewed their marriage vows and moved back in together for the sake of their daughters. Macy pulls at the fabric of the shirt stretched across her belly and thinks about her unborn child. Doing what's best for your children isn't always possible.

She switches on the television and scrolls through the channels, only stopping when she finds the local news. Unable to name the victim, the reporters have interviewed anyone who's ever known Grace Adams. Several photos flash across the screen. Grace is a tearful toddler, clinging to an unseen adult. Grace is a sullen preteen, posing as an angel in a Christmas Nativity scene. Grace scowls, dressed as a witch for Halloween. Grace is an anxious teenager, her uneasy smile captured in a high school yearbook.

All the while a dramatic voiceover reduces her life to bite-size chunks. *A sickly child raised by a single mother. Abandoned at seven and adopted by her aunt and uncle. A heart transplant. The only witness to a brutal murder.* There's nothing new to report, so after a few minutes the same headlines are repeated.

Macy presses the pause button on the remote and stares at a photograph taken six months earlier at Grace's high school graduation. Grace stands perfectly still, her dark eyes gazing past the photographer, but all around her there's chaos. Her classmates laugh, hug, and throw their caps into the air, but Grace looks as if she's alone on the stage. Macy switches off the television and shrugs out of her blazer, tugging off her shirt and trousers before hanging them up on the back of the desk chair. Barely able to see her own feet, she pads toward the bathroom feeling tearful and fat. The only thing that seems to help is hot water.

3

Jared eats his breakfast cereal dry, washing it down with black coffee. The view outside his back door is flat white punctuated with the slim dark trunks of pine trees. He watches his two springer spaniels chase each other through the snow, darting beyond the woodpile and skirting the length of chain-link fence that surrounds his backyard. They do this again and again, never growing tired of the repetition. He envies their persistence.

He had a disturbing dream about Grace Adams and he can't shake the images out of his head. A bony little creature with no curves to her at all, she had an angry mouth that drew blood when she tried to kiss him. He woke up feeling anxious in ways he didn't understand.

Jared's cell phone rings, and he lowers the volume of the television. "Hi, Mom," he says, pacing the cluttered kitchen.

His mother sounds nervous when she speaks. "I know you're probably getting ready to go to work but I needed to hear your voice."

"I take it you saw the news."

"It's so upsetting that things like this happen in Collier. Your father and I worry about you."

"You know I can look after myself." He picks at a whiskey bottle's label, takes a shot glass out of the dish drainer, and sets it down on the counter.

"Do you know who the woman was?"

"Yeah, but I've got to keep it to myself for now."

He slouches on a stool at the breakfast bar and sips his coffee but he keeps one hand around the neck of the whiskey bottle. His mother asks him for more details and he tries to be patient. "I'm not going to tell you anything. You'd have nightmares." He glances at the television. "Yeah, I've got it on too. Nothing new."

"According to what I've heard, Grace Adams has been in and out of Collier County Hospital for years. Do you know her?"

He thinks about his dream and hesitates. "No, I don't know her."

For a while he listens quietly, twice lifting the bottle to pour, twice emptying the shot glass. "Yeah, Lexxie and I are still coming for Christmas." His mother had pressed his grandmother's engagement ring into his hands the last time she met him for lunch. He knows what's coming next.

She almost whispers. "So I guess you haven't popped the question yet."

"I promise you'll be the first to know when I do." Claiming he has to get to work, Jared says good-bye and hangs up.

Instead of leaving the house he turns the volume up on the television and pours more coffee. Young people are caught on camera for the first time in their lives. Microphones practically stick to their lips. Prepared to claim Grace Adams as their best friend, the kids of Collier crowd around the reporter, telling stories dating back to when they wore their Sunday school best. One girl says she saved a seat for Grace on the school bus every morning. Another declares they talk regularly on the phone. Another says she visited Grace's house the week before the murder.

The screen blinks and a newscast goes live to a female reporter stationed in Grace's front yard. Bundled up for cold weather, the reporter gazes into the camera. Her expression is muted by a thick layer of makeup. Snow falls heavily and she brushes it away from her hair. Behind her, Grace's home on Summit Road is wrapped up in snow, power cables, and yellow crime-scene tape. The narrative is disjointed. The reporter speaks too quickly and has to wait for the information to come through her earpiece.

"This is Connie Evans reporting live at the scene of what police are describing as a particularly brutal murder."

She turns and points to the Adams residence.

"At approximately 10:35 yesterday morning emergency services received a desperate plea for help from a residence in this Northridge neighborhood."

She presses her earpiece and nods a few times, holding up a finger indicating that the viewers should be patient.

"Reports are just coming in. The police hope to interview Grace Adams later this afternoon. As of yet there is no word from the police as to the identity of the murder victim. They are appealing to the public for any information that might be pertinent to the case."

Text from the live news feed moves like a ribbon across the bottom of the screen: *Grace Adams remains at Collier County Hospital. Police to interview her today. No suspects. Police: "a particularly brutal attack." Stay tuned for a press conference later this morning.*

Jared looks at his watch and frowns. He's late for work, but can't be bothered to make a move. He lights another cigarette and yawns. The phone started ringing at two in the morning and it didn't stop until he gave up and answered it a half hour later. At first all he could hear was Hayley crying down the line. It took him ages to calm her down.

Jared takes a long drag off his cigarette and swirls the last dregs of his coffee. His ongoing affair with Hayley has to end. It's been two weeks since he saw her at his family's summer cabin out at Olsen's Landing, and he's been trying to distance himself ever since. He can no longer deal with the stress of not knowing if or when he'll see her again. It's better to end it, to not see her at all. Jared picks up his cell phone and scrolls through the texts. Aside from a couple from his girlfriend Lexxie, most of the messages and calls are from Hayley. One way or another he has to let her go.

When his dogs stretch up against the fence and howl, Jared grabs his deer rifle and walks over to the back door. He squints into the low morning light. The chain-link fence that surrounds his little patch of land stretches up the hillside. The dogs stand in the far corner barking into the trees. The view behind his home is no different from the one behind Grace's house. The trees are the same. The light is the same. The snow has fallen from the same sky. It makes him uneasy.

The road Jared takes to work is as twisted as the narrow creek it follows but he knows every curve, transitioning smoothly in and out of the gears. Sleet falls heavily, sliding down his windshield before being flicked away by the wipers. He speeds up and races past a gritting truck, honking at the driver as he takes the final turn. The road opens up and descends into the washed-out river valley.

Logs, harvested in the higher elevations, once floated down the Flathead River. His father told him about the islands of tree trunks, occasionally jammed together so tight that it looked as if you could walk all the way across the swollen river. These days the river runs empty, its milky glacier spill carrying little more than debris. The view of the valley is monochrome in the winter months. Other than a blue signpost indicating a turnoff to Walleye Junction, there's nothing of color in Jared's sightline.

Though it was originally a coal-mining town, the logging industry took over as Collier's main source of employment in the mid-1800s. The streets are wide and accommodating, but unless you count the business loop, which only cuts out the south side of town, there is no way to bypass Collier. Part of Route 93 goes straight down Main Street, and where Route 93 goes so go the big eighteen-wheelers travelling back and forth over the Canadian border. Most of the time Collier smells of exhaust fumes.

Stopped at a red light in front of the high school, Jared waits for the cross traffic to clear. His old school sits just off the road but visibility is poor. He can barely make out the low brick classrooms. In front the parking lot is filling up but around back the sports fields sit lazy and white. An old lackluster marquee announces an upcoming basketball game and the date of the winter formal. Back in high school he'd gone to the winter formal with Hayley. It was during their senior year, and they'd been in love. But that was in January. By June he'd somehow lost her to Brian Camberwell, a truck driver nearly twice her age. Jared did not see much of Hayley the following year, but people liked to talk and pretty much everyone was saying she was doing a lot of drugs. Four years later she was in court and after that she was in rehab.

Jared checks his pack of cigarettes and finds it lacking. He pulls into the gas station at Olsen's Landing and parks in front of a little grocery store that squats low in a sea of plowed tarmac. The parking lot is empty except for a disused station wagon jacked up on cinder blocks. Stubborn brown grass grows out of the snow on the front hood. A gust of wind blows the sleet sideways and picks at the corners of a red, white, and blue banner stretched across the store's roofline, but a tattered American flag droops wet and idle from its pole.

Jared searches his coat pockets for his knitted cap, puzzled when he can't find it. He remembers giving it to Grace, and his mind goes still. He stares beyond the windshield wipers that tick back and forth, keeping time with the music playing on the radio. Posters advertising specials for everything from hot dogs, to ammo, to buckets of lard cover the front of the store, but Jared doesn't see anything except for that scar running the length of Grace's sternum. He'd almost touched it, pulling his fingers back just in time. He can't figure out why he'd done such a thing.

The anxious little bell set above the entrance to the store announces Jared's arrival. A woman with a weathered face and a tight ponytail watches him as he stomps his feet and shakes off the cold. She relaxes when he pulls his hood back and waves hello.

"Hey, Jared, figured you'd be in at some point this morning." She glances up at a fat little television that sits high above the counter bleating for attention. She lowers the volume and turns to her customer.

"Mornin', Trina," he says, clearing his throat. "Where's that daughter of yours? Doesn't Sissy usually do the early shift?"

By way of explanation, Trina juts her chin toward the television news. It's been fifteen minutes since he turned off his set at home, and they're still saying the same things. "She's a little nervous about being here on her own and I can't say I blame her." She turns away from the TV and meets Jared's eyes. They'd grown up together and until she'd dropped out of high school at fifteen, they'd always been in the same classes.

He asks her to heat up a breakfast burrito and she pops one in the microwave.

She sniffs into a wadded-up tissue. "Saw Carson yesterday. He told me that it was you guys that found them out in the woods."

Jared spots Trina's daughter Sissy lumbering up the aisle, her pregnant belly pushing out in front of her, a fair indication of the impatient child it's bound to be. He says good morning, noticing the Coke in her hand and the blue circles under her eyes.

Sissy barely raises her face to look at him. "Mornin', Jared." She lifts the hinged board and heaves herself behind the counter to join her mother.

Jared asks for a pack of Marlboros. A twelve-gauge shotgun rests on the shelf behind Trina and Sissy. Hovering above the barrel, a patchwork of photos of young men in uniform is tacked to a pinboard. At the last count more than a couple dozen Flathead Valley boys were away fighting in the war. He points to the picture of Sissy's fiancé. "Heard anything from Dwayne?"

Sissy's eyes open a fraction. "We talked last night. He sounded real good." She leans over the counter and flicks through a fashion magazine. In her bleached hair, black roots run two inches deep. She gives her mother a short look. "Ain't heard a thing from Daddy, though."

Trina wears a tight-lipped smile but Jared can see the tension around her eyes. Carl has been gone for over a year, and running the store, fishing camp, and gas station on her own is nearly killing her. She's Jared's age but it looks like time is wearing her down twice as fast. Jared does the math. Trina will be a grandmother before she's thirty-three.

Trina punches the cash register with her chubby fingers. "National Guard, my ass. All he wanted was a few weekends a year away playing soldier with his buddies."

Jared tries a smile. "Carl will be home and driving you crazy before you know it."

Trina stares up at the television again. "They've just extended his tour. Another six months on top of the year he's already been away." She picks up the remote and turns up the volume. There's another photo of Grace Adams. She's sitting among her classmates wearing an unsteady smile and clothing that would look more at home on a 1950s housewife. Compared to everyone else she shrinks from the lens.

Jared points to the television and asks Sissy if she knows Grace.

Sissy struggles onto a stool and peers at him from behind a counter display selling condoms. "Yeah, I've known that freak all my life." She pulls her chewing gum from between her teeth and twirls the long strand around her finger. "A total loser."

Not sure he has the appetite for this, Jared stares down at his breakfast burrito. Steam comes out the side of the greasy waxed paper. He sounds apologetic when he speaks again. "She seems okay to me. She's just a bit different, that's all."

Sissy smirks and wipes her nose with the back of her hand. "Yeah, she's different, all right."

The bell over the door rings again and a few high school kids he recognizes slouch into the shop. Sissy sits up at the counter and calls them over. Within seconds, they're all laughing at some inside joke about Grace Adams.

Trina throws Jared a sympathetic look.

"You take care, Trina," he says, exiting the shop. "See you soon."

Jared drives east along Main Street, tucking into the burrito between shifting gears. Music plays on the radio but he's not paying attention. He turns it up when a song is interrupted by a news bulletin.

"Detective Macy Greeley of the state police has been brought in to assist local law enforcement, increasing speculation that interest in this case goes beyond Collier. Among the local community there have been no reports of missing persons for several months and here at WXKB we've received unconfirmed reports that a car with Canadian plates has been discovered in the Northridge neighborhood where the murder took place. Authorities have still been unable to interview the only known witness, Grace Adams."

The area near Collier's Town Square is known as Old Town, and for a few blocks along Main Street faded yellow ribbons are tied to every lamppost. Most of the businesses set up along the covered walkways cater to tourists who are passing through town on their way to Canada or the casinos on the nearby Indian reservations, but that's just in the summer months. Collier's winters are lean. Aside from a pizzeria and a bakery most of the shops only sell souvenirs. The locals don't bother much with Old Town. The prices are too high, and most of the crap they stock is made in China.

Up ahead there's a police roadblock. The towns of Walleye Junction and Wilmington Creek have sent in reinforcements. It's freezing cold, and the sleet shoots down at a forty-five-degree angle, but the officers are huddled outside questioning everyone. Traffic is thick with eighteen-wheelers and early-morning commuters. Like everyone else's vehicle, Jared's truck slows to a crawl. A hundred feet farther on he's pulled over by a cop bundled up in a long down coat and wearing a cowboy hat.

"ID and registration" is all the cop says, looking Jared full in the face with unblinking blue eyes.

Jared hands over his driver's license, registration documents, and his paramedic badge. "You from Walleye?"

The police officer nods before looking over Jared's paperwork. "Sorry about that," he says, his mouth barely breaking out from a hard line. "We have to check everyone coming through."

"No need to apologize. We appreciate the help."

"Least we can do."

Collier County Hospital is a dense block of cement that crowds the landscape as uncomfortably as a heavy meal. The stunted trees in the parking lot barely rise above the rooflines of the cars and a high barbed-wire fence separates the hospital from the Flathead River and train tracks, which run along the edge of town. The parking lot is a sea of slush but the temperature is dropping. The snow swirls in Jared's head-lights like summer pollen. He eases into an employee parking space and cuts the engine.

The lobby is unusually full, and he recognizes only a few of the faces.

The receptionist spots him and laughs as she fusses with her spray-mounted hair. "Hey, honey. When are you going to make an honest woman out of me?"

Jared pretends he hasn't heard her say the same thing to him at least once a week for the past twelve years. "If your husband hasn't managed yet I don't think there's much hope for you." At the elevator he stops and turns to face her, going off script. "Say," he says quietly, walking back to the desk with his coat tucked under his arm. "The girl that we brought in yesterday, Grace Adams, have you heard if she's going to be okay?"

The receptionist takes a quick peek around, making sure no one is within earshot. "I've got reporters prowling everywhere. From what I've heard she's up on the top floor in the private wing. Moved her out of ICU late last night."

Jared raps the desk with his knuckles and thanks her.

Long, low-ceilinged corridors crisscross the hospital in a confusing maze. Over the years departments have been moved or shut down but no one has bothered to change the signs. Patients wander the hallways in their hospital gowns and slippers and families go round and round trying to find their sick relatives. Jared thinks of Grace up on the top floor, where they would have given their prize patient a private room overlooking the rooftop courtyard, and heads for the elevator.

4

The smell hits Grace first—disinfectant, meds, and sweat. Sound comes second. A heart monitor reminds Grace she's still alive while her aunt Elizabeth's familiar snoring provides another sort of comfort. Elizabeth is sound asleep, sitting in her usual chair, gold cross around her neck and wrinkles etching her face like fine lace. Grace runs her fingertips along the tubes taped to her left arm and closes her eyes again.

Her mother's last words are the first ones she remembers. *You'll have to be careful. They're still looking for the money.*

Panic swells in Grace's chest until it feels as if her ribs might snap one by one like violin strings. She holds her breath, counting down from ten. All she can see is her mother lying broken on the forest floor. Grace opens her eyes and is relieved when the memory dissolves in the glare of the overhead lights.

Her thoughts dart to her chest. There are no bandages. She wasn't the one bleeding. She'd been so cold. Those big snowflakes fell from the sky by the thousands. She gazed straight up into them, some in sharp focus, others blurred like white cotton balls, wet and pressed behind glass. It was like resting within a snow globe. She sets up the little tableau and changes her mind. It was nothing like any snow globe she's ever seen.

On a side table, bottles of her prescription medicine crowd in with floral bouquets and get-well cards. Still wrapped in cellophane, the flowers smell of nothing. She reaches for a card attached to a bunch of pink carnations and notices Jared's knitted cap. She picks it up, kneading it in her hands before bringing it to her nose. It smells of cigarettes and coffee. It's warm in the room but she slips it on anyway, pulling it down over her dark, lank hair. The wool itches her forehead so she takes it off for a second so she can smooth her bangs underneath its brim. She steadies her hands by tucking them under her armpits and tries her best not to cry.

What was it her mother always used to say? *You don't look pretty when you cry.*

Something catches her eye, and Grace sees a stranger's face swallowed up by the shadows beyond the door to her room. She tries to piece together the bits she's seen but can only draw a caricature in her head—a sullen expression, pale complexion, and an angular jaw, but nothing more detailed. It was definitely a man.

"Who's there?" she says, a little too late and projecting her voice no farther than the end of her bed. She hopes no one answers.

Grace squints, searching, giving up when she decides that whoever it was, is now gone. She pulls down Jared's cap, almost concealing her eyes. Her heart sinks when she hears the familiar squeak of Sam Fuller's cart, its one wheel still ungreased. As regular as a heartbeat, the noise rises above the din of foot traffic and voices of the hospital corridors. The squeaking cart stops outside and Sam walks in carrying a tray. His smile is a wall of veneered teeth. His wire-framed spectacles perch on an elongated face covered in liver spots and little else. He's as bald as an egg. He looks from Grace to the tray and back again, his elastic face changing its message more than once. The smile is gone.

"You're not George," he says in a low voice. He squints his filmy eyes at Grace, inspecting her like she's a specimen trapped under glass.

Grace shakes her head and wishes him gone.

As if he's expecting to find the missing patient hiding behind curtains, Sam cranes his neck around the room like a curious lizard. Grace follows his eyes, imagining George's shadowy profile behind the backlit drapes. Sam hovers with the tray held in midair, his old gnarled hands trembling. Grace decides it best to help him on his way.

"Maybe George has gone home," she suggests. Her unused voice rakes against her throat and she falls into a fit of coughing.

His wire-framed eyes tilt forward and look down his nose at her. "George is never going home."

She pulls her blanket up so it rests beneath her chin. "I'm sorry, I don't know where he is. I've just woken up."

"Grace Adams," he says when he finally recognizes her from past visits. "You're the girl from the woods?" His milky eyes go wide and he backs away a step, sucking his lips in around his teeth.

"What day is it?" she whispers.

Sam walks toward Grace again, the tray at waist level, friendly once more. "Same day it's been all morning. Tuesday, just coming up to noon."

I've lost a day, she thinks. Grace sinks down farther into the bed. She wants Sam to go look for George somewhere else. The woods, the snow, her mother, the crows; it's all coming back to her. Inside her chest, panic awakens like a giant spongy moth. She puts her fingertips to its powdery wings before it can take flight.

Instead of leaving, Sam holds up the tray and lifts the metal lid. The plate rattles and gravy pours across the rim. "We've got some nice mashed potatoes and roast beef today. I'm sure George wouldn't mind if you took his order."

She imagines lumps in the mashed potatoes the size and texture of mothballs. "No, thank you."

He leans in so close she sees the crescent moons of sweat under his arms. His eyes are cold. "Is it true what they're saying? That a woman was butchered."

Grace clutches her hands tightly in her lap. They've been scrubbed clean. All she can remember is how dark and sticky they once were. She holds them out in front of her, checking them over carefully. All trace of her mother is gone. Grace doesn't meet Sam's eyes. She can tell from his breath he's been picking at the mashed potatoes. They hear voices down the corridor and Sam backs away.

"You sure you don't want some?" he asks once more, tilting his long face at the plate before looking at her chest. "You need your strength."

She says *no, thank you* again and after a pause, Sam scurries off to look for George in other rooms. His cart rattles back down the hall, the one wheel still squeaking.

Grace's hands tremble as she sips water from a paper cup. The taste is metallic on her tongue. Her thoughts jump to the gate key where it's hidden in the silk-lined pocket of her kimono. It's lying among the bracken, invisible under a thick layer of newly fallen snow. In the night animals could have dragged it away; or worse, he could have it.

Grace sees Jared standing at the door and blinks several times, hoping to erase the previous day from her thoughts.

Jared knocks lightly on the doorframe. "Feeling better?"

They regard each other across the small distance. Grace notices how his eyes droop down at the corners and wonders if he always looks this tired.

She wants to speak, say something coherent, but tears come too easily when she asks after her mother. "She's dead, isn't she?" is all she says.

"I'm sorry" is all he says.

Grace closes her eyes and pretends she's elsewhere, but instead of fading, Jared's footsteps come closer. When she looks up, Jared is reading her chart. He gnaws at a cuticle, and his forehead pinches up into a series of questions as he sifts through the pages. He takes his time flipping backward and forward then repeating his actions until he's satisfied.

"You look young for your age," he says as he hangs the clipboard back in its place.

She shrugs. This man has seen her breasts, her scar, and her medical history. He knows everything. She knows less than nothing.

"How old are you?" she asks, picking at the tape on her arm, feeling the hairs tug from their roots.

He tells her he's thirty-two. "When I first saw you I thought you were much younger, but you're nearly eighteen."

Grace looks out the window. It's snowing again. A long time ago her mother promised to take her away from Collier. In the intervening years Grace has often hoped her mother was someplace really warm, like hell. Other times Grace was more forgiving. Kneeling next to her aunt on Sunday mornings, she'd pray for her mother's soul.

Jared gestures toward Grace's aunt. She is squeezed into the same lilac tracksuit she's always worn during Grace's hospital stays. A small gold cross sits flat against her white turtleneck. Her silver hair is pulled back into a loose knot.

"That's my aunt Elizabeth," says Grace, thinking back on the number of times she's awoken in the hospital to find her aunt sitting next to her bed. "She's learned to sleep through almost anything."

Jared drops his voice to a whisper. "I imagine she never lets you out of her sight."

Grace wipes away a tear and keeps her own counsel. The previous morning had been an exception. After breakfast she'd chased her aunt out of the house, swearing that she was going to spend the day resting in front of the television. Her aunt had laughed before telling her niece not to swear. Grace thinks of everything bad that's happened since. She closes her eyes and counts down from ten again. She can hear Jared's footsteps. He is coming closer still. All she can smell is cigarettes and coffee. The stale scent of booze is gone. He reaches out to touch her, and her eyes open wide.

He wraps his fingers around her shoulder, giving her a reassuring squeeze. "Don't be so hard on yourself. Going out in the woods like you did. That took guts."

Grace doesn't know what to say. Talking will only bring tears, and she doesn't want to cry.

Jared removes his hand, but Grace can still feel the pressure of his grip. He tells Grace that she couldn't have saved her mother.

Grace doesn't agree, but instead of arguing, she asks him if he would like his hat back. She's hoping he says no.

He bends forward to adjust it so it sits evenly on her head and says she can keep it.

Elizabeth stirs in her sleep, and they both stop moving. For a few seconds his fingers sit in frozen benediction on Grace's forehead. Elizabeth's neck is arched back and the loose skin on her throat trembles with each breath. Like an A-frame house about to slide off its foundations, the book *The Pilgrim's Progress* rests unsteadily on her lap.

Grace lowers her voice. "They always hated each other."

Jared folds his arms across his chest. "Who do you mean?"

"My mother and my aunt."

"That's a shame. Do you have any other family?"

"No one."

"What about your father?"

Grace blinks up at the lights. The tears are flowing again. Jared hands her a tissue and apologizes.

"No, it's okay," she says quietly, her words muffled by the tissue pressed to her face.

"No, it's not. I had no business asking."

"It's always been everyone's business. My dad could be anyone." Her face reddens. "My mother never told me his name."

"She was probably looking out for you."

She puts her hands flat against her face and holds them there. "My mother never looked out for me."

There is a beeping noise and Jared slips his pager out of his pocket. "I'm really sorry, but I have to go."

Grace is too upset to speak.

46

Jared passes her the entire box of tissues. "Look, I'm here at the hospital most days. Why don't you call me if you need someone to talk to?"

She almost manages to say thank you.

Jared hides his hands away in his trouser pockets and gazes outside. His stare is vacant, but his jaw looks like it's set as tight as a snare. "You know, you scared me out in the woods. You were so still, I thought you were dead. When you started screaming, I think my heart stopped."

"I seem to have that effect on people," she says, not meaning to be funny, but realizing how it must sound. She rubs her sore eyes.

He leaves her then, promising to visit when she's feeling stronger.

"I'd like that," she confesses in a low voice only she can hear.

Grace reaches forward to take her aunt's book, but Elizabeth springs up from her chair just as Grace's fingers touch the spine. The book falls, its flat cover slapping hard against the floor. Her aunt lets out a small cry, and her pale eyes dart about the hospital room as they try to find a safe place to land. The thread-like veins in her cheeks glow brightly against her ivory complexion. Behind her reading glasses her small cornflower blue eyes water. She calms down when she sees Grace but starts to panic all over again when she remembers why they are in the hospital.

"Oh, Grace," she says, reaching out for her niece's hands, rubbing them with her own because she always finds them cold. She breathes deeply again and presses the flat of a palm to her bosom. "Oh gosh, what a dream I just had." She looks at her niece once more just to be sure. "But you're okay. You're still here. You're okay." A tissue appears out of nowhere. She lifts her glasses and dabs her moist eyes before blowing her nose.

Grace hands her aunt a paper cup filled with water and tells her to drink. "Do you remember your dream?" she asks.

Elizabeth's brow wrinkles. "It was too upsetting to talk about," she says. The cup trembles in her hands and some of the water spills on her lap. More water drips down her chin. Her stubborn mouth refuses to function as it normally would. "I think I need to eat something. It's been a long time since breakfast."

"I want to go home."

"I don't think that's going to be possible for some time." Elizabeth points at Jared's hat. "It's hot in here, why are you wearing that ugly thing?"

Grace's voice goes up sharply. "It's not ugly."

Elizabeth places a hand on Grace's arm. "I'm sorry. It's been a long night. I couldn't sleep so the doctors gave me something. I feel so groggy."

"You look tired."

"That's because I am tired. How are you feeling?"

Grace thinks she should ask the same question of her aunt. She's slowed down over the past few months. Some mornings she can barely get out of bed. Grace bites her lip. "Are you sure you're okay?"

Elizabeth breathes uneasily, rubbing her hand up and down the center of her chest as if pressing into the flesh would help the air move along. She shivers in the heat of the room. "I just can't get it out of my head. You must have been terrified." She lays a hand on one of Grace's forearms but doesn't let it settle. "Your mother and I had our differences but you must know how very sorry I am. I feel awful we never reconciled."

"She sent her love."

Elizabeth fingers the gold cross at her neck. "Pardon?"

Grace makes it up as she goes. "It's one of the last things she said to me. Please tell Elizabeth I love her."

"You have no idea what a relief that is to hear."

"She looked ill. I didn't recognize her."

"We'll know more soon enough. I imagine they'll tell us everything soon enough."

"I wish she'd told us she was coming back."

Her aunt draws in a deep breath like she's preparing to dive into a pool then she asks in that clear Methodist voice of hers, "Did you know him? The man who attacked your mother. Had you seen him before?"

Grace snaps her eyes shut.

But her aunt snaps right back.

"Don't you dare," she says, shaking Grace back into the room. "You need to tell me what's going on."

Grace barely moves her lips. "Nothing's going on."

"Then why were you so eager to get me out of the house?"

"No reason. I just thought you could use a break."

"Grace, your mother died. The police are going to want to question you."

Grace fumbles with the call button sitting next to her on the bed, twisting the cord around her fingers like she always does. "Why would they want to talk to me? I don't know anything."

"On the phone you said that you saw it happen. You must know what he looks like."

Grace tries to remember.

"Well, can you describe him?"

"It happened so fast."

Elizabeth squeezes her niece's arm but her short fingernails gain no purchase. "You have a good eye, Grace, a memory for detail. I know you can help in some small way."

Grace stares down at her aunt's swollen knuckles. Last spring the doctors cut off the wedding ring she'd worn for forty-three years. Her aunt had it mended so she could hang it on a chain around her neck. Grace keeps forgetting to ask her why she doesn't wear it anymore.

Distracted, Grace asks her aunt if her hands hurt.

"Grace, I've got more important things on my mind than my arthritis." Elizabeth strokes Grace's arm gently with an outstretched hand. "They had to do a biopsy on your heart to check if everything is okay. Because of the stress you were under they were worried about rejection."

On impulse, Grace reaches up and puts her hand to her new heart. All she knew about the donor was that he'd been young and healthy when he'd died in a hunting accident. Dr. Gibson had looked sad when

Grace had asked about sending a card to the family. Apparently they didn't want to know Grace.

Elizabeth tries to reassure her niece. "It was just a precaution. Everything is fine."

"I'd been thinking about her a lot lately."

"Your mother?"

Grace gazes outside the windows into the fading afternoon light. "I've been remembering more about when I lived with her."

Elizabeth stiffens. "Well, you've had a tough time lately. It's to be expected that you'd be thinking of her."

Grace picks at her raw cuticles. Her face reddens when her aunt puts out a hand to stop her. "Had you heard from her?"

Elizabeth tears at the rim of her paper cup. "No, sweetheart. Why would you ask such a thing?"

Grace's eyes slide in her aunt's direction. "You'd tell me?"

"Of course I'd tell you."

"I'm sorry."

There's a knock at the door and Elizabeth looks up and smiles. "Dustin Ash, how long have you been standing there?"

Dustin brushes back a strand of graying hair that has fallen from his ponytail and steps in the room. Tall and slim, he has a habit of stooping. He smiles apologetically and holds up a pink teddy bear that has a bandage wrapped around its head. It wears a T-shirt that says GET WELL SOON.

"I'm sorry to disturb you, but I had to see for myself that Grace was okay."

Elizabeth peers beyond Dustin toward the door. "I'm surprised you got past security. I hope someone is still out there."

"Don't worry, Grace is well protected."

Elizabeth is close to tears. "You've always been so good about looking after us."

"Old habits die hard."

Elizabeth turns to her niece. "Do you remember when you got lost out at Darby Lake? You must have been seven or eight at the time."

"No, I don't think so." A few days earlier Grace told Dustin she was too old for stuffed animals but he seems to have forgotten already. She takes a quick glance up at him. He doesn't look as angry as she thought he might be.

"Of course you remember," Elizabeth insists. "We searched for hours. The sheriff even came out to help."

Dustin raises his deep-set eyes. "It was pitch-dark when I found you asleep under a tree. You seemed to be the only one that wasn't worried."

Elizabeth's words are sharp. "That's because she didn't understand the danger she was in. I still don't know what possessed her to wander off like that."

Grace can still hear them shouting her name. Flashlight beams had darted through the woods like fireflies. She'd gone looking for her mother. She had seven dollars and twenty-three cents in her pocket and a map she'd stolen from her uncle's truck.

Dustin tilts his head. "I'm just grateful I was there when you needed me."

Grace looks at Dustin and their eyes meet for the briefest of seconds. She owes him so much.

When her uncle Arnold was still alive he threw a party at the house on Summit Road every year for his employees and their wives. After one too many beers her uncle had humiliated Grace in front of his friends so she'd gone off and sulked, sitting out on the back porch of an unfinished house a few hundred yards away. She was eleven, but felt four, and aside from a few geeky girls she'd met in Sunday school she was friendless.

Walter Nielson came looking for her. He sat down next to her on the step and patted her knee in a friendly way. It seemed as if he'd been working for her uncle as a truck driver since the beginning of time. He'd also known Grace's mom. Grace trusted him.

He held out his beer. Just like his body, his fingers were big and fat. "Go ahead," he said, offering it to Grace. "Have some. Will do you good to have some fun."

Grace hesitated but he insisted so she held the beer with both hands and put it to her lips. In that moment he took the opportunity to put his hands up her dress. She sat frozen with the bottle in her mouth, swallowing hard and pretending she wasn't there and *it* wasn't happening. In her mind she floated above the porch, watching Grace and Walter from her perch among the latticework of two-by-fours tracking through the unfinished roof. But Walter didn't go away, and his hands stayed where they were. He had one hand inside her panties and the other one was down his own trousers. His face was twisted up into shapes she'd not seen on a man before. He pushed his way on top of her and groaned into her neck, his hot breath on her cheeks, his swollen lips eventually closing over her mouth. She looked past him up into the darkening sky and thought about the number of ways she could die. Walter mumbled into her neck that she was his baby girl and she imagined jumping off the north bridge into the Flathead River, slipping into the dark water, never to be found again. There were all kinds of ways she could die. Walter, however, seemed impervious. She didn't know how to get away from him.

It was Dustin who came to her rescue. Shaped like a whippet, he was surprisingly strong. He grabbed Walter by the throat, pounding his big round head hard into the pavement and threatening to kill him if he ever so much as looked at Grace again. Walter staggered off toward the woods. That was the last time Grace saw him. He died in an alleyway in Boise a week later. Someone bashed his head in with a baseball bat.

Dustin clears his throat before handing Grace the teddy bear. "I brought you a little present. I know it's a bit childish, but I guess a part of me doesn't want you to grow up."

"Thank you," she says, setting it on her lap. "It's very sweet of you to come by."

"It's the least I could do. How are you feeling?"

Grace holds the bear close to her chest. "Fine, thank you."

Elizabeth lets out a heavy sigh. "Quit lying, Grace. You're not fine." She looks up at Dustin. "You know she's lucky to be alive. She saw the killer."

Dustin gazes directly at Grace. "Is that true?"

"I didn't see him properly," she says, her face reddening. "He was too far away."

Elizabeth huffs about, looking on the floor for her handbag. "Are you sure you don't remember anything else about him?"

Grace wipes some tears from her face. "I could tell he was big because he made my mother look really small."

Elizabeth offers a mint to Dustin before popping one into her mouth. "Big, as in fat?"

"I'm not sure. He was wearing one of those puffer jackets."

Dustin sits down on the edge of the bed and pats Grace's leg. "Weren't you scared?"

Grace closes her eyes. "I'm sorry, I don't want to talk about it anymore."

Elizabeth takes her niece's hand and tells her not to worry. "Grace, I'm going to get something to eat. You want anything?"

Grace imagines lumpy mashed potatoes and says a quiet no.

Trying to stand, Elizabeth fights like a child trapped in a stroller. Her arms and legs reach forward, but gravity keeps her rear end trapped in the seat. She shuffles one hip at a time before pushing up with her chicken-winged arms until she's standing solid in her beige orthopedic shoes.

Elizabeth breathes heavily. "What about you, Dustin?" She slings the thick strap of her handbag over her shoulder and manages a smile. "Would you like to join me?"

Dustin glances over at Grace. "If it's okay with Grace, I'll stay here and keep her company until you get back. She shouldn't be on her own."

Elizabeth leans over and kisses her niece on the forehead. "I won't be long," she says before heading for the open door.

Dustin sits quietly for a few minutes. His head is dipped and Grace thinks he might be praying. He looks up and his eyes are moist.

"I'm really sorry," he says.

Grace watches his hand settle on her leg again. "You shouldn't be. You didn't do anything wrong."

5

Flying like goose down, snow swirls around the hospital's parking lot in dizzying spirals. Even though it's not yet noon daylight is dying. There is nothing to guide Macy to the main entrance. She slowly makes her way along the row of parked cars, stopping every so often to look around. A cold wind blows hard, kicking up more snow. Ahead of her the large gray building emerges from the gloom before vanishing just as quickly. She drops her head into the wind and plows through the parking lot toward it.

Ray calls her when she's halfway there. "I'm at the hospital now," she says, holding the phone to her ear and carefully making her way along what feels like a raised walkway.

"What did you find out from Grace Adams?"

"I just got here, Ray. I've not had a chance to interview her."

"It's nearly eleven. What have you been doing?"

"Have you seen the weather forecast? It took me a half hour to drive two miles."

The hospital is a large, six-story structure, but the snow is so thick she can't see it anymore. A horn sounds, and she jumps, almost dropping the phone. The iced-over headlights are just a few feet away. She waves and keeps walking, taking hold of the side of a pickup truck parked nearby and edging along it so she won't get off track again.

"I'm going to have to call you back," she says, slipping the phone into her pocket. She stands up straight and glances around. There's a low rectangle sign in the distance. She's nearly on top of it when she realizes she's arrived at the emergency room entrance. Somehow she's missed the main entrance and come to the far side of the building.

Outside on the pavement a woman wearing a private security uniform stands hunched smoking a cigarette under an overhang. Her thick body is bundled in a dark jacket and hat. In her large, bare hands the cigarette she's holding looks like a matchstick.

The woman laughs, setting off a coughing fit. "I was just about to come out and rescue you."

Macy dips her chin into her coat and tries to smile. She can feel the cold seeping through her thick boots. "It's really blowing now."

"Just wait. We're supposed to have a real storm move through the valley in a couple days' time."

Macy shivers. "It's nice to have something to look forward to."

"You're the detective they were talking about on the news?"

Macy draws herself farther into her jacket and does a three-quarter turn. She looks the woman over for a few seconds and decides it's best to keep it friendly. "Guilty as charged," she says.

"Going in to have a little talk with Grace?"

Macy wraps her arms around her body for warmth. "That's the idea."

"Well, good luck with that. She's an odd one."

Macy leaves the woman alone with her cigarette and heads inside. In the waiting area a few people sit scattered among the rows of seats. Each time Macy's eyes fall on someone they turn away. Some stare at the floor, some at a television playing music videos, and others turn back to their newspapers. Macy asks the nurse standing at the admissions counter where she can find the elevator. Instead of answering right away the nurse makes Macy wait while she finishes reading a report. The woman's name tag is decorated with hearts, and her hair, which is pulled back in a severe ponytail, is secured with a bright pink ribbon. She closes a file and puts it to one side before staring at Macy blankly.

"Sorry," says Macy. "I'm a little lost. Could you please direct me to an elevator?"

The nurse points a pink fingernail at Macy's cell phone. "You can't use phones in here."

"Then it's a good thing I'm leaving." Macy smiles, but her eyes are cold. She tilts her head and shows more teeth. "The elevator?"

On the second floor Macy stops outside the cafeteria doors and peers in through the windows. Warren sits at a table holding a cup of coffee aloft like he's reading what's written on its base. A petite woman occupies the chair across from him with her back to Macy.

As Macy approaches, Warren rises from his chair and reaches out a hand to greet her. "I see you found your way here easily enough."

The woman sitting across from him doesn't look up from her meal. She raises a small bite of food to her mouth and stares straight ahead. She chews slowly and carefully. When she's finished Warren clears his throat and introduces Macy to Elizabeth Lamm.

Macy observes Elizabeth closely. It's impossible to reconcile the woman in front of her with the one she met previously. Eleven years earlier Elizabeth had a helmet of hair and wore tailored jackets and skirts. Loyal to the end, she always appeared at her husband's side whenever he was called in for an interview with the police. Macy shrinks back and prays she isn't recognized.

Elizabeth Lamm's cornflower blue eyes snap up and catch hold of Macy. "I remember you," she says quietly, holding out a hand. "It's been a long time."

Macy takes hold of the hand. It is warm and powder dry but there is none of the strength in the grip that was there before.

Elizabeth withdraws her hand and drops her gaze. "And now I suppose you're here to pick apart my family again."

Macy peels off her scarf. "I don't have a lot of choice. Leanne was your sister."

"Please don't call her my sister. Leanne lost any claim to sibling fealty years ago."

"Regardless, nobody deserves to die like that."

The blue eyes catch Macy again. "We're all entitled to our own opinion."

"What about Grace?" she says, taking an empty chair. "Does she have an opinion?"

Elizabeth Lamm puts down her fork and stares at Macy without speaking.

"You know I'm going to have to speak to her."

Elizabeth drops her eyes to her plate. "That's out of the question. She needs to rest."

"Has she said anything to you?"

"She said she didn't get a good look at him."

Macy waits, but nothing more is forthcoming. She tries a new angle. "I understand you only just started going back to work."

"Yes, it's only a part-time job but I'd taken as much time off as I could while Grace was recuperating from her operation. Yesterday was my first full day in weeks."

"How did Grace seem when you left the house?"

Elizabeth hesitates. "She seemed excited, which was a nice change. She's been given a new lease on life. Some days she's euphoric."

"And other days?"

"Less so. It's been a huge adjustment for her."

"I can imagine."

"With all due respect, I don't think you can."

Macy slips her notebook out of her bag and puts it down in front of her. The room is empty save a table in the far corner. The doors open and Jared and the nurse she'd spoken to earlier walk into the room and head over to the self-service area. Even from a distance Macy can tell they're a couple. For some reason she's relieved to see that Jared looks miserable. The woman next to him is chatting gaily while he's slumped so low it looks as if he's trying to disappear.

Macy turns her attention back to Elizabeth. "Are you comfortable speaking here or would you rather go somewhere more private?"

"Here is fine. I've got nothing to hide."

"Tell me more about Grace's state of mind. You've said she was excited yesterday morning. Did you know she was wearing a red nightie when they found her out in the snow? According to the first responders she was nearly naked."

Elizabeth's cheeks redden. "I truly have no idea. It belonged to her mother."

"Did she say if she was meeting anyone? Had anyone been coming to the house?"

"She's only been out of the hospital a couple of weeks. No one has visited aside from my girlfriends."

Macy looks at Warren. "Did you tell her about the roses?"

Warren clears his throat. "No, not yet."

Elizabeth looks up at the sheriff. "Roses?"

Macy keeps her voice low. "We found a bouquet in one of the garbage bins. They were still wrapped in their packaging. If you don't know anything about them, we have to assume the killer brought them with him."

Elizabeth's hands start to shake. "I don't understand. Why would he bring roses?"

"Grace might have a stalker." Warren presses his palms flat onto the table. The knuckles on one of his hands are swollen and bruised. "Leanne may have come across him spying on Grace. Maybe she confronted him."

Elizabeth drops her voice to a whisper. "So this may not have had anything to do with Leanne?"

"We're just speculating at this point."

Macy opens her notebook and flips through until she finds what she's looking for. "I heard there was an incident with a teacher named David Freeman when she was fourteen."

Elizabeth sighs. "The whole thing was blown out of proportion."

"So what did happen? There's usually some grain of truth to these things."

"There's really nothing to tell. It was an innocent schoolgirl crush." Elizabeth shifts awkwardly in her chair. "There was talk that Grace was having an affair with a married man but thankfully his name was never revealed."

"Charges were filed."

"And charges were dropped. They both denied the whole thing. The only mistake he made was thinking he could handle it on his own. He didn't know how to cope with Grace. She could be very needy with anyone who showed her kindness. The doctors weren't sure how long she had left to live. It was a difficult few years for her."

"Does she have any friends we could speak to?"

Elizabeth remains silent.

"You know I can find out who Grace's friends are without your help."

Elizabeth closes her eyes. "Grace has no friends."

Macy writes down the words "no friends" in her notebook and underlines it three times. "So why don't you tell me about Grace's present state of mind?"

"She seems calm but really, it's hard to tell."

"I need to talk to her."

Elizabeth looks at Warren for support but he agrees with Macy. "Sorry, Elizabeth, there's a killer out there and Grace is our only witness."

Elizabeth stands up with difficulty and tells them she wants to go upstairs to prepare her niece. Warren offers to go with her.

"Grace knows me," he says. "I'm sure she'll be fine if I offer to sit with her."

Macy turns to face Warren. "I didn't realize you were so close to the family."

Elizabeth takes Warren's arm. "Warren and Arnold were both deacons at the church."

Warren leads Elizabeth away. "Arnold was the one who took it seriously. I was a lapsed deacon at best."

A female doctor meets them as they're leaving the cafeteria and they stand huddled together in the open doorway speaking in low voices. Macy strains her ears but there is too much noise coming from the kitchen to hear what is said. For a second it looks like Elizabeth might cry. She holds on to the doorframe for support and is eventually led away by the doctor. The doors swing shut and Warren is left standing alone.

Macy walks over to him. "What's going on?"

He runs his fingers through what's left of his hair. "Grace has had a panic attack. They've had to sedate her."

Macy stares at the closed doors. "What's the name of her doctor? I should probably speak to her."

"Dr. Sonya Gibson. She's been looking after Grace for years." He pauses. "You probably won't be able to interview her until tomorrow."

"Yeah, I figured that. I think I'll head over to Wilmington Creek. I want to speak to David Freeman."

"You know he has an alibi for yesterday. He was teaching all morning."

"I've got to start somewhere. From what I've read about the complaint made against him, David Freeman is the closest thing Grace has had to a friend in the last ten years. She may still be in contact with him."

"I'm going to head upstairs to look in on things. I'll let Dr. Gibson know you'd like to have a word with her."

Macy walks back to the table and sits down. Resting her head in her hands, she tries to think through everything she knows about the original case. Unable to sleep in the strange motel room, she'd combed through the files, making fresh notes on her laptop for hours and only stopping when the grinding noise of truck traffic along Main Street announced a new day. Her thoughts on the killer's motives keep snagging on the bouquet of roses and baby-doll nightie.

She hears the lightest of footsteps and looks up to find Jared standing over the table.

He pulls out the chair across from her. "You were a million miles away."

Her notebook sits in front of her, a schematic of the original case in full view. She eases it closed and hopes he hasn't had the chance to see what's written there. "Not quite a million miles away," she says, looking around the cafeteria. Everything inside is beige and outside it continues to snow. She wishes she were a million miles away.

He gestures to her empty cup. "Another coffee?"

"No, thank you. I'm fine."

He sits across from her anyway. "I spoke to Grace Adams this morning."

Macy arches an eyebrow. "And?"

"She seems a little lost."

"Lucid, though?"

"Yeah, but you'll see. She's not like the other kids around here."

Macy puts her notebook in her bag and stands. "From what I can tell that's probably a good thing."

"Are you going to interview her?"

"They've had to sedate her. She's had a panic attack."

Jared rubs his chin. "She's okay, though?"

"That's what I'm going upstairs to find out."

Outside in the corridor Macy spins around trying to find her way. "Aren't there any signs in this hospital? I can't even find an elevator."

Jared steers her to the left. "I'll take you. We don't want Montana's finest getting lost."

Macy turns on her heel and grins. "So, Jared, was that the other woman?"

Jared pushes the button for the elevator. "Excuse me?"

"The nurse you were sitting with in the cafeteria. Was she the one you were seeing when we were dating?"

"I've only been with Lexxie for a little over a year."

Macy presses him. "But you were seeing someone else when we were together."

"No," says Jared, following her into the elevator. "There was no one else."

Macy laughs. "Don't bullshit me, Jared. I'm a detective."

"You're a detective that can't find the elevator." He turns and looks at her. "Anyway, you're all set now. You're having a baby. Life is good."

Macy concentrates on the ascending numbers. Two floors to go. "Yep, all set."

"We could have dinner tonight. It would be nice to catch up."

Macy thinks about it for a second before declining. "I'm going to be too tired. Provided the roads are clear I have to drive over to Wilmington Creek. By the time I get back I know I'll just want to go to bed."

"Look, I just got off work so I'll drive you. My folks live over that way and I have some stuff I need to drop off at their place."

Macy can't help but look grateful. "Are you sure?"

"I'm happy to do it."

Macy keys his number into her phone and agrees to call him as soon as she's finished talking to Grace's doctor.

By the time Macy and Jared are on the road the weather has lifted, but everything is powdered white and there is no sky. The world ends in a low mist that hovers just above their heads. Jared isn't bothered by the poor road conditions. He drives fast, cutting in and out of lanes and passing trucks when they are going too slow for him.

"So where are we going?" he asks.

"Wilmington Creek High School."

"Home of the fighting bears. I know it well."

Macy shifts the elastic waistband on her trousers so she's more comfortable. Her unborn child seems to be resting right on top of her intestines, making it impossible to eat more than one mouthful of food at a time. When she's finally settled she glances over in Jared's direction.

"So are things serious between you and Lexxie?"

"That depends on who you ask. She's serious. I'm not."

"Why does that not surprise me?"

Jared checks the wing mirror and moves into the right lane. Up ahead there's an exit for Wilmington Creek. "What did the doctor have to say about Grace?"

"Given patient-doctor confidentiality, not much. Apparently, Grace has suffered panic attacks in the past but not usually this extreme. This time they decided it best to sedate her."

"I can't say I'm surprised. What happened yesterday was horrible. I don't see how she'll ever get over it."

"Thankfully, there was a family friend with her. He said it came on quite suddenly. Her heart started racing and she couldn't breathe properly."

"Have you ever had a panic attack?"

She thinks for a few seconds before answering. "Maybe once or twice back in high school. What about you?"

"No, I'm not the type. It's one of the perks of never being serious."

"You just keep telling yourself that."

Her phone rings and she glances at the screen before leaving it unanswered.

"Aren't you going to get that?"

She turns off the sound. "It's my mother. We spoke earlier today so it can wait."

"She's probably worried about you."

"She's got no reason to be."

Jared takes a left onto a driveway lined with a low, snow-covered hedge. A billboard marks the entrance to the modest high school campus. The single-story classrooms are spaced out amongst the trees. The gym is the only building that is of decent size. It's situated next to a clearing dotted with snow-covered picnic tables. Jared and Macy drive through a parking lot full of pickup trucks and older four-door sedans. Other than a smoking section, located in the corner next to the Dumpsters, there's not a soul in sight. The students there barely acknowledge Jared's truck as it crawls over the compacted ice.

He pulls up in front of the main building and peers in toward the reception desk. "Do they know you're coming?"

"Yeah, they know. I called earlier." She looks at Jared. "Thanks again for doing this."

Jared reaches for the cigarette he put aside earlier. "Given what a shit I was in the past it's the least I could do. I'll wait out here until you're done. By the way, I called my parents. They're expecting us for lunch."

Macy stares at him. "You've got to be fucking kidding me. We date for three years and I never meet them and now we're having lunch."

He tilts his head toward her belly and grins. "Just do us a favor. Don't tell them the baby's mine."

David Freeman stands in the small lobby waiting for her. Slightly balding and carrying a bit of extra weight around the middle, he's wearing a suit and tie. He looks her in the eye when they shake hands.

"Welcome to Wilmington Creek High School, Detective Greeley."

Macy thanks him and asks if there's someplace private they can talk.

He guides her into his office and shuts the door behind them. "I hope this isn't about one of my students."

Macy takes the chair on offer. "Actually, it's about a past student. I assume you've heard Grace Adams witnessed a murder yesterday morning."

He stops moving. "Am I a suspect?"

"We checked. We know you were here."

Instead of sitting, David leans against the desk. He pulls up his trousers at the hem and scratches his ankle. "In that case what can I do for you?"

"Let's consider it homework. I need to learn more about Grace Adams but there are very few people who are close to her."

"Getting close to Grace Adams nearly cost me my job."

"I've looked into the allegations made against you when you were her teacher at Collier High School. There was no evidence of inappropriate behavior. You went to your superiors and told them your concerns about Grace prior to the charges being leveled."

"Unfortunately, it's a known hazard in the teaching profession. I'm just thankful the accusations were never made public. It would have ended my career."

"You transferred schools shortly afterward?"

"I thought it would be easier for everyone concerned if I moved on. I don't regret it. This is a smaller school but has more opportunities. I'm already the vice principal. I'm making a real difference."

"So you don't blame Grace for what happened?"

"No," he says, shifting his weight. "She was special. Really bright but very troubled. She used to eat lunch in my classroom because she felt safe there. I'm not sure if you have access to her school records but it's all there in black and white. Grace was the victim of a prolonged campaign of bullying."

"Any particular kids come to mind?"

"Yeah, a couple of them were my accusers, Sissy Olsen and her boyfriend Dwayne Harris."

"Do you have any idea why they made false charges?"

He puffs out his cheeks. "I flunked them in English."

"That's all it takes?"

"You'd be surprised."

"Given what I do for a living, nothing surprises me anymore."

"I imagine not."

"So during lunch you and Grace discussed literary classics?"

"That and other stuff. She'd talk a lot about dying. According to the doctors she didn't have long to live."

"Did you ever discuss her mother?"

"Not directly, but it came up in her short stories and poetry. Even for a teenager, they were fairly dark. She wrote about a young girl trapped in a trailer for three days waiting for her mother to come home."

Macy glances up at him from her notebook. "Actually, that really happened."

He puts his hand on his forehead and closes his eyes. "Well, now I know why it was such a good story."

"In the story, did the mother come back?"

"Nope, the father came home instead."

"That's the part she made up. She doesn't know who her father is. I imagine she was looking for a replacement and found you."

"Yeah, that's what the school psychologist said. Anyway, things between me and Grace were fine for a while. She kept a respectful distance."

"What changed?"

"At some point something happened. Her whole personality shifted. She became very clingy and at times inappropriate. She started calling me at home. Sometimes I thought she was following me. I let the principal know. We talked to the family." He looks away and pokes through a pile of papers on his desk. "It just got worse."

"And she was fourteen at the time?"

"That sounds about right."

"Did you ever suspect abuse?"

"Of course, but then I'd meet her with her aunt and uncle and there were no indications there were any problems. I thought maybe it dated back to when she was with her mother."

"Have you had any contact with her family at all?"

"Grace called me last Friday."

"Had she been in touch with you previously?"

"No, this is the first time I'd spoken to her in four years."

"What did she want?"

He scratches his cheek. "You know, I'm not really sure. She apologized for her behavior back when she was my student. She said she was better now and that there was an opportunity to put things right."

"No specifics?"

"At first I thought it had to do with the heart transplant. New lease on life and all that sort of thing, but since I heard about the murder I've been replaying the conversation in my head over and over again." He pauses. "Have you identified the victim?"

"It was Grace's mother, Leanne Adams."

"Jesus Christ," he says, dragging his hands across his face. "She finally came home."

Macy stands up and hands him her card. "For now I want you to keep what I've told you to yourself. We've not released Leanne's name to the press yet."

David's head bobs up and down nervously. "Of course. How is Grace?"

"I've not had a chance to interview her so I'm not sure."

"I remember her as being very fragile."

"I suspect she still is." Macy points to her card. "If you think of anything else I want you to give me a call."

6

Jared sits on his sofa, strumming his guitar and singing to himself in a low voice. Every so often he writes down a couple of chords, doubles back, and repeats. His dogs are sleeping at his feet, snoring in the half-light. The television is on, but the volume is turned down. Jared flips through the channels regularly. One minute it's football, the next a basketball game. He's got money on both.

The dogs put their heads up at the same time, letting out a low growl before racing toward the front door, teeth bared and barking. A car's headlights fill his front windows with fractured light. Jared moves beyond his reflection in the glass and peers out into the night, watching the lights dim. The engine cuts and a door slams shut and there's Hayley taking a final pull off a cigarette before flicking it into the snow. She's carrying a handbag and a bottle of whiskey and wears nothing more than a pair of tight jeans and a T-shirt. Outside it's below zero and the temperature is dropping.

Jared had tried to put her off coming to see him, but she wasn't having it. *Come on,* she purred into the phone, *you know you want my company. And don't tell me that Lexxie's there. I know she's working.* He leaned against his refrigerator drinking his beer, trying to be nice, but he was still telling her she shouldn't come. She teased him then, saying he should quit being such a *fucking Boy Scout*. He laughed, which was probably his biggest mistake. Trying to rectify the situation, he reminded her that she was married. It was her turn to laugh. *Since when has that ever mattered to you?* She hung up and Jared was left listening to a dial tone. He tried to call her back a few times but predictably her phone went straight to voicemail. He knew she was on her way.

He pulls the door open expecting her anger, but she's jumping into his arms and kissing him hard on the mouth before he can even say hello. Jared feels how easy it is to slip into this habit they have and hates himself even more. He makes his face immobile, closing his mouth on hers and pushing away. He has to end this.

Jared looks her straight in the eyes when he speaks. "I told you on the phone. We can't be doing this anymore."

Hayley cracks a smile and swings the neck of the whiskey bottle between her fingers. "I need a drink if you're going to get all serious on me." She sashays into the kitchen, making sure to give him a good view of her ass.

Jared leans against the doorframe and watches her pour.

"Ice?" She reaches for the freezer door, her shirt riding up in front, showing off her pierced navel.

"Fuck if I know," he grumbles. "Look in the freezer." This game they play is exhausting.

Hayley stands in the middle of the kitchen holding an ice tray, an uncertain look on her face. "What's going on?"

Jared rests his head back against the wall and frowns. "I don't want to do this anymore. You're married. You've got kids. Us sneaking around like this." He knocks his head against the wall to emphasize his point. "It's not fair to Lexxie. She deserves better from me."

Hayley's eyes light up and her voice grows more animated with each word. "What if we just tell everyone we're together so we can quit sneaking around? We could sleep in the same bed every night. You could finally get rid of that boring girlfriend of yours." She walks up to him and slides a chilled finger down his cheek. "You'd like that."

"Hayley, that's never going to happen and you know it."

"But I love you."

"It doesn't matter."

Hayley digs her fingers into his shirt. Her voice is low and demanding. "And you love me."

He can't look at her. "Not anymore."

"Don't say things that aren't true," she whispers, unsure. "Now you're just being mean."

"Fuck." He loosens her grip and grabs his drink off the counter. "We've done this so many times. You're never going to leave Brian."

She pulls a cigarette out of a pack and casts around for a lighter. "I have to see you. Seeing you is the only thing that keeps me sane."

"And what about my sanity?" he asks. He finishes off his glass of whiskey and pours another. He raises his voice for the first time. "I can't give you what you want anymore."

Leaving the cigarette unlit, Hayley takes the bottle from him and moves to the living room. She curls up on the sofa and stares at the silent television, not saying a word.

"Are you going to say anything?" he asks.

Hayley pours another drink.

"You understand what I'm saying?"

Hayley's eyes snap at him like they're baby birds wanting to be fed. She won't cry. He's never seen her cry. It's her temper that worries Jared.

Her voice comes out as a hiss. "So all these times we've been together. I don't mean jack to you?"

Jared sits across from her on the coffee table and places a hesitant hand on her knee. He squeezes it gently and tries to hold his nerve. "Of course it's meant something to me. I like spending time with you. I care about you." His hands fly up in the air. "Which is why we can't sleep together anymore. It confuses everything." He stops for a moment and lowers his voice further. "We should just be friends."

Hayley's lip curls when her eyes light on his. Her glass trembles in her hand as she puts it to her lips. "Friends?" She laughs high and uneven. "Brian doesn't even let me talk to you and you've got Lexxie sniffing around all the time. How are we supposed to be friends?" She puts down her drink before taking his hand and pressing it to her cheek. "I promise I'll be better. I won't call so often. I won't come by at night. You just have to let me know when I can see you again, that's all."

Hayley scoots up to the edge of the sofa so they're closer, one of her knees nestling between his legs. She lowers her voice to a whisper and tilts her head upward so she's looking straight at him. "It's the not knowing that makes me a little crazy."

Jared closes his eyes and she puts her hand to his face, stroking his eyelids with her fingertips. He curves his cheek into her cupped hand and makes a noise that almost sounds like crying. Her lips move across his lower jaw and onto his mouth. He pushes her away but she only holds on tighter. She crawls onto his lap, wrapping her legs around his waist, rocking against him with her hips.

Jared lifts her onto the sofa, stretching out on top of her, giving in like he always does. Losing to her arms, to her frantic need for him, to the lightness of her touch. This thing wins every time. An endless loop. Tomorrow he'll sink down to a lower level. Tomorrow she'll fall off the edge of his world. Tomorrow will come no matter how good it is tonight.

Later, wrapped up in Jared's bedding, they're almost asleep. Hayley curls around him, her legs entangled with his. She's nestled in the crook of his arm, resting her head on his shoulder. Her breathing is soft and one of her hands sits flat on his chest. Jared kisses the top of her head, imagining the thoughts worming around inside her.

Out of habit he asks if she's okay.

"Yeah, I suppose so. Brian's been away ice fishing so it's been quiet."

Jared brushes the hair out of his eyes. Hayley's husband works as a long-haul trucker and is often out of town for weeks on end. "I thought you told me he was working. When is he back?"

She yawns. "Tomorrow maybe. I'm not sure."

"So he could come back tonight?"

"No," she mumbles. "I spoke to him earlier. Definitely tomorrow."

Jared stares at the ceiling. It's quiet outside. As far as he can tell no cars have passed down his road in hours. "How are your girls?"

She props up her chin so she can look at him. "They're fine. My sister is with them." She hesitates. "Brian is being weird lately."

"What do you mean?"

"He's on edge."

Jared runs his hand over her shoulder. "Has he hurt you?"

She shakes her head. "We had one of his friends over for dinner the other night and Brian drank too much. The next thing you know he's threatening to kill this guy if he doesn't stay away from us."

"Sounds like he's jealous."

"Maybe, but it's not like the guy tried to feel me up in the kitchen."

"Brian calmed down though?"

"Yeah, eventually, but I was so embarrassed. Dustin is the only friend Brian has that I actually like. God knows what would happen if Brian found out that he stops by sometimes to help me out when he's on the road."

"Maybe Brian should be jealous. This guy sounds perfect."

She digs her chin into his chest. "You're perfect."

"I'm not."

She raises her voice. "You are for me."

"Hayley, I'm sorry, but I'm not. We've talked about this."

Hayley lowers her head back into the crook of his arm and closes her eyes. For a long time neither of them says a word.

"Hayley, this has to be the last time," he says, feeling her soft body go rigid. "I'm not ever doing this again. It's over between us." Jared kisses the top of her head and holds her a little tighter.

A few hours later he wakes up in an empty bed.

"What in the hell were you thinking?" Jared leans forward in his truck, hunched over his steering wheel like a gargoyle. Sucking hard on a cigarette, he strains his neck, peering under the thick layer of frost that hasn't had time to melt from his windshield. His vision is myopic at best. Words fire like shots from a gun; short blasts followed by guilty silence. He takes furtive glances at his passenger.

Hayley isn't listening. She rests her cheek against the cool of the window, her damp hair sticking to a face as gray as river stone. Her lips are open and she draws shallow breaths too quiet to count. She's no longer holding her wrists above her heart as directed. Two well-bundled appendages sit askew on her lap, jumping up and down with every bump in the road. The white gauze is soaked through with her blood and taped with such violence her fingers are turning blue.

Jared hits ice and the back end of the truck fishtails to the left, coming close enough to kiss a high cement retaining wall. His expression grim, he turns the wheel a fraction and the truck is on course once more. The road dips and the truck leaps upward, briefly losing traction. A chunk of ice breaks free from his windshield and slides away. His vision cleared, Jared sits up in the driver's seat. On the right-hand side of the road, the Flathead River runs close and deep, a thirty-foot plunge just beyond the guardrail. As he takes a curve he catches sight of the icy water and thinks about how he'd like to be clean again. Covered in Hayley's blood, his hands stick to the molded plastic of the steering wheel.

He looks at Hayley again and lowers his voice, his pulse, and his expectations, addressing his passenger with more patience than he feels. "Hang in there. You're going to be fine."

His headache is a slow-traveling bullet moving forward from the back of his skull. The exit wound is his left eye. It twitches. He swallows back the sick in his throat and holds the wheel a little tighter.

At the hospital Jared swings his truck onto the ramp marked EMER-GENCY ENTRANCE. A sign looms ahead: EMERGENCY VEHICLES ONLY. He ignores it and heads straight for the sliding glass doors, screeching to a halt and laying on the horn with the flat of his bloody palms.

Before help has time to arrive, Jared's out of the truck and pulling open the passenger door. Hayley half falls out, her bandaged limbs hanging limp, her torso caught in the seat belt. She's lifeless but breathing. The doors slide open behind him and there's a rush of movement. The voices are all familiar, but there's a strain in their words, like they're holding back on all the questions they really want to ask. Hayley is unresponsive when they load her onto a gurney.

The doctor on duty doesn't waste time with small talk. "Fuck, Jared, what happened?" Compared to outside, the interior of the hospital feels like a sauna.

Jared keeps his head down, shying away from the fluorescent lights that line the ceiling. "She called me this morning in a panic so I went to check on her." He pauses, filling in the blanks as he goes. "God, that must have been a little before seven. I don't know how long she'd been bleeding when I found her."

They move past the nurse's desk and he spots his girlfriend, Lexxie, holding an admissions clipboard in her hands. He focuses in on it, imagining the spot where she will take pen to paper and seal his fate.

"When did this happen? Where are her kids?" Lexxie runs alongside them. She looks back toward the doors, expecting to see the entire family traipsing into the ER. "Where's Brian?"

Jared doesn't answer. Hayley's eyes pop when the gurney is jostled. She reaches for his hand. Beside him he hears Lexxie mumble something under her breath but he can't make out the words.

"Brian's away, isn't he?" Lexxie finally manages to catch Jared's eye. A quiet look of disapproval hangs around her neat features but she doesn't raise her voice against him. She directs her frustration at Hayley instead. "Hayley," she shouts. "Where are your children?"

At the mention of her kids, Hayley heaves her body up from the gurney and grabs Jared's collar. Wide-eyed and scared, her face is only inches from his. He's seen that look in addicts but never in her. She smells of booze and cigarette smoke. Lexxie drops the clipboard and helps pry Hayley off him one finger at a time. Fabric rips and Hayley's left holding a piece of his collar but nothing else.

Jared backs away and watches her flop about the rolling platform like a landed fish. She twists around her neck so she can see him, screaming his name. The shredded fabric from his collar flutters to the floor. Jared staggers a few feet farther and leans heavily on the nurse's desk. He looks down at his work boots, noticing that they too are splattered with her blood. He closes his eyes and waits for the thick surgery room doors to deaden her cries.

Lexxie slaps her clipboard down on the counter. "Looks as if you've had some morning." She gestures to his bloody hands as she slides around to the other side of the desk. "Anything you want to tell me?"

Jared flicks his eyes up at her. Her gray eyes blink back at him. He can tell she's trying her best not to cry. He knows she'll hate herself later if she causes a scene.

He has nothing he can say in his defense. "I'm sorry."

"Saying sorry really doesn't cut it."

Jared can't believe what he's about to ask of her until he does. "I need your help."

There's a high note in her voice that wasn't there previously. "You're asking me for help?"

"You've met Hayley's husband."

"Everyone's met Brian," she says, filling in Hayley's admission form, her pen audible as it scratches hard against the paper. "They're an accident-prone family."

He watches her closely for any sign of sympathy. "He can't know I brought her in. He can't know I was with her."

Like she's weighing the two possibilities in her head, she nods imperceptibly and fills in the admission form with a flourish. Afterward she shows him the evidence of their pact.

Jared's jaw goes slack. "You've been here working all night. You can't put down that we brought her in together. Are you nuts?"

"I can't very well leave it blank."

"Lexxie, anybody checks and they'll know you've lied. You could lose your job."

"Well, you better hope nobody checks."

He starts to speak, but she cuts him off.

"And just so you know, this is the last time I put up with this shit. I swear I'll call up Brian myself and tell him all about you and Hayley if this happens again." All business, she checks the clock on the wall. "Just go, your shift is starting soon."

Jared stands his ground. "Brian will kill her if he finds out. You can't go making threats like that."

"Yes, I can." Lexxie's eyes flick upward as if she's expecting patience to be delivered from on high. "You don't think it's too much to ask. Do you? A little loyalty. I'm supposed to be your girlfriend, for God's sakes. I'm the one spending Christmas at your parents', not Hayley."

Jared places his elbows on the counter and presses his fingers hard into his forehead. The pain he's feeling is much sharper now.

Lexxie leans in and speaks softly. "Are you okay?"

His voice is muffled. "I feel like my head is going to split open."

She puts a hand on his shoulder. "I'll get you something."

The staff locker room smells of cleaning fluids and wet towels. Jared heads straight to a small bathroom, locking the door behind him. For a long time he stands immobile, white-knuckling the sink. He wishes that somehow he could go back to when Hayley first drove up to his house the night before.

The bathroom door muffles Carson's words. "Hey, Jared," he says in a voice that never fails to sound comical. "You okay in there? Lexxie told me what happened."

Carson waits a few seconds, and Jared imagines Carter's head tilted toward the door expectantly. He's a shade taller than Jared and several years younger. His blond hair is cut short, making his sharp chin and long nose even more pronounced.

He knocks on the door. "I brought you another shirt."

Jared splashes his face with cold water, but it does nothing for him. He puts his hand in front of his mouth and blows and whiskey's sour breath wafts right back in his face. His reflection in the mirror is a confession of sorts; his hooded eyes, bloated complexion, and unshaven cheeks are all evidence. Jared leans against the closed bathroom door and lights a cigarette. His face relaxes after a couple of drags. He blows smoke up at the No Smoking sign. He asks if Hayley's mother has arrived yet.

"Haven't seen her," says Carson, just inches from Jared, leaning on the other side of the door, a mirror image minus the cigarette and hangover. "Lexxie pointed me in your direction. If I didn't know her better, I'd swear she's on the verge of a nervous breakdown."

Jared takes another drag. "What was I thinking?"

"When a woman like Hayley crawls through your window in the middle of the night I imagine *thinking* doesn't really come into it."

Jared bangs his head against his side of the door. "Yeah, it's not like we ever do much talking."

"I imagine not. So what happened this time?"

"I told her it was over. Brian is going to kill me when he finds out."

"That's not going to happen."

"Lexxie threatened to tell him everything and this time I think she just might do it." Jared opens the door and Carson falls inward, holding two cups of coffee.

"Damn, Jared, a little warning."

Jared watches the locker room swim for a few seconds too long. He puts his hand to the door frame and gulps for air. If he didn't know any better, he'd think he was six feet underwater. Carson places the coffee cups on the bench and puts a reassuring hand on his partner's bare shoulder.

"Hey, buddy," he says, searching for life signs in Jared's eyes. "Are you in there somewhere?"

Jared blinks. "Whatever Lexxie gave me for my headache is giving me the spins."

"Why don't you go lie down," says Carson, taking hold of Jared and leading him to a cot that sits in the back of the locker room. "I'll tell dispatch you're not well enough to work this morning."

7

Macy stands in the shadow of the open doorway watching Grace Adams. She's never seen someone sit so still. She's nothing like the little girl Macy met eleven years ago. Macy remembers a skinny kid who couldn't stop moving. Grace wore a summer dress a couple sizes too big, and her bangs had been so random, Macy thought she must have taken pinking shears to them. Eleven years on and Grace is the very model of composure. Her pale face is unblemished and her shoulder-length black hair hangs perfectly straight. It's only when Grace looks up that Macy sees something familiar. The girl's eyes are still haunted. Macy takes a deep breath and reminds herself to take it slow. Somehow she's going to have to earn Grace's trust.

Macy knocks twice. "So who's Sam?" she says in a voice that is not from Collier.

Not waiting for an answer, Macy closes the door behind her and walks across the floor in her flat black boots. Making an exaggerated groan she leans over and picks up a pink teddy bear with a bandaged forehead from the floor. She turns it over in her hands before placing it on the bed next to Grace. She pokes through the get-well cards on the side table, picking one up and scrutinizing the message on the front cover. All the while she's observing Grace from the corner of her eye. The girl's dark eyes follow her every move, but she never once changes her pale expression. Macy decides she looks like a doll.

"There's an old guy named Sam out there looking for someone named George," Macy says by way of explanation. With difficulty she settles down in the vacant chair.

Grace stares at her. "Do I know you?"

Macy only says, "Not yet," before pulling a small notebook from her bag. She takes a pen out of the breast pocket of her blazer.

"Are you a reporter or something?"

"No, but I am something." She looks directly at Grace. "You haven't been talking to reporters, have you?"

"No, ma'am. I haven't been talking to anyone."

Macy pulls a bifold wallet out of her jacket pocket and flips it open. It's a man's wallet and it's well worn. Macy shows Grace the police badge. Grace reaches out and touches it, running her fingertips along the design stamped into the metal. Macy notes that Grace's nails are chipped and bitten to the quick. She is not so changed after all.

"Just like in the movies. You see what it says here?" She points to the engraved inscription.

"Detective," reads Grace. Her eyes widen and Macy notices how she backs away a fraction. "You're a detective?"

"Yes, I'm a special investigator for the state. My name is Detective Greeley but you can call me Macy."

"You're pregnant?"

"I am."

Grace tilts her head to the side. "You're not from around here."

"I'm normally down in Helena but I've got a nice room at the Collier Motor Lodge I'm calling home for the time being. Have you ever been to Helena?"

Grace lowers her voice. "The hospital there is much nicer than this one."

Macy doesn't disagree. Collier County Hospital seems like the sort of place people come to die. "I've got a few questions."

"About what happened?"

Macy flips through her notebook until she finds a blank page. "You don't remember me, do you?"

"No, ma'am."

"I met you eleven years ago just after your mother left town. I was investigating the deaths of four young women. They would have been about the age you are now. Are you sure you don't remember?"

"Did you ever catch the men who killed them?"

"No, I'm afraid I didn't, but that doesn't mean I've stopped trying."

Grace places her hands palm down on her lap. "Sam was the head janitor here for thirty-three years but he's retired now."

"He didn't seem very retired to me."

Grace almost smiles. "That's because he couldn't stand being away. From what I've heard, he practically lives at the hospital now."

"Is he still the janitor?"

She makes a face. "I think he's a bit of everything. He helps out whenever they need him."

"Sounds like a nice guy."

"Sometimes he gets on your nerves but I think most people are fond of him."

"Your doctors say you had a panic attack yesterday. They had to sedate you. Are you feeling better now?"

Grace nods.

"You're sure?"

Grace looks toward the door. "Shouldn't my aunt be here with me?"

Macy folds her hands on her lap and looks Grace in the eye. "Grace, you're nearly eighteen."

Grace focuses straight ahead and grips the bedsheets. "I didn't know him. The man who attacked my mother, I didn't know him."

"We found the car your mother drove. Canadian plates but it's not registered to her." Macy has spoken to the Canadian authorities. She'll make a trip over the border if anything interesting comes up about the owner.

"I don't understand."

"It's nothing for you to worry about. It just means we have to work a bit harder trying to figure out where she's been all these years. There is a possibility her return is somehow linked to her murder."

Grace fidgets with the tubes stuck into her arm.

Macy speaks softly. "Did she say anything?"

"She didn't say anything important."

"After eleven years? You'd think she'd have something to say."

"She said she loved me and she was sorry for being away."

Macy takes Grace's hand and squeezes it. "But Grace, that *is* important. Had she been in touch at all?"

"She always sent me money on my birthdays." Grace presses a tissue to her eyes and rocks back and forth. "It had been so long I didn't recognize her."

"There was probably a good reason for her to stay away all these years. Do you remember anything about the night she left?"

"I've never understood any of it. I don't know why she left without me. I don't understand why she never came back." Grace's hands begin to shake.

Before continuing Macy gives Grace a few minutes to calm down. "Did your mother say anything about the man who attacked her?"

Grace stares off into the distance and remains silent.

"Grace," says Macy, waving a hand in the airspace between them when Grace's eyes start to droop. "You in there somewhere?" Dr. Gibson had warned her that Grace had a tendency to fall asleep when she was stressed. *There's nothing really wrong with her,* she said. *We're sure it's just a defense mechanism.*

"I don't like trying to remember," says Grace.

"Just start by telling me what happened earlier that morning. We'll slowly work our way toward the difficult part," says Macy, making notes in neat little rows.

Grace lowers her gaze and speaks in a monotone. She tells Macy that she cleaned up the kitchen after her aunt left for work. "I made breakfast for her. She's been so busy looking after me I decided it would be nice to do something for her. I usually don't have much energy in the mornings."

"Did you hear the garbage truck come?"

"Yeah, but by then I was up in my room getting dressed."

Macy stops her. "When they found you in the woods you were only wearing a red baby-doll nightie. Why was that? Were you expecting someone?"

"When I went outside I was wearing my kimono. It's long and it covers everything."

"Kimono?"

"It belonged to my mother. I like to wear it sometimes."

Macy makes some notes. "Where is it?"

"Out in the woods; I used it to try to stop the bleeding."

"It's out in the woods?"

"I saw the paramedics throw it to one side. There are keys to the back doors and the garden gate in the pocket."

Macy raises a hand and asks her to hold that thought. She pulls out her cell phone and barks instructions. The woods and the house need to be checked. They should be looking for a key and a silk kimono. She repeats the word "kimono" several times and then spells it for whoever is listening. She also tells them to dust the back gate for fingerprints if they haven't already.

Macy's voice is gentle when she speaks again. "Sorry about that, Grace. The missing keys worry me." She checks her notes. "So, you saw everything from the window up in your room."

Grace presses her fingertips to her eyes and bends forward. "I'm not sure why I looked out the window."

"Did you hear something?"

"Maybe. I might have just seen something move. Sometimes we get elk moving along the hillside beyond the back gate."

"Do you know what time this was?"

"A little after ten, I guess. I wasn't really keeping track."

"Who did you see first?"

"My mother. She was walking through the trees real slowly. She was stooped over and looked really old."

"You didn't recognize her?"

"I just figured she was a vagrant, living in one of the empty houses in my neighborhood."

Macy arches an eyebrow. "It's not really a neighborhood if you don't have neighbors."

"Sometimes at night I can see their fires."

"Well, it's been cold and they've got no place to go."

"That's what my aunt says."

"The police are searching all the houses and clearing them out."

"They'll be back."

"Do you often get homeless coming to the house?"

"Sometimes, but we don't give them anything. There are too many. My aunt and I volunteer down at the mission instead."

"That's very kind of you."

"My aunt is the one who is kind. I just go along because I've got nothing better to do."

"When did you see the man?"

Grace turns away and looks out the window. The whites of her eyes look raw under the lamplight. "He was hard to see at first."

"Why's that?"

"He was wearing a camouflage coat. He was practically standing in front of my mother when I first saw him."

"So he didn't look homeless."

"No," she said, her eyes widening. "He was wearing proper winter gear. His hat had earflaps and his face was covered."

"Did he wear a ski mask?"

"I think it was black."

"Can you describe him?"

"Not really, I couldn't see his face."

"What about his build?"

"He was tall, possibly stocky, but with the big coat on it's hard to be sure. He was much taller than my mother. He towered over her."

"Did he move in any particular way? For instance, did he have a limp?"

"No, nothing like that."

"Was he carrying any flowers?"

Grace places her fingertips to her throat and holds them there. For a few seconds she says nothing. She stutters when she speaks again. "I don't. I don't remember anything like that. Why?"

Macy looks at her notes. "It's just something we found. It may be unrelated."

"I thought the man and my mother knew each other." Grace describes how they'd faced each other in the woods. "They might have even said a few words. I'm not sure. It happened so quickly. My mother backed away and started screaming. He went up the hill after her."

"When did you realize it was your mom?"

Grace looks away again. "When he attacked her she screamed my name. I wasn't sure at that point but I had to find out."

"So you went out looking for her?"

Grace says a quiet yes.

"You had no shoes and were only wearing a silk kimono and a baby-doll nightie."

"Yes, ma'am."

"You must see how crazy that sounds."

"I could hear her moaning. I couldn't just leave her out there on her own."

"Weren't you frightened that the man who attacked your mother was still around?"

Grace blinks for the first time. "I saw him disappear over the ridge. He was long gone by the time I went out in the garden."

"It was still pretty brave to go out there."

"That's what Jared said."

"I interviewed him. He said he spoke to you."

Graces slips a dark knitted cap between her fingers. "He gave me his hat."

"That's sweet," says Macy, making a note to tell Jared to watch himself.

They both look up to see Lexxie standing in the doorway. Macy keeps her voice low. "Doesn't anyone knock around here?"

Lexxie gestures toward Grace. "Excuse me, I've got a few things to do in here."

Macy flashes her badge. "We're in the middle of something. Can you come back in half an hour?"

Lexxie gives Grace a little wave and heads out the door, promising she'll be back soon.

"She's one of the nice ones," says Grace.

"Aren't they all supposed to be nice?"

"Not to me they're not."

"Why do you suppose that is?"

"My mother mostly."

"Your mother has been gone for eleven years. You would have thought they'd have moved on by now."

"Collier never moves on."

Macy keeps her eyes on Grace. "Well, at any rate, it's good to know Jared is with someone *nice*."

"What do you mean?"

Macy tilts her head toward the door. "Lexxie is Jared's girlfriend."

Grace hands tighten around the cap. "I didn't know."

"Well, now you do." Macy seesaws her pen with her fingers. "Did you know the fire trail behind your house ends at Dray Creek Lane?"

"Until the day before yesterday I'd never been on the trail."

"No matter. Anyway, there's evidence that a car was parked near the trailhead. There's a nice big rectangle where the snow isn't quite as deep as everywhere else. Went out and found it myself. So I'm thinking the killer parked there and then hiked the rest of the way to your house. It's only a little over a mile."

"Why would he do that?"

"I'm asking myself the same question. No one uses the road much except during hunting season. He would have been confident he could come and go unseen. We're clearing away the snow and looking for tire tracks. Who knows what we might find?"

Macy picks up her phone again, scrolling through the numbers to find the one she needs. "Hello, Colin. This is Detective Macy Greeley. We spoke earlier."

"What can I do for you?"

"I need you to track down the sketch artist. His name is Robert and I think he's hanging out down in the cafeteria. I'm just finishing so bring him up here in ten minutes."

"Is he the guy who looks like a liberal?"

"Yeah, but try to be nice to him anyway."

Macy hangs up and gives Grace a friendly smile. "I know you said you didn't see him very well, but Robert is good at what he does. He can probably help you remember details you've forgotten."

Grace shrugs.

Macy looks at her notes. "I've got it written here that your uncle ran a trucking company? Cross Border Trucking?"

"Yes, ma'am. We didn't find out until after he died that things weren't going too well."

"Your doctor told me that your uncle was against you having the operation."

"I guess he had his reasons."

"Didn't you find it a little odd?"

"I don't know. I suppose so."

"You're lucky your aunt didn't feel the same way."

Grace runs her palms downward across her face, eventually making two tight little fists, which she rests against her chin. "I'm not feeling so lucky these days."

"Were you close to your uncle?"

"We used to go on camping trips together. He was always very protective of me."

"And yet he didn't want you to have a lifesaving operation? Strange." Macy pulls out a business card and places it on Grace's lap. "You're to call me if you remember anything new."

"Do you think you'll find him?"

"I hope so. I seem to have a knack for finding people. That's why they've brought me up from Helena." Macy rises from her chair.

"I think my mother rang the front doorbell."

Macy bites her lip. "What makes you say that?"

"When I was up in my room it rang several times, but I was on my own in the house so I ignored it."

"That's understandable."

"But not so lucky."

"No," Macy admits. "Not so lucky."

Macy leaves Grace with the sketch artist and slips into the hospital chapel for privacy. Warren answers on the third try.

"Sorry, it's a bit hectic over here."

"Please tell me you found the house keys."

"I wish that were the case. As far as we can tell the killer used them to get into the house last night."

Macy starts pacing between the pews. "What's been taken?"

"We're not sure, but Arnold Lamm's office has been thoroughly searched. It looks like an entire file cabinet has been cleaned out. Then upstairs in Grace's room there's been some vandalism."

"What do you mean by vandalism?"

"There's a fairly strange message written on the wall. A forensics team arrives any minute. I'll have them get started immediately."

Macy slumps down in a pew and stares up at the cross above the altar. "This is a major screwup."

"Not our finest hour. I was out there searching the hillside along with everyone else. I don't know how we could have missed it."

"Stranger still is that the killer thought to come back for it."

"He might have stuck around for longer than we realized."

"At this point there's no way of knowing. He may have just got lucky." She looks at her watch. "I'm going to speak to Grace's doctors. It makes sense for her and her aunt to come have a look. They can tell us if anything is missing."

"Elizabeth isn't going to take the news well."

"I imagine not. I'll call you when I have a better idea when I can head up there. In the meantime, let me know if you find anything."

"Will do," he says before ending the call.

8

Jared stares at the low basement ceiling and watches the tail end of the fluorescent lights blink on and off. His eyes follow a line of exposed piping and he counts three disused fire sprinklers. Cobwebs hang off thickly wrapped cables like tinsel that's lost its shine. The narrow bed where he's been sleeping in fits and starts is hidden in the back corner of the men's locker room, a concrete wall to one side and the backside of a bank of lockers along the other. Unwelcome images have run through his dreams in loops, doubling back to overtake him just as he thinks he's broken free. A discarded shoe and a red stain in the snow—that's how he found Grace and her mother. That's what he saw. His dreams of Hayley are more frantic. No matter what he does, the gauze he uses to wrap her wrists keeps falling apart like wet tissue. He can't stop the bleeding.

The two pills Lexxie gave him had looked harmless, but in the intervening hours, he's passed in and out of unwanted dreams and memories. In his lucid moments he knows there is something worrying about how he feels, but his concerns fade each time he drifts off into pleasant numbness.

Jared listens to the sharp tapping of a woman's heels on the hard-tiled floor. He smells her before he sees her. It's a fragrance that reminds him of a flower but he doesn't feel confident enough to give it a name. But he'd know those heels anywhere. Somehow, Hayley's mother has managed to find him.

Pamela Larson is dressed in a powder blue jacket and skirt. Her blouse is white and crisply ironed and there is not a stray blond hair on her head. It's been thirty-two years since she gave birth to Hayley and her twin sister Angie, but the only place her age shows is in her hands; they're a contour map of raised blue veins. She gives Jared a worried smile and sits down on the edge of his narrow bed.

"You okay?" she asks, reaching out to touch him lightly on the forearm with a chilled hand.

Jared doesn't know if he's okay or not. He only wants to fall asleep again. He sits up, inching his way toward the wall, but her hand doesn't slide away like he wants it to. He notices her nails are painted pale pink. *Talons,* he thinks.

"How's Hayley?" he asks, rubbing his damp face.

"She's confused. She's lost a lot of blood."

Jared pictures his bathroom floor. He already knows too much about the blood she's lost. "Is she awake?"

"She's awake and talking."

"What's she saying?"

"She's saying what I tell her to say." She digs her nails into Jared's arm.

He winces. "And what's that?"

"That she was upset and called you so you came and took her to the hospital." She eases her grip and pats his arm. "You saved her life so she's grateful."

"Not so sure about that." Jared leans back and closes his eyes.

Pamela doesn't skip a beat. "Which part? Saving her life or her being grateful?"

"Both, I guess."

Pamela rolls her eyes.

Jared's sluggish mind has difficulty putting together a coherent sentence. "I mean she did it because of me, and the way she fought when I tried to help makes me think she really wanted to die."

"That's nonsense. If you really want to kill yourself, you don't do it in a paramedic's house." She lays her hands flat on her powder blue skirt. The diamond on her wedding ring is the size of a pecan. "Brian is the reason she did it. Not you."

"If Brian finds out that Hayley spent the night at my place, I'm as good as dead." Jared thinks for a slow second. "Ditto for Hayley."

Pamela puts her hand back on Jared's forearm, gently this time. "Then he can't ever find out. The police and the doctors have no reason to question our version of events. So relax. You're a hero."

Jared won't look her in the eye.

Pamela tells him that she's heard about what happened behind the Adamses' house.

"It's been a difficult couple of days for a lot of people."

"Still, that's all anyone in this town is going to be talking about."

"I can't get what I saw out there out of my head," he says, his eyes welling up. "And a day later I find Hayley on my bathroom floor."

"That girl Grace. She's an interesting one. Those clothes she wears."

Jared can only imagine her red nightie and the scar running down her chest like a zipper. "What do you mean?"

"She dresses like my grandmother. I imagine she smells like an old folks' home."

"I don't know how she's managing. I'd be a wreck if I saw my own mother murdered." Jared backtracks when he remembers he's supposed to keep some things to himself. "I shouldn't have said . . ."

"That woman had a lot of nerve showing her face in this town after what she did to my family." She digs her fingers into Jared's arm again. "Do you know anything about Leanne?"

Jared pulls away. "I've heard rumors."

"They're not rumors. That woman was a nightmare. Leaving Grace behind was the kindest thing she's ever done for that child."

"She was lucky her aunt and uncle took her in."

"There was nothing lucky about it. Elizabeth couldn't have children. She probably had her sights on Grace from the day she was born. I have to hand it to her though, she got what she wanted in the end."

"What about Hayley's kids? Are they okay?"

"I went and picked them up this morning. Isobel had her younger sisters up and dressed for school. She'd even made breakfast. That's quite a lot for a nine-year-old to accomplish before nine in morning."

"I didn't know," he mumbles into his shirtsleeve, noting that the fabric feels pleasant on his cheek. "Whenever I asked after them, she'd always say her sister was staying over."

Pamela purses her lips. Her disappointment in her twin daughters is familiar territory for anyone who lives in Collier. "Angie's in Chicago. She claims to have been shortlisted for a spot on the Chicago Bears cheerleading squad."

Jared laughs, but Pamela's face remains immobile.

"I'm sorry," he says, forcing his features to mirror hers. He ends up looking lopsided.

"Sometimes I wonder if that girl ever looks in a full-length mirror. She's twice the size of Hayley and can barely get her fat ass off the couch to answer the phone."

Jared wants to sleep again. He yawns, hoping Pamela will get the hint. "I would have never let Hayley stay over if I knew the kids were on their own."

"A girl like Hayley, you should have checked."

"They might take her kids away," he says, thinking the courts already have enough reasons to declare her an unfit mother. "Or Brian might leave her and claim full custody."

"We'll lie and say they were with me." She presses harder into her thighs. The blue-veined rivers swell on the backs of her hands. "The police will want to talk to you."

Jared keeps his mouth shut.

"You okay with lying?"

He yawns again. He thinks of asking the time but forgets. "I have to be, don't I?" He remembers Hayley's car and his eyes widen. "Her car is still at my place."

She fidgets with her phone, frustrated there's no coverage. "I'll deal with that. I'll also tell everyone that her father and I cleaned up her place."

Jared relaxes.

"I think Brian gets off on threatening her with losing the kids if she causes too much fuss."

Jared doesn't know how many times Hayley has left her kids on their own, but he imagines it's been every time she's stayed over. She's not a good liar. He should have seen through it. "She's not exactly mother of the year."

Pamela's head snaps up. "You think I don't know that. She's desperate, that's all."

They get real quiet and Jared almost falls asleep. Pamela's voice revives him, pulling him back into the room like a collared dog. "She should have never taken the fall for him on those drug possession charges. No judge in their right mind would give her custody of the girls."

"He must have bullied her into doing it. Everyone knows he's been bringing stuff over the border for years."

"He would have gone to jail. Hayley could have made a clean break. I can't believe she was so stupid."

"What about the physical abuse?"

"She's never reported it. Not once."

"Has anyone managed to contact Brian?"

"When the authorities tracked him down he said he'd been ice fishing up near Calgary."

"You didn't call him?"

"We don't talk, or rather he no longer takes my calls."

Jared keeps his thoughts to himself.

She looks around the little bunker he's sleeping in, noticing how awful it is for the first time. "Why are you still here? You should go home."

"What time is it, anyway?"

Pamela shakes her wrist so her watch sits right. "Nearly three. If you don't mind me saying so, you don't seem right."

"I think Lexxie may have slipped me a mickey."

"I imagine she's pretty angry with you."

"This might be a deal-breaker."

"Rumor is you're planning on marrying her."

"My mother's been talking too much. How she manages to spread gossip all the way from Wilmington Creek is beyond me."

"So it's true."

"Lexxie is getting impatient and I'm not getting any younger."

Pamela jostles him a bit more to keep him awake. "This place is depressing. You should get out of here. I can give you a ride."

"Can't quite face the mess."

It takes Pamela a few seconds to realize what he's talking about. "Shoot, I didn't think of that." She picks up her phone and starts to scroll through her address list. "I've been calling in favors all over town. One more isn't going to hurt."

"There are already enough people who know Hayley was at my place. Let's not add to the list."

"Are you sure?"

"This is my mess. It's up to me to clean it up." He sits up and rubs his face. "I'm going to have to work this evening. I need a shower and a cup of coffee."

"You really should go visit Hayley. She'd like to see you."

"I can't risk it. Brian might be there."

"You'll be fine. Brian said he won't be back until morning."

"I thought you said you hadn't spoken to him."

Pamela hesitates. "He left a message."

9

GRACE called, GRACE cried, GRACE shattered my deafness,
GRACE sparkled, GRACE blazed, GRACE drove away my blind-
ness, GRACE shed Her fragrance, and I drew in my breath,
and I pant for GRACE. GRACE brought Thee down from heaven;
GRACE stripped Thee of Thy glory; GRACE made Thee poor
and despicable; GRACE made Thee bear such burdens of sin.
Nothing whatever pertaining to godliness and real holiness can
be accomplished without GRACE. One who loves a pure heart
and who speaks with GRACE will have the king for a friend. It is
by GRACE you have been saved. For sin shall no longer be your
master, because you are not under the law, but under GRACE.

The words covering the wall above Grace's bed are written with a thick black marker and stand three inches high. The animal posters that once hung there have been ripped into pieces. They're scattered on the floor, crackling underfoot. Macy spots the torn chestnut mane of a once coveted mare, its silky brown eyes no more. She steps forward in shoes sheathed in protective covers and starts reading to herself.

A few feet away Warren clears his throat. "According to the brains down in Helena, most of the words have been lifted from the writings of Saint Augustine and John Bunyan. They've promised to send us the full text in the morning."

Macy doesn't turn to face him when she speaks. "Did you find the pen he used?"

"Yes, but no prints. He must have been wearing gloves. We're pretty sure he used a pen he found here. Grace's desk is filled with art supplies. There's a black marker missing from a set."

"And aside from the office downstairs, this was the only room that was disturbed?"

"That's what we're thinking, but we'll know for certain after Grace and her aunt have a look." With his gloved hands he picks through a stack of sketchbooks on the desk. "Are you sure it's such a good idea bringing them up here?"

Macy gazes out a window that overlooks the backyard. The wooded hillside is lit up with portable lights. She has told them to search the whole area again. A half-dozen police officers fan out through the trees in a single line.

"I need Grace to make sense of what's been written on this wall. Given her name is written sixteen times, I'm guessing it's personal."

Warren checks his phone. "They should be here any minute. I'll go downstairs to meet them."

"Elizabeth is pretty angry."

"That's an understatement. She didn't want us in her house and now it's a crime scene."

"I don't want her up here. I think Grace will be less inhibited on her own."

"I'll get Elizabeth started downstairs. She's gonna have a fit when she sees the mess in the office." Warren tilts his head toward the wall. "I wasn't expecting to find something like this."

"Neither was I."

"It makes me wonder if Grace was the intended target all along."

"The fact that Leanne is stabbed to death her first day back in Collier in eleven years is too much of a coincidence to ignore. What happened out in the woods was definitely about Leanne." She points to the wall. "This, however, is about Grace."

"So he wants to kill her too?"

"Perhaps, but this looks more like something a stalker would do."

"Well, I'll leave you to it then." Warren turns to go but stops. "By the way, you should have a look at Grace's sketchbooks. It's not just drawings. There's a lot of writing. Poetry, stuff like that."

"Thanks, Warren, I'll go through them when I get a chance."

Macy climbs up onto the bed and stands with her arms stretched high. The first two lines of text are well out of reach of her fingertips. The bed is made of solid oak and there are no drag marks in the carpet, which would indicate it was recently moved. The killer would have had to stand on the bed. She steps away and inspects the writing carefully. The lines are almost perfectly straight and the curves consistently uniform. It doesn't look like any handwriting she's ever seen before. He took his time. There are no spelling mistakes. The grammar is perfect. Reading Grace's name comes too easily; GRACE strikes Macy in the eyes over and over again. The wall demands her attention. GRACE, it hisses. He wrote her name sixteen times. GRACE.

Aside from the window and desk, there's a closet, two large bookcases, a chest of drawers, and a full-length mirror framed with delicate fairy lights. Macy runs her eyes over the books, stuffed animals, and dolls and is struck by everything that is missing. There is no laptop, television, or phone. The only hint that Grace might be a teenager is a modest stash of CDs and a small radio. There's only one photo sitting on the chest of drawers. Macy picks it up. Elizabeth, Arnold, and Grace stand in front of Mount Rushmore. Grace must have been around ten years old. She squints into the camera.

Macy pulls open drawers one by one. The contents are carefully folded.

Grace's undergarments are the only things that appear to have been disturbed. Macy reaches into her coat pocket and pulls out an evidence bag before plucking a silver strand of hair from where it is caught on the clasp of a bra. She holds it up to the light. It's a couple of inches long so it could belong to Elizabeth. She puts it into the bag and rummages around but she can't find anything else of interest. She closes the drawer and shifts her attention to a tube of lipstick sitting next to the framed photo.

She pulls off the cap. The color is blood red, and it's hardly been used. There's a plastic bag from Collier Drug Store. Along with more cosmetics there's a bottle of hand lotion and a box of tampons inside. Macy unfolds the receipt. None of the cosmetics are listed and the date indicates it's a recent purchase. She pictures Grace walking along the aisles filling her pockets with blusher and mascara while her aunt stands in line at the pharmacy filling Grace's prescription for immunosuppressants.

Warren knocks on the half-open door and Macy steps out into the hallway. Grace doesn't look well. Her skin has a yellowish tint, and she casts her eyes about nervously. She's propped up between Warren and Jared, but leans more heavily on Jared. Jared sways on his feet, and they almost topple like bowling pins. Macy takes Grace firmly by the elbow and guides her into the bedroom.

"This isn't going to be easy, Grace, but I need your help." She looks the young woman in the eye. "Are you sure you're feeling up to this?"

Grace's chin bobs up and down silently.

"You just say the word and I'll get you out of here."

Grace catches sight of the writing over Macy's shoulder and hesitates. "My mother's killer did that?"

"We think he broke in last night."

Grace can't take her eyes off the wall. Her mouth moves with the words but she makes no sound. Halfway through she starts to tremble. By the time she's finished she's crying.

Macy continues to hold Grace's arm. "Grace, does this mean anything to you?"

Instead of answering, Grace slips from Macy's grip, collapsing into a heap on the floor.

Jared kneels down next to her. "Warren, could you go get Carson?"

Macy catches Warren's eye. "Elizabeth doesn't need to know about this."

Jared elevates Grace's legs and takes her pulse.

"Is she going to be okay?"

"I think so." He looks up at the wall and Macy can see his eyes trace across the lines. "Why did you bring her here? Couldn't you have just shown her a photograph?"

"Jared, please don't tell me how to do my job."

Carson follows Warren into the room.

"What have we got here?"

"I'm pretty sure she fainted." Jared pats Grace on the cheeks and calls her name several times.

Carson sets his bag down on the floor. "Did she hit her head on anything?"

"Not that I saw."

Grace opens her eyes and blinks a few times.

Jared almost smiles. "Hey, Grace. You okay?"

She stares up at him. "What happened?"

"You're not well. We need to get you back to the hospital."

Grace's voice comes out in short bursts. "I don't want to go back. I'm here now. I want to help."

Jared looks up at Macy. "What do you think?"

"I think I'm not going to tell you how to do your job."

Grace waves Jared's hands away and tries to sit up. "It was just a shock, that's all. I'll be fine now."

"You need to take it very slowly. Can you do that for me?" He eases her forward and she sits cross-legged on the floor. "Wait like this for a few minutes. I don't want you to pass out again."

Grace shifts her position so she's facing the window. Her eyes sweep across the area under the desk. "Did he take anything?"

Macy follows her gaze. There is nothing on the floor. "As far as we know all he's done is leave you a message on the wall. Does it mean anything to you?"

Grace doesn't look up at the writing. "No, I've never seen anything like that before."

Warren steps into the center of the room and points up at the wall. "Grace, are you familiar with Saint Augustine and John Bunyan?"

"No, sir."

He purses his lips. "John Bunyan wrote *Pilgrim's Progress*. Your aunt was reading it the other day."

Taking hold of Jared's outstretched hand, she rises to her feet. "I didn't notice."

Macy's words come out sharper than intended. "Grace, I need you to start paying attention now. I want you to have another look at what he's written on the wall and then tell me whether you've seen it before."

Grace bows her head. "Yes, ma'am."

Macy glances over at Jared and Carson. "Do you mind waiting out on the landing? It's kind of crowded in here."

Grace won't let go of Jared's arm.

"It will be okay. Jared will be right outside and Warren and I are here with you. You're in safe hands."

Grace holds on to the back of the desk chair and looks up at the wall again. She sways as she reads. Macy keeps her eyes on Grace the entire time.

"I'm sorry. It means nothing to me." Grace turns away and picks up the first sketchbook in the stack. She glances at it for a second and then places it facedown on the desk.

Macy comes over and stands next to her. "Are you absolutely sure, Grace?"

"Yes, ma'am."

Macy picks up one of the sketchbooks and flips through it. Drawings and little notes fill the pages. "You're very talented."

"Thank you."

Macy watches Grace flip through the stack three times, her movements growing more rushed with each pass.

"Is something missing?"

"No," says Grace quietly. "They're all here."

"I want you to go through the room and tell me if anything is out of place." She gestures toward the chest of drawers. "Why don't we start here?"

Macy picks up the tube of lipstick and holds it out in front of Grace. "Is this yours?"

"Yes, ma'am."

"You bought it?"

Grace hesitates. "A while back."

Macy twists it open. "It looks brand-new."

"I haven't had reason to use it."

Macy puts it down and opens the top drawer.

Grace's eyes widen. "He's gone through my things."

"That's what I thought."

She lowers her voice to a whisper. "I'm pretty sure he's taken some of my underwear."

"Take your time, Grace. I'll need a description of everything that's missing."

Grace's hands tremble as she sorts through her clothing. "He's taken Thursday and Saturday."

"Excuse me?"

Her face reddens. "It's the days of the week." She holds up a pair of pale blue underwear. "They're written here on the back. Monday, Tuesday, Wednesday, and so on."

Grace goes through the rest of the drawers and the closet, but everything seems to be in place. They both stop in front of the bookshelf and stare up at the collection of glass-eyed dolls. The dolls appear to be as pristine as the day they were bought. Grace picks one up and its blue eyes roll back in its head. The porcelain skin is pure white. The hair is done in plaits and she wears a traditional German dress.

"That's a lot of dolls," says Macy.

Grace puts the doll back on the shelf, taking care to place it in the exact position it had been in previously.

"They were gifts from my uncle. Whenever he went away on a trip, he'd bring one back for me."

"It looks like they've never been played with."

"They're not meant to be played with. They're collectibles."

On the other bookshelf a brand-new teddy bear sits front and center. Grace picks it up and turns it over in her hands but makes no comment. The rest of the stuffed animals appear to have been ravaged by a family pet. Many have been patched up but a few are still missing body parts.

Macy picks up a particularly homely kangaroo. "Did you have a dog?"

"My aunt has allergies so we couldn't have pets." She takes the kangaroo from Macy and gingerly puts it back on the shelf. "When I was younger I used to rescue unwanted stuffed animals. I liked to sew them up and give them a home."

"Where did you find them?"

"Flea markets, garage sales. Places like that. My aunt hated it. The first thing she did was throw them in the washing machine when I brought them home."

Macy points to the new teddy bear. "What about this one? It doesn't look like a stray."

"It was a gift." She glances up at the ceiling light before turning to Macy. "Who changed the bulb?"

"Had it gone out?"

Grace sits down on the bed and closes her eyes. "When I was in the woods with my mom, I could see right into my room. It blinked a few times and went out."

Macy glances over at Warren. "You need to check that bulb for prints."

They hear Elizabeth out in the hallway shouting at someone. Her voice rises up from the floor below. "Grace, are you up there?"

Warren makes for the door and steps outside to meet her. "Elizabeth, we're almost done in here. You need to give us a few more minutes."

"I've given you as much time as I'm going to. I want you out of my house."

"You know we can't do that."

"I heard that Grace fainted. She needs to go back to the hospital immediately."

The landing is crowded. Jared, Carson, and two police officers hover at the top of the stairs. Elizabeth tries to sidestep Warren so she can look inside Grace's bedroom but Macy steps out with Grace and shuts the door firmly behind her.

Elizabeth takes hold of her niece's hand. "You poor thing. We're taking you back to the hospital."

Macy steps between them. "I'm sorry, Elizabeth, but I still need to ask you a few questions."

"Can't it wait until morning?"

"I promise to be brief."

"It's late."

"It's not late. It's only a little after six." Macy gestures to Jared and Carson. "Grace will return to the hospital with the paramedics. I'll run you over there when we're through here."

Elizabeth crosses her arms in front of herself. "It doesn't seem like you're giving me a lot of choice."

"Like I said, I promise to be brief." She looks at the two police officers. "I need another few minutes up here with Warren. Could you take everyone downstairs and make sure Elizabeth is comfortable? Get her a cup of tea or something."

Warren follows Macy back into Grace's room and shuts the door behind him.

"Macy, I'm not going to tell you how to do your job, but Elizabeth isn't used to being bossed around like that. It may make things easier if you're gentle with her."

"I'm not here to hold her hand. I'm trying to figure out who killed her sister."

"And I'm just trying to help. I've known Elizabeth a long time. If you want her to cooperate you're going to have to use a bit more charm." Warren looks around the room. "Did you find anything?"

Macy hands him the evidence bag containing the silver strand of hair. "This was in Grace's drawer. Maybe whoever did this left it behind?"

Warren holds the bag up to the light. "Impossible to tell. It may belong to Elizabeth."

Macy walks over to the window. "Grace must have stood here and watched. You can see her handprints on the glass."

"It's a good fifty, maybe sixty yards to where we found them. I'd be surprised if Grace could give an accurate description."

"But it would be close enough for her to recognize someone she knew."

"You think Grace knew who the killer was?"

"It's not making much sense but this feels personal."

"You know, there was a lot of press about Grace's heart transplant. Her name and picture have been in the papers. She's a pretty girl; someone may have fixated on her. Someone could have made it personal."

"If the office downstairs hadn't been ransacked, I'd agree with you. But whoever broke into the house was looking for something specific."

"Given a filing cabinet has been cleaned out, I'd say they found it." He pauses. "You worked that case involving the four Eastern European girls?"

"I did."

"Arnold Lamm was a suspect."

"He's still a suspect."

"This could be related. Leanne left town at around that time."

Macy heads for the door. "I need to go talk to Elizabeth."

"Remember what I said."

"It's been noted. I promise to be gentle."

. . .

Macy sits across from Elizabeth at the dining room table sipping a cold cup of coffee. Through an open archway she can see officers moving about inside Arnold Lamm's office. The filing cabinets and locked desk drawers have been pried open with a crowbar. Papers printed with Cross Border Trucking's letterhead are scattered across the floor. It's all being documented as evidence.

Macy pushes a box of tissues in Elizabeth's direction and offers to make her another cup of tea.

Elizabeth wipes her eyes and says she's had enough tea for one day. "I knew Grace wasn't well enough to deal with this."

Macy looks at her watch. "She's back at the hospital by now. They'll take good care of her."

"She shouldn't have come out here in the first place."

Macy wants to disagree but apologizes for the missing house keys instead.

Elizabeth waves her off. "I can't blame that on you. You weren't here."

"But I'm here now. Everything is my responsibility." Macy waits a few seconds. "Can you shed any light on all this?"

Elizabeth throws her hands up in the air. "I don't understand any of this. My sister and I were never friendly. Our mother tried everything but Leanne would never meet us halfway. She seemed to take pleasure in making me miserable. As far as I'm concerned the only thing she ever did right was leaving town."

"Tell me about Grace's childhood. I've read the files from social services but I'd like to hear your thoughts firsthand."

Elizabeth pulls her cardigan around her. "In the years before we adopted Grace, we only saw her a handful of times. Our friend Dustin kept tabs on her, making sure she was taking her medication, sneaking her money for food. Things like that. He'd make a point of stopping by Leanne's place unannounced."

"Is Dustin the man I met at the hospital yesterday?"

"That's possible. He was with Grace. He and Leanne were friends but he didn't approve of how she lived. He was more than willing to help us keep an eye on things. We were worried Grace didn't get enough to eat. We'd see her from a distance sometimes. She was painfully thin."

"It must have been difficult for you to sit back and do nothing."

"When Leanne went off the rails completely, Dustin would take them in but they'd never stay long. My sister always had a stubborn streak. Once she was stable and Grace was fattened up she'd be out living in that dreadful trailer again."

"Did Grace ever have any close friends? Someone from her past who we could talk to?"

Elizabeth's eyes well up. "Leanne had a bad reputation in Collier. Affairs with married men, drink, drugs, things like that. I'm afraid people took it out on Grace. She was bullied in school."

"Didn't it get any easier for Grace when her mother left town?"

"We were hoping it would, and believe me when I say we tried hard once she was here with us. I'd organize things through my friends, but I got the impression she found other children boring. She preferred the company of adults."

From her chair, Macy can see straight into the kitchen. The refrigerator is covered with family photos. Grace looks cheerful in every single one and yet all the photos they've shown on the news portray her as an unhappy child. "When did Grace's health problems start?"

Elizabeth relaxes. "As a toddler she was diagnosed with leukemia. She survived but her heart was damaged. She was in and out of the hospital for years. Arnold and I have paid for all her medical insurance and expenses from the time she was born."

"How did you manage that?"

"Arnold did what he had to do. I didn't ask questions."

"How did Leanne feel about the arrangement?"

"She told Grace her father was paying for everything."

"But Grace doesn't know who her father is."

"It was a horrible thing to do. It gave Grace hope. She was crushed when she found out we were paying for everything, but the damage was already done. She's obsessed with finding him."

"Do you have any idea who he might be?"

"I've had my suspicions, but now Leanne is dead and Grace may never know the truth."

"I'd like to hear your thoughts. It may be important."

"It's all based on rumor. It's nothing more than gossip."

"I'm not going to hold you to it."

Elizabeth hesitates. "Near as I can tell my sister only had one serious relationship and that was with Toby Larson. I've always had an inkling he was Grace's father."

"The used car salesman in the television ads?"

"That's him. At the time he was married to Pamela Larson. Still is."

Macy makes some notes. "So it was an affair?"

"I'll never understand what Toby saw in my sister. He's such a good man. Since Arnold died he's made a point of coming up here to check on us. He was supposed to come over this week to have a look at Arnold's truck. I was going to give it to Grace but now I'm not so sure."

"Does Grace suspect Toby is her father?"

"I'm sure she does but we've never discussed it openly." Elizabeth runs her finger across the rim of her cup. "You see, Grace knows Toby is just one in a long list of possibilities. She says she doesn't remember much about the years she spent living with her mother but I think she remembers plenty. There were a lot of men going in and out of that trailer."

"Did Toby's wife know about the affair?"

"Oh yeah, Pamela knew. Toby likes to make light of it but I hear she nearly killed him the night he tried to leave town with Leanne."

"When was this?"

"Eleven years ago. It was the same night Leanne left Collier for good."

"Is Pamela the type of person to hold a grudge?"

"Maybe you should ask her yourself." She looks at her watch. "She should still be at the hospital. If we leave soon you just might catch her."

"Does she work there?"

Elizabeth clenches and unclenches her swollen hands. "No, she's at the hospital for personal reasons. Her daughter Hayley attempted suicide this morning."

"I'm sorry, that's awful."

"With Hayley it's always been awful. I don't know how Brian has put up with her all these years. Arnold warned him but he went ahead and married her anyway. God knows what she gets up to when he's out on the road."

"Her husband worked for Arnold?"

"Yes, occasionally, as an independent contractor."

"Grace told me her mother sent her money on her birthdays?"

"Yes, but don't read too much into it. Every year she'd stuff a wad of dirty bills into an envelope with a birthday card. There was never a note or return address."

"It sounds like Leanne was afraid of letting people know where she was living."

"It may well have been the case, but she still could have included a note. Those cards could have come from anyone. Do you have any idea how that made Grace feel?"

"Did Leanne try to contact you?"

"No," she says, staring back at Macy. "And if she had I would have told her to stay away."

"Were Grace and her uncle close?"

Elizabeth looks down at the table, smoothing the linen with her fingertips. "He doted on her, took her on fishing trips."

"So they'd spend a lot of time alone together?"

Elizabeth's head snaps up. "What are you implying?"

Macy glances at her notes. "Grace may have told her uncle more about her relationship with Leanne than you realize. I want to understand why Leanne left town so suddenly and why she was desperate enough to leave Grace behind."

"Arnold wasn't the type to have heart-to-hearts. I don't think I ever saw them hug." She gestures to a framed photo of her husband standing arm in arm with a friend. "Grace took that photo when she was about thirteen. She always looked forward to their trips. They'd spend a lot of time planning them."

In the picture Arnold Lamm holds up a massive fish by the gills, but there is something odd about the composition. It's only when Macy gets up to inspect it that she realizes there was once a third man in the photo. She points to the man standing with Arnold. He wears sunglasses and grins into the camera. His hair is cut short, making his head appear unnaturally round.

"Who's this?"

"That's Hayley's long-suffering husband."

Macy steps away from the picture. "That's one big walleye."

"Arnold broke the state record that year. That fish weighed nearly eighteen pounds."

"I suspect you got pretty bored with cooking walleye."

"No, not at all. Coming up with new recipes was part of the fun. We even tried smoking some but it didn't turn out very well."

Macy takes a deep breath. "Elizabeth, I'm sorry, but I have to ask you what you know about your husband's business dealings?"

"Why? What does that have to do with what's happened?"

"Other than Grace's room, your husband's office was the only part of the house that was disturbed. There's evidence to suggest Leanne's killer has taken away the entire contents of one of the filing cabinets."

"My husband was away a lot for work. He had a whole life I knew nothing about."

"He was in business for thirty-three years. That's most of your married life. I have a hard time believing you were never involved."

Elizabeth looks down at her hands. "I know what you're trying to do and you're not going to get away with it. Arnold was cleared of any wrongdoing."

"Did he have any enemies?"

"The trucking industry is a rough business. I'm sure Arnold had enemies. I just have no idea who they were."

"Did Arnold keep cash in his office?"

"I didn't find anything like that when I cleared out some stuff a few months ago. Why?"

"We found evidence that there was once a manila envelope secured with masking tape to the bottom of one of the overturned drawers. We don't know if it was recent or not so we don't know if whoever broke in found it."

Elizabeth presses a tissue to her eyes as she starts to cry. "I'm sorry, I'm just so worried about Grace."

"I know you are, but please try to think. Do you remember seeing a manila envelope? It would have been letter sized?"

"No, I don't recall seeing anything like that."

Macy puts her palms flat on the table and thanks Elizabeth for her time. "I'd best get you back to the hospital. Grace will be expecting you."

Elizabeth blows her nose before reaching for her purse. "I've been meaning to ask. Did you find Arnold's gun?"

"No, we haven't found any firearms. Why?"

"Arnold knew I hated the things but after he died I found a box of shells in the garage so I know he lied and got one anyway. Since he passed away, I've been looking for it everywhere. I don't want it in the house."

10

"What the fuck are you doing here?" Brian Camberwell was never one to waste his time on small talk.

Jared was about to knock on Hayley's door but now Brian is right behind him, pressing up against his back. Cellophane-wrapped flowers crackle and pop. The smell of aftershave and sweat fills the hospital corridor. Brian's words glance off the top of Jared's head, raising the hairs.

"I asked you a fucking question. You're high if you think I'm letting you anywhere near my wife." Brian puts his palm flat on the door.

Beyond Brian's thick knuckles, Jared sees Hayley propped up in bed looking more dead than alive. Her dark-circled eyes are closed, and he has to remind himself that she's only sleeping. Her two heavily bandaged wrists are stretched out on either side. When Jared notices the gauze is covered with the pale pink ribbons, he almost smiles. Jared has spoken to the doctors. He knows the exact number of stitches required— eighteen in one wrist and twenty-five in the other. He presses his forehead to the cool glass and comes close to crying instead.

Jared's voice is weary. "I'm just checking on her."

With a beefy grip, Brian spins Jared around and shoves his back into the door. It rattles in its frame but holds. Unlike Jared, Brian is broad, bordering on fat. His thick forehead overhangs his eyes, putting his entire face in shadow. Jared watches the ceiling lights blink on and off above Brian's shoulders. The flowers are crushed between them and the cellophane bag pops open. The cheap yellow blooms are level with Jared's chin. His eyes flick up at Brian and he holds the other man's gaze. There was a time when they'd been civil, but then Hayley happened and everything changed. They've not spoken to each other in years.

Brian steps away, putting a little space between them. "I don't want you anywhere near her."

Jared pretends to sniff the air. "You know what," he says, pushing hard against Brian. "You fucking stink."

The blow to the side of Jared's head knocks him flat on the ground and for a few seconds the world goes black. Brian grabs at Jared's shoulders, trying to pull him up to his feet, but Jared won't stay upright. His vision is blurred and he thinks he might be sick. Brian's steel-toed boots are dangerously close. Jared imagines them breaking his ribs and shattering his skull. Brian kneels down and shouts at him, but to Jared the words sound like drumbeats in a well. Looking beyond the yellow carnations scattered across the floor, Jared sees Lexxie running down the hall toward them. A couple of burly orderlies he doesn't recognize race after her. Jared curls up tighter and hopes he'll disappear.

"Get your hands off him!" Lexxie pulls at Brian's shoulders, flinching when Brian twists around and raises a fist.

The orderlies pile onto the little group and Jared is caught between Brian's solid back and the door. The two orderlies wrestle Brian away. One of them has him in a headlock. As the pressure increases, Brian's face turns a murderous shade of purple. His curses fade when his words lose oxygen. He bows his head and but for his eyes, he's finally still. He breathes through his fat mouth and glowers at Jared.

But then Lexxie is high on her toes and right up in Brian's face, her words rat-a-tat-tatting like gunfire.

"You ungrateful shit," she yells, her red mouth widening and the tendons in her neck as sharp as razors. She jabs a finger in Jared's direction. "This man saved your wife's life."

Brian tries to muscle his way toward Jared again but goes slack when Macy steps between them.

Macy flashes her badge in his face. "Let's all calm down now, shall we?" She puts a hand on Lexxie's arm. "Nice work, darling, but I think I'll take it from here." She gazes into Brian's purple face. "You gonna play nice now or do I need to take you in for questioning?"

Brian mumbles something she can't quite catch.

"Louder and with more respect, if you don't mind."

Brian apologizes and Macy gives the signal to the orderlies to release their grip. She glances over at Jared, who's being attended to by Lexxie.

She takes out her notebook and looks up at Brian. "You gotta name?"

"Brian Camberwell, ma'am."

"Aside from assault and battery, what is it that you actually do, Mr. Camberwell?"

"I'm a long-haul trucker, ma'am."

"Does this look like some roadside bar to you, Mr. Camberwell?"

"No, ma'am."

"I shouldn't have to explain it to you, Mr. Camberwell, but you're in a hospital. This is where the sick come to be mended. It's not a place for barroom brawls." She gazes over at Jared, who looks unsteady on his feet. Someone has brought him an ice pack and he's got it pressed to the side of his face. "Hey, Jared. You want to press charges?"

"I'd rather forget the whole thing happened."

"That's very generous of you. Somehow I doubt your friend here would extend the same courtesy." She nudges a crushed flower petal with her toe. "You got somewhere you need to be, Mr. Camberwell?"

He juts his chin out toward Hayley's door. "I'm here to visit my wife."

Macy turns to Jared. "I take it you had the same destination in mind?"

"Like I told him. I'm just here to see how she's doing."

Lexxie steps forward theatrically. "Jared saved Hayley's life." She beams with pride and rocks back in her thick-soled nursing clogs.

Macy's eyes flit from Lexxie to Jared and back to Brian again. "Seems you need to adjust your attitude, Mr. Camberwell." Macy snaps her notebook shut and walks over toward Hayley's door. She peers in the window for a few seconds before coming over to stand in front of Brian. "It seems you're lucky Jared came along when he did."

Jared leans back against the wall, catching what little he can of the conversation above the ringing in his ears. Lexxie is covering for him, telling them she'd stayed at his place and that they'd brought Hayley to the hospital together. He feels too ill to be grateful. He's also wary. Everyone at the hospital knows she pulled an all-nighter in the ER.

Jared's voice breaks as he speaks. "I think I'm going to head out now. It's been a long day and I just want to go home."

"What's going on?" Not more than a few feet away Hayley stands on unsteady feet, propping open the door, a portable IV drip-feeding a bandaged arm. Her eyes sweep across the scene, taking in the scattered yellow carnations and Jared before finally landing on her red-faced husband. She steps away and tries to shut the door on all of them.

Brian grabs the top of the door before it closes. "Where the fuck do you think you're going? I've been driving straight through for the past twenty-four hours. Sitting for so long my ass is on fire. I want some answers and I want them now."

Macy clears her throat. Flanked by two uniformed officers, she is no longer alone. "I'm warning you, Mr. Camberwell. I've got you in my sights now. Keep this up and I'm hauling you in."

Brian glances down at his wife's bound wrists and his voice loses its edge completely. "What makes you think it's a good idea to call him for something like this? Call your mother, for god sakes. She'd have sent the cavalry."

In one quick movement Lexxie marches over to Jared and plants a kiss on his cheek. "We couldn't believe it when we got the call from Hayley yesterday morning. Could we?"

Jared can't look at Hayley.

Hayley dips her chin and speaks to her husband. "Please, Brian, I'm not feeling so good. Can we talk about this later?"

Brian swallows her up with an embrace. He kisses her on the top of the head repeatedly and rocks her back and forth in his arms.

"I've just been so worried about you, baby." He looks up at Jared. "No hard feelings, man."

Jared hangs back, trying his hardest to keep his composure. He gives Brian the slightest of nods. Then they're gone, disappearing into Hayley's room and closing the door behind them with a soft click.

"You okay?" Lexxie asks, touching the side of his swollen face.

Jared winces and pulls away. "Yeah, I will be."

She lowers her voice. "I warned you to steer clear of Hayley."

He gives her the type of smile that could mean most anything. "I've never been too good at listening."

Macy interrupts them, flashing her badge again. "Police business. I need a quick word with Jared." Macy takes Jared by the elbow and steers him toward a bank of chairs. "Seems like you've had better days."

Jared sinks into a chair and closes his eyes. "Understatement was always your specialty."

"Among other things."

"It's late. What are you still doing here? You must have dropped off Elizabeth ages ago."

"I needed to check that the security arrangements were adequate. We're going to have to keep a close eye on Grace for a while." Macy tries to scoot around so she's sitting less awkwardly, but her belly keeps getting in the way. "Out of curiosity, does Brian Camberwell work for Cross Border Trucking?"

"On and off for years. He and Grace's uncle went way back. Why?"

"No reason. I just wanted to confirm he was the same guy."

"As far as I know there's only one asshole named Brian Camberwell."

"So how long have you been sleeping with his wife?"

He doesn't waste her time with denials. "Too long. We also go way back."

"The third party in our relationship?"

"Sorry."

"She's Pamela Larson's daughter, isn't she?"

Jared glances up toward Hayley's door and frowns. His head is aching but he's starting to think along straight lines. He's beginning to wonder if Brian really did leave a message for Pamela.

"Yeah, she's her daughter, all right."

"So what's the scoop on Pamela?"

Jared rubs his temples.

"Jared?"

Jared looks up and sees Macy staring at him. Even though she's heavily pregnant she's still attractive. She's certainly more interesting than Lexxie. "I always fuck everything up."

"Not everything. Not yet, anyway. Look," she says, leaning in and lowering her voice. "Collier has this weird small-town vibe, and I'm not from here. I could really use your help."

"I'm not sure how I do that."

"It's quite simple, really. Pamela Larson. Goodie or baddie?"

Jared doesn't hesitate. "Baddie," he says, remembering how she'd smiled thinly when she told him Brian wouldn't be back until the morning. "Definitely the biggest bitch I've ever met."

On the drive home Jared catches sight of only a handful of cars. Aside from a few stragglers, Collier is ghost white and emptied out. He stops in at Olsen's Landing to fill his tank and buy a few basics. Gusts of wind kick debris and snow across the forecourt. His tank is nearly empty and the pump is painfully slow. He huddles next to his truck, keeping out of the freezing northerlies as best he can. From somewhere close by muffled sounds of an argument rise up above the wind. The voices are animated and angry but he can't make out the words. He twists his head around trying to figure out where it's coming from. Looking out toward the fishing camp that borders the parking lot, he sees dark blue shadows fall across the six inches of fresh snow. Jared waits for someone to appear, but the shadows recede, taking the raised voices with them. For a long time nothing moves unless it's being slapped about by the wind.

Behind the counter a spotty teenager gives Jared a sullen look. The television plays music videos at full volume so Jared has to raise his voice to be understood.

"Any news about Sissy's baby?" he asks.

The word "hospital" is all that's forthcoming.

Jared asks the boy if he knows if anyone is staying in the summer cabins out at Olsen's Landing.

The boy shrugs. "Some guy who just moved back here."

"Why would anyone live out there?"

The boy yawns. "Fuck if I know. Ask Trina."

Jared points a thumb in the direction of the parking lot. "When I was out front, I thought I heard shouting."

Bored with the conversation, the boy lets his eyes drift to the television and stay there. "Big deal. Someone's always shouting in Collier."

As Jared crosses the Flathead River, a pickup truck pulls in behind him from where it had been parked in a lay-by. Keeping close to Jared's back bumper, the truck follows Jared all the way home, blocking him in the driveway. Jared's got a gun stashed in the glove compartment, but he grabs a crowbar out from under his seat instead. Weapon in hand, he jumps out of the cab. Hayley's father steps out of the other truck, one unsteady foot hitting the packed-down snow at a time. Toby Larson is long in limb and body and as usual he's smartly dressed. Jared anticipates the scent of whiskey long before he can actually smell it.

Toby gestures to the crowbar. "Are you going to invite me in or bludgeon me to death?"

Jared holds his ground. "You coming here isn't such a good idea."

Toby rocks gently as if he's standing in a boat. "Your sofa is just as hospitable as any in this backward town." He points at his gold watch. "Plus, I've missed the Denver-Phoenix game and I'm hoping you've taped it."

"Why are you really here?"

Toby clasps his hands in frustrated prayer. "Don't be so naïve. When it comes to our girls, Pamela tells me everything. I know you and Hayley have had this little dalliance going on for years and I'm well aware that she tried to end her life in your bathroom."

"That alone seems like a pretty good reason for you not to come into my house."

As if he's taking an oath, Toby holds up a hand. "Don't worry, if I need to relieve myself I shall piss off your back porch like all the other rednecks in Collier."

Inside the house Jared stands in his darkened entryway, waving his fingers in the air in front of the light switch. The smell is wrong. There is an artificial freshness to it. He flicks on the lights and stares.

Toby puts his chin over the top of Jared's shoulder and looks out over the room. "What a delightful little place you have."

Jared keeps glancing around, seeing how so many things have been cleaned, shifted, or completely removed. He's only been away for fifteen hours.

"Someone has been here." Jared remembers fragments of the conversation he had with Pamela. He tries to recall what exactly they agreed.

"Well, if you've been burgled they've done a neat job of it. Perhaps you could give them my number." His laughter sounds bitter.

Turning down the hallway, Jared switches on lights as he moves through the house. Everything has been dusted, polished, and swept. Outside the bathroom, he hesitates before pushing the door open. Hayley isn't on the floor anymore, but for a few seconds her pale face is all he sees. There is no blood. All trace of Hayley has vanished. All he can smell is bleach. He reaches for his cell phone. Pamela answers on the third ring.

Jared peeks down the hallway in time to see Toby pass into the living room. He's carrying a beer. *So much for coffee,* Jared thinks uneasily.

"Jared," she says in a low voice. "Everything okay?"

"Did you arrange to have my place cleaned?"

"No, why?"

"Cause someone's cleaned the whole house." Jared enters his bedroom. The bed is made. He pulls the quilt away. "They even changed my sheets."

"That's odd." Pamela's voice sounds like she's speaking from the inside of a closet. Jared thinks he can hear people arguing in the background. "I really can't talk right now."

"Toby is here."

"At your house?"

"Yes, in my house, on my sofa, drinking my beer." Jared wanders into his kitchen.

"Look, just keep him company."

"He's drunk. And he's acting weird. Hayley just tried to kill herself and he's making jokes."

He can hear Pamela sigh.

"That's how he deals with any difficulty. You should have seen him at the hospital. The man is a wreck. If it were me in intensive care, he'd be celebrating, but this is his baby girl we're talking about."

"I don't have time to deal with him right now."

"Of course you have time," she says mockingly. "Your house is spotless. What else do you have to do this evening?"

"That's not helpful."

"I've got to go, but we'll talk later."

Jared drops his phone on the counter and goes outside into the garage to see about his dogs. Their food bowls are half full. Jared raises his arms in frustration. His dogs cock their heads to the side and follow him into the house. He arrives in time to see Toby coming in from the back porch. Hayley's father is zipping up his trousers and whistling.

"You keep a very clean house, young Jared." Toby helps himself to another beer before heading back to the living room.

Jared sits down on the reclining chair and his dogs come over and put their chins on his lap. He watches the game but is far too distracted to follow what's happening.

Toby points a lazy finger at the coffee table. "Someone left you a note."

Jared picks it up and immediately recognizes Lexxie's handwriting. *Surprise! Lexxie xx* is all it says.

Jared goes around opening his newly organized kitchen cupboards. He stares in disbelief at the row of alphabetized spices and wonders if she's taking drugs. She can get her hands on Ritalin easily enough.

Toby grunts at the television. He's not happy with how the game is going. "Are you going to watch the game? Your pacing is distracting me."

Jared is too busy inspecting his refrigerator to answer. Rows of low-fat yogurts stare back at him. He grabs a handful of ice and wraps a dish towel around it. The side of his head still smarts from where Brian hit him. The whiskey bottle isn't out in the open like it usually is. He roots around the cupboards again and finds it way in the back, stashed behind the cereal. He pours some in a glass and adds some ice from the dish towel.

Toby fills in the empty airspace. "Never did understand what Hayley saw in Brian."

"That makes two of us."

"I imagine you were too nice for her."

"Yep, I've been told that more than once."

"Given you're employed, not addicted to meth, and have all your teeth, I imagine you're Collier's most eligible bachelor."

"Hardly."

Toby takes a long swallow of beer and concentrates on the TV screen, sitting slightly forward when one of his used car advertisements comes on. He sings along to the jingle, but he's dead serious when he speaks again.

"I've always liked you, Jared."

Jared sits back down. "Why are you here?"

"You mean aside from the usual reason of hiding from Pamela."

According to Hayley, her father keeps a mistress in an apartment a couple of blocks off Main Street. Her name is Annie and she's almost half Toby's age.

Jared drops his head back onto the cushions and closes his eyes. "You've got other places you can hide."

Toby agrees but makes no attempt to leave. Instead he starts talking about the night he almost left Pamela. Jared pretends to watch the game but he's taking in every word.

"It would have been okay in the end. Pamela wouldn't have missed me and the girls were old enough to cope."

"So why didn't you go?"

"I made the mistake of trying to do the honorable thing. I told Pamela my plans. She hid my car keys. You know where we live. We're miles out of town. By the time I got to my girl, she was long gone." He shakes his head sadly. "And now Leanne is dead. Pamela sent me the news via text. I swear the only thing missing from that message was a smiley face."

"Are you talking about Leanne Adams?"

"I am indeed."

"No offense, but from what I've heard she was a bit of a wreck."

"Saint Jared, we can't all live in glass houses." He gestures to the game, which has now swung in favor of his team. "This isn't a morality tale. This is life. If you really want something, you have to fight for it."

Jared keeps his mouth shut. He's not stupid. He knows Toby is talking about Hayley. He holds the ice against his head and sips his whiskey.

Toby leans in closer to Jared. "A little advice from a man who got it all wrong. Don't marry Lexxie unless you love her. Don't settle. It will only make you miserable in the long run."

"I'm already miserable."

"You're still young. You have no idea what misery is." Toby swings a long leg up and kicks Jared, upsetting a half-empty beer on the coffee table. It spills onto Lexxie's note, blurring the ink. "So, young man, what do you intend to do about it? One way or another that fucker Brian has to be taken out of the equation."

Jared turns off the television and faces Toby. "That's your point? You want me to kill him?"

"Jesus no, nothing that extreme, but I know he's still dealing in some pretty shady stuff. If you hear of anything we can use against him, I want you to let me know. The right type of information can send a man packing."

Jared takes away the ice pack and touches the side of his head lightly with his fingertips. The swelling hasn't gone down. "I don't think that's a good idea. Brian isn't one to negotiate."

11

Grace gets out of bed and walks over to the window. The temperature drops the instant she opens the thick curtains. On a clear day the view from the hospital would stretch to the Canadian border, but tonight Grace has difficulty seeing past her own sallow reflection. It's four in the morning and she's hardly slept. When she closes her eyes all she sees is her bedroom wall. Every word opens an old wound. She doesn't understand why he'd want to hurt her like that. She pulls the drapes shut and gazes out into the dimly lit corridor. A patrol officer named Gareth sits just outside. He has a thermos of coffee and a well-thumbed paperback to keep him company. He's not been reading though. For the past few hours Grace has been eavesdropping on the endless phone conversations he's been having with his girlfriend, but now he's gone so quiet Grace wonders if he's finally switched off his phone.

Grace pads toward the half-open door and peeks outside. The lights are low but every so often a bright fluorescent strip slips out from beneath a doorway. The glow sets a shine to the linoleum floor, metal carts, and gurneys. The cleaning crews are gone, but there's a smell of disinfectant and bleach about the place. Gareth's thermos and paperback sit on the floor next to his empty chair.

"Gareth," she asks, hoping he's nearby. "Is everything okay?"

A loud thumping noise rises up from the far end of the corridor. It takes Grace a few seconds to realize it's nothing more than hot water forcing its way through narrow pipes, which rattle and rock inside the hospital's walls. Above the racket, she can hear crashing sounds coming from the stairwell.

"Gareth?" she repeats, stepping out into the hallway to have a better look.

A shadow lurches past the small windows cut into the heavy double doors leading to the stairwell. Grace runs forward a few paces and ducks behind a laundry cart parked in a dark alcove. There's a hard smack and seconds later the doors open. The footsteps are soft at first but grow in volume as they draw near. Grace pulls in tighter to the laundry cart and rests her cheek against the rough fabric of the bag. The man passes close enough for her to reach out and touch him. She watches his dark silhouette stop in front of her room before disappearing inside. Moving silently, Grace makes her way to the stairwell, only letting the door close behind her when she's sure it will make no sound.

She nearly trips over Gareth. He's sprawled out in the middle of the landing. Grace kneels down and whispers his name but he doesn't move. She leans in and feels his warm breath on her cheek. She starts to look through his pockets for his phone but stops when she notices that his gun is no longer in its holster. She slides away from Gareth and looks through the crack between the double doors. There's someone standing in the shadows just beyond the nurse's station. He's reading a board listing the patients' names and room numbers. Grace puts a hand to her mouth. She needs to run but she doesn't want to leave Gareth. She starts crying when she hears Sam's cart out in the corridor. He's coming from the direction of the elevators and passes within a few feet of her hiding place.

Sam's voice is sharp. "It's the middle of the night. You've got no business being up here."

Grace edges over to the gap in the doors and peeks out into the hallway again. The cart is abandoned. Sam is standing right outside the door with his back to her. He shifts his weight from one leg to the other. Beyond him is the man who'd gone into her room. She strains her eyes. His face is covered so she can't make out his features. His voice is not familiar.

"You just get out of my way, I don't want no trouble from you."

"Stay right where you are. I'm calling security."

Next to Grace, Gareth begins to stir. He moans softly but his eyes remain closed. She tries to speak, to warn him to be silent, but she's too afraid of making any noise. She stands with her back pressed up against the wall. The stairs are so close. She eases her way toward them. Outside in the hall, Sam is begging the man to put down his gun.

Grace's shoulder scrapes against a fire alarm. Her gaze fixes on Gareth. He's trying to sit up. Their eyes lock just as the first shot rings out. The sound is deafening. Window glass splinters into a thousand shards. She grabs the alarm and pulls hard on the black lever. Red emergency lights flash on and off throughout the stairwell. The sirens scream at her as she runs. She takes the steps two at a time. She doesn't stop until there's nowhere left to go but the basement.

Grace slides out into the corridor in her stocking feet. Unlike the rest of the hospital it is brightly lit. She needs to find a safe place to hide. With no warning a door on her right opens. There are no dark alcoves so Grace stands in the middle of the hallway, completely exposed. A young man hurries into the hall. Unaware that Grace stands a few feet away, he focuses all his attention on the elevator doors. Grace stares at his profile, memorizing the roundness of his cheeks and the gentle slope of his nose. She wants to speak, to call out for help, but by the time she's found the courage the elevator doors open and he's gone. She takes a few hesitant steps and reads the sign on the door from which he so suddenly appeared.

MEN'S LOCKER ROOM

Grace puts her ear to the door and hears no one moving about inside. Cautious, she goes in. Rows and rows of lockers stand tall like soldiers. Every last one is padlocked. She stops when she spies Jared's name. She touches the tape's raised lettering and runs her fingertips across it as if it were Braille. She tilts her forehead to the cool metal door and thinks of all the things she'd like to say.

"Where are you now?" is all she manages.

Grace eventually finds a narrow bed hidden back in a corner, out of sight from the rest of the room. She pulls a curtain shut and turns off the lights. She only wants to close her eyes for a few minutes. The basement walls are thick and keep everything at bay. She presses her back into the soft mattress and sinks into a groove, fitting perfectly but sleeping fitfully. The pipes lining the ceiling shudder and pop. Doors open and shut. Voices drift in and out. Grace wakes, groggy and unaware of the time. She's been dreaming of the messages written on her bedroom wall. Her eyes fly open. Someone has come into the locker room and turned on all the lights. She pulls the blankets over her head and pretends to sleep.

"Grace," the unfamiliar voice says softly, nudging at her shoulder, once, twice, three times. "Wake up. A lot of people are looking for you."

Grace listens, taking in the sounds, none of which are quite right. Refusing to open her eyes, she waits patiently. She wants another voice.

This time the voice speaks to someone else. It twists around and calls out over an invisible shoulder. "Call upstairs and tell them we've found Grace in the men's locker room."

"What the hell?"

This voice she knows. Jared is there with her.

"Yeah, don't ask," says the stranger. "Came in and found her sleeping here. Nothing to do with me."

"Don't worry. I'll deal with it."

12

Macy dips under the crime-scene tape stretched across the corridor and almost pitches forward when she tries to stand up straight. She rests a gloved hand against the wall until she feels steady on her feet. The area is alive with the hum of electricity buzzing through the overhead lights, and broken glass crunches beneath the soles of her plastic-coated shoes. She spots Warren and suppresses the urge to yawn as she makes her way toward him.

"Any sign of Grace?" she asks. It's just past six in the morning and she's already been working for a couple of hours.

"She was hiding in the men's locker room down in the basement. They're bringing her up now."

"Thank God for that. I thought we had a kidnapping on our hands. Has someone called Elizabeth?"

"No, I thought I'd let her sleep a bit longer. Near as I can tell, she didn't leave the hospital until after midnight. I imagine she's exhausted."

"Where's she staying?"

"A patrol officer dropped her off at Martha Nielson's house over on Spruce."

Macy stares at the double doors leading out to the stairwell. Aside from the broken window she counts two bullet holes. There's blood splattered on the walls and smeared across the floor. Dark shoeprints fade and then vanish as they move away from where Sam Fuller fell.

"Sam Fuller is still in surgery," she says. "What was his actual role here at Collier County anyway? Grace told me he did a bit of everything."

"Sam is an institution around here. I think he's been working at the hospital since it opened in seventy-two. He runs errands, delivers food. He'll do whatever is needed."

"What was needed last night?"

Warren looks at his notes. "A patient named Candice Brown misplaced her reading glasses yesterday. Apparently, Sam spent all evening looking for them and after finally tracking them down in the cafeteria, was on his way to return them."

"He must be well past retirement."

"They can't get him to stay away."

"I wish I loved my job that much. How's Gareth?"

"He has a concussion but they didn't find anything alarming on his CT scan. He's pretty pissed off that he let everyone down."

"We've got three witnesses and they're all still breathing. That's a refreshing change."

"Who do you want to speak to first?"

"Gareth, but, I need a cup of coffee first."

Gareth is propped up in a hospital bed wearing a dark blue sweatshirt. He readjusts the ice pack on the back of his head and winces. "I was stupid. I should have called it in the moment I realized something wasn't right."

Macy observes him over her cup of coffee and decides he'd be better-looking with a beard. Without one his chin vanishes just below his lower lip.

She takes a sip of her coffee. "So you heard a noise in the stairwell and went to investigate."

"Yeah, but he jumped me the second I walked through that door. I managed to hold my own for maybe a minute but then he smacked my head hard against the railing."

"Was his face covered?"

"He was wearing a black ski mask." Gareth removes the ice pack and frowns. "It was like getting hit by a linebacker."

"So, he was a big guy?"

"No, I'd say he weighed less than I did. He was really wiry and very strong. I got the impression he was fairly tall but it was hard to tell."

"How much do you weigh?"

"Two ten, give or take a few pounds." He glances over at Warren. "It's blind luck nobody got killed."

"I don't think you were in any real danger." She writes down some notes in her book. "He just wanted you out of the way."

"What makes you say that?"

"I'm almost positive he's local. You might even know him." Macy hesitates. "Was there anything he said or did that struck you as familiar?"

"He didn't say anything so I can't help you there. I'll tell you one thing though; he had some pretty nasty BO. Really pungent."

Macy looks over at Warren. "Does this sound like anyone you've come across before?"

"A lot of men in Collier fit the physical description. At the moment I just can't think of any of them that stink."

Macy circles the word "pungent." "What happened when you came to?"

"The first thing I saw was Grace looking down at me. I could tell she was scared. She kept glancing at the door above my head. Seconds later the shooting started. She pulled the alarm and ran. When I checked the hall, the shooter was gone."

Warren tips his hat back. "He must have used the stairs at the other end of the building. I doubt he'd have risked the elevator. A couple of guys are going through the security tapes."

Gareth closes his eyes. "I'm not feeling so good."

Macy starts to get up. "I'm not surprised. You shouldn't sleep, though."

"No chance of that happening. The nurses come in and prod me every ten minutes."

Warren puts a hand on Gareth's shoulder. "Have you called your wife yet? You don't want her hearing about this from anyone but you."

Gareth's eyes start to well up. He rubs his face. "I'll do that now."

Out in the corridor Macy tries to fall in step with Warren and ends up trotting.

"I came across a guy named Brian Camberwell yesterday evening. He was here visiting his wife. I showed up just after he whacked Jared on the side of the head."

"Yeah, I heard about that. Are you figuring him as a suspect?"

"According to Jared he was away when Leanne was killed. Ice fishing or something like that. I think we should do some further checking, though."

"Brian weighs at least two hundred fifty pounds, and as far as I remember he doesn't smell."

"Does he have a record?"

"No, but he should have one." Warren lowers his voice. "He's assaulted his wife on more than one occasion."

Macy pictures Hayley. She'd looked so vulnerable standing next to her husband. "Why doesn't she report it?"

"I have no idea, but she's going to end up a statistic if she doesn't do something soon."

"Anything else?"

"He's probably dealing, but I'd say he's pretty small time. He's not too bright so it's kind of surprising he's not been caught yet. He somehow manages to stay just below the radar."

Macy puffs out her cheeks. "Did they find any prints up at the house?"

"There was a partial on the back gate, otherwise it was clean."

"That's not much to go on."

"No, it isn't."

Macy stares up at the cross above the altar in the hospital chapel and tries to be patient. According to the officers stationed at the door, Grace Adams has been on her knees praying for a half hour.

Macy slides into the pew next to Grace and picks up a copy of the Book of Common Prayer. "Grace, I'm sure Sam will be fine. You've done enough."

Grace scoots up onto the bench seat and drops her hands on her lap. Her eyes are raw from crying. Macy hands her a tissue and waits.

"I feel like it's my fault."

"Don't be ridiculous. You're not responsible any more than Sam is."

"I didn't see his face. It was covered with a black ski mask."

"Like the one your mother's killer wore."

"I think so."

"Was it the same man?"

"It's hard to say. It was dark and I didn't have a great view. I had to peek through the crack between the doors. Sam was in the way most of the time."

Macy thinks of the shattered glass and splintered wood. "It's probably a very good thing Sam was in the way. Did you think he looked the same size as the man in the woods?"

"Maybe, the distance was different. He seemed tall."

"What about his voice?"

"It was kind of high in pitch. He sounded really nervous."

"Did his voice sound familiar?"

"No, not at all."

"What was he saying?"

"I didn't catch most of it, but he did yell at Sam to get out of the way."

Macy puts a hand on Grace's arm. "Warren will send in a detective and they'll take a full statement from you. I'll go check on Sam and let you know how he's doing."

Grace thanks her before once more clasping her hands together in prayer.

13

The elevator doors open on three and Carson is standing in front of Jared, a shit-eating grin on his face. Jared moves to the side and Carson squeezes into the crowded elevator.

"Darlin'," cracks Carson, tongue firmly in cheek. "Which way are we going today? Up or down?"

"Down. The meeting is canceled. Want to grab some breakfast?"

"So I rushed to work for nothing?"

"Looks that way." Jared and Carson step out of the elevator on the second floor and head for the cafeteria. "The sixth floor is a mess."

"Yeah, I heard Sam got shot." Carson grabs a tray and shuffles along the line with Jared.

"You don't know the half of it."

No sooner have they taken their seats than Lexxie appears, breathless and beaming from ear to ear. She sits in the chair next to Jared and takes hold of his arm. "What did you think of your surprise?"

Carson sips his coffee and winces because it's too hot. "You should know by now that Jared hates surprises."

"Well?" she says, ignoring Carson.

Jared hesitates. He can't afford to be as honest as Carson. "It's not that I didn't appreciate it. It just seemed a bit too much."

Lexxie's laugh fails to convince. "I'm sorry, I guess I got a little carried away." Her pager goes off and she reads the message. "I have to go. Everything is a mess here today. Did you hear that Sam went nuts and tried to shoot a cop?"

"Don't go saying stuff like that. Gareth didn't get shot, Sam did. The poor guy just got out of surgery."

She lowers her voice. "Well, that's the story that's going around."

Carson scowls. "You of all people should know that most of what's said in this hospital is total bullshit."

"What do you mean *me of all people?*"

"You're a smart girl, you'll figure it out."

She reaches over and steals a piece of toast off Jared's plate. "I'm going to ignore you, Carson," she says, taking a bite. "So Jared, enlighten me, what actually happened?"

"I have no idea. I wasn't there."

She throws the rest of the toast back on the plate and gives him a quick peck on the cheek. "You're tired. We'll talk later."

"Yeah, I'll call you."

Carson waits for Lexxie to leave the cafeteria before speaking again. "What's she going on about?"

Jared no longer feels like discussing what happened. "Lexxie shouldn't go around saying that stuff about Sam."

"I imagine she's not the only one. So, what did happen?"

"It looks like someone came after Grace Adams. They knocked Gareth out and took his gun. When Sam got in the way, he was shot."

"Where was Grace when all this was going on?"

"Thankfully, she ran."

Carson leans back in his chair and folds his arms. "All that happened on the sixth floor?"

"Yep."

"That's insane."

"Speaking of insane, do you want to know what Lexxie's surprise was?"

"She's pregnant?"

"Don't even joke about stuff like that."

"So what did she do?"

"Cleaned my house."

Carson's spoonful of granola freezes midair. "Did she clean up your bathroom?" He puts down his spoon. "Seriously, did she clean up where Hayley . . ."

Jared says a quiet yes and attempts another stab at his breakfast.

"Damn, that's some serious bunny-boiler behavior."

"My life is a fucking mess, but at least my sheets are clean. To top it off Hayley's dad followed me home."

"Have you seen his latest commercial?"

"Came on while we were watching the game."

"They showed it like five times. My kids already know the words to his new jingle by heart." Carson starts singing, but so low that only Jared can hear him. "Do you think he writes this stuff himself?"

"Apparently his first love was musical theater. Inheriting a used car dealership from Pamela's parents must have been a bit of a setback."

"So what did Hayley's old man want?" Carson gives Jared the once-over, noticing the bruise on the side of his face. "It looks like he popped you pretty good."

"Brian did that."

"Now there's a guy that shouldn't be left to wander freely."

"Brian is a fucking criminal and everybody in this town knows it. Toby and Pamela are practically offering me their used car empire if I take Hayley back."

"What do you want?"

"What do I want?" Jared looks up at the ceiling. "I have no idea."

Carson raises an eyebrow. "Existential crisis?"

"Something like that. I sure as hell don't want to run a used car dealership."

"I imagine the commercials would take on a darker tone."

Jared pushes his plate away. "You know Grace Adams hid in the men's locker room last night?"

"Down in the basement?"

"Yep."

"Why would she hide there?"

"She was scared. I doubt she was thinking straight."

"Maybe she was looking for you."

"Nah, she just needs a friend, that's all."

"Don't say I didn't warn you." Carson checks his pager and pushes out of his chair. "We've got a call out at the trailer park. We'd better scoot."

As expected there's a sheriff's patrol car parked out in front of a double-wide unit, but even before they step out of their rig, Jared knows something is amiss. From inside the mobile home comes the sound of children screaming. A man dressed in nothing more than a white T-shirt and a pair of boxers runs out of the house and leaps off the porch. He's covered in blood splatter and yelling something over his shoulder Jared can't catch. It's only when he comes around the side of the police car that Jared realizes the man is carrying a gun. Jared hears Carson shout *Jesus* but it's far too late. The man is already on top of them, his gun trembling in a shaky fist.

Jared eases his EMT response kit to the ground. When he stands again he raises his arms up high and nods at Carson to get him to do the same. All the while Jared is looking over the man's shoulder back at the trailer, scanning for more threats or someone hurt. The kids are still wailing but no one else has followed the man out into the yard.

The hand with the gun jumps around, pointing first at Jared and then at Carson. The man doesn't seem to notice the cold. His bare feet are blue-veined and dirty black against the snow-covered sidewalk. His eyes dart around and his mouth looks like it's working hard to form words but as yet nothing has come out. For a moment it appears that he's forgotten he's got a gun in his hand before he once again points it at Carson.

Jared clears his throat. He's spotted a gray-haired neighbor with a rifle trained on them, and the last thing he wants to happen is for him and Carson to get caught in the crossfire. He clears his throat a second time and the man in front of them shifts the gun in Jared's direction. It's then that Jared can see that it's standard police issue. Jared cocks his head to the side, gesturing to the mobile home.

"Those your kids in there?"

The question confuses the man. He blinks a few times and his dark eyes shift back to the house from which he's just escaped. He takes the time to dig wax out of his ear with his index finger before answering.

He stutters when he speaks. "Yeah, they're mine . . . That trailer is mine." He points the gun at the pickup truck trapped in the covered driveway beyond the sheriff's patrol car. He starts laughing but it doesn't sound like he's happy. "And that's my truck too."

Jared pretends to admire it. "Nice truck."

The man is near tears. "Damn nice truck. All paid for too."

"You got a name?"

"Brady," he says, low and polite. "Brady Monroe."

"Well, Brady Monroe, you should know we're paramedics."

Brady scowls. "Course I know that. I ain't stupid."

Jared backtracks slowly, though he wants to sprint. "Nobody's saying that you're stupid. It's just that me and my buddy Carson ain't got no guns. We're just here to help." Jared looks down at Brady's shirt. "You've got blood on you. You hurt?"

Brady rubs his left hand across his T-shirt like he's trying to hide the stains. He shakes his head.

Jared directs his gaze at the trailer again. "If you're not hurt, then maybe there's someone inside that could use our help. Like I said before, we're just here to help."

Brady sweeps his gun from Jared to Carson. "You can go in," he says to Carson, before training the weapon on Jared again. "But you're stay-ing here."

Jared decides Carson is about to pass out. He does his best to speak to his friend as calmly as he can but he knows he's not fooling anyone. "You go on in and see what you can do. We'll just stay right here and talk some more." He tilts his chin toward his breast pocket and tries to catch Brady's eye. "Mind if I smoke?"

The man is watching Carson so Jared keeps quiet until the door to the mobile home closes. He has mixed feelings about having Brady's attention again.

Jared asks once more. "Mind if I smoke?"

"I'd rather you didn't. Secondhand smoke's a killer. Sets me to cough-ing." He holds his gun up higher and starts crying. "Been after my wife to quit."

Jared can hear the sounds of police sirens in the distance. "You hear that?"

Brady casts his eyes about like he's trying to find an exit, but comes up empty. "Reckon they're coming for me."

Jared purses his lips. "Got anything you want to say?"

"I didn't do what she's said I did."

Jared already thinks he knows who *she* is but he asks anyway. "Who's she?"

Brady gestures toward the trailer. The children have stopped crying. "My wife." He holds the gun with one hand and runs his fingers through his greasy hair. He's bone thin and his scraggly beard is peppered with gray. The gun is by his side pointing at the ground and the man is shifting his weight from foot to foot. "It's cold out here."

"Damn cold."

Brady Monroe regains focus. "She's saying that I did it. That I killed Leanne Adams."

Jared doesn't know quite what to say to that. He hesitates, picking out little movements in the distance. The police and armed neighbors have surrounded the trailer. He knows there are guns trained on them from everywhere. He thinks there might be a dead cop inside the trailer and that everybody with a radio knows about it. Brady Monroe is as good as roadkill, and he might be too if things don't go well.

Out of ideas, Jared asks the obvious question. "Well, did you kill her?"

Several times Brady opens his mouth to speak but nothing comes out. All Jared can see is bad dental work and a cyst the size of a marble on the man's tongue. Brady yells so he can be heard from quite a distance. "Hell, no, I did not kill that woman." He points the gun at the trailer. "That bitch in there wants the kids, the trailer, and my truck. She wants everything." His voice trails off. "Well she ain't gonna get none of it now."

Jared fails to swallow with his bone-dry throat. "So why don't you tell me your side of the story?"

Brady levels the gun at Jared again. There are tears streaming out of his eyes. They dampen his pockmarked cheeks, catching in shallow craters that glisten like tiny silver coins on his leathery skin.

Jared tries to speak again but he stutters over simple words. His legs may buckle beneath him any minute. There are little sounds and movements all around them—the cocking of rifles and the low crackle of radios. In the distance he picks up the thumping of helicopter blades coming from the direction of the hospital. He's hoping it's not a ride he'll need to take.

A foamed outline of spittle forms around Brady's dry lips. He licks them with a papery tongue and Jared imagines the scraping of sandpaper on flesh. Brady looks as if he's trying hard to work out his thoughts so he can make himself better understood.

"That's the thing," Brady says, laughing and crying all at once. "I lose the kids either way. I lose everything no matter what. That bitch knew she had me. I bet she was smiling like a pig in shit when she called the police."

"That bad?"

Brady nods and bites into the fleshy part of his thumb pad. His nails are broken and black. He leans in and Jared fights the desire to lean away from the stench coming off him.

"You see, me and a couple of guys got a lab out near where Leanne died. I was working there that whole day." He looks around and gasps like he's only just realized what has brought him to this point. "I can't go telling the cops that. Now, can I?"

Jared can see the problem clear enough. He tries hard to breathe, think, and force out words in a logical order all at the same time. "This is the time to make things right. The past is past. You need to figure out how to move forward with what you've got."

Brady isn't listening. He wipes his nose across his shoulder. "I can't believe Leanne was stupid enough to show her face around here again. Damn near ruined everything, as far as I can tell. After what she did there was no way he was gonna let her live. No way at all. Taking all that money. Crazy bitch."

"I'm worried about your kids," says Jared, trying again to make headway. "They need to know that it wasn't you that killed her. You need to put down the gun so we can go talk to them."

Brady seems to see the sense of this and for a few seconds the gun stops jumping up and down. "I still have nightmares about those girls we brought over here. Especially the young ones. It wasn't right what we did. But I wasn't like the others. I swear I never did what they did. Never. It's important that my kids know that too."

Jared lowers his voice. This isn't what he was expecting to hear. "What girls are you talking about, Brady?"

Brady raises the gun to his mouth and shoves the barrel deep into his throat using both his hands. Tufts of coarse black hairs line the backs of Brady's fingers, the hairs blunt and thick like they've grown back after being shaven or burnt. Brady's hands and forearms are lined with deep blue veins. His nostrils tilt upward and inflate like tiny inner tubes. He muffles his words into the gun's barrel. Greasy tears stream down his cheeks and he repeats himself several times, growing more desperate with each pass, but Jared cannot understand a word he's saying. Jared says *pardon me* several times, leaning in because he really means it. Jared wants Brady to keep talking. He wants to understand.

Brady pulls the trigger and they both collapse onto the snow. Jared lays there feeling like he used to after a week of football tryouts in high school. Everything hurts. He opens his eyes but keeps them locked on the sky. It feels like a train is thundering through his head. He imagines the cops and their fast-approaching footsteps but the gunshot's echo and a thick layer of snow muffle the sound. Above him heads bob in and out of view. They're all saying the right sort of things but Jared can't be bothered to listen anymore. The man who introduced himself as Brady Monroe is startlingly silent but his kids are screaming again. People will tell them lies just to quiet them down. They'll say everything is going to be fine when nothing is fine anymore. Something about Collier is broken and can't be fixed. It's not their fault; it's just the way things are now. He wonders if he should tell Brady's kids the truth—that he couldn't hear their daddy's last words. Above him the sky is white going to gray but all he can see is the splatter of blood and brain and bone.

14

Macy's truck bounces along the deep ruts cut into the frozen surface of the narrow country road. Hidden among the trees, the house is only a few minutes' drive from Route 93. She parks among the other sheriff's patrol cars that line the soft shoulder, getting as close to the little house as she dares. The residence looks harmless enough, but when she climbs out of the truck she gets her first whiff of the madness coming her way. The stench of cat urine is overpowering. She's visited enough meth labs to recognize it immediately. Anhydrous ammonia, an ingredient more commonly found in fertilizer, is also used in methamphetamine production. It's not only toxic, it's highly explosive. In the distance she can see a crew suited in protective gear going in and out of what's left of the house.

It didn't take long to track down Brady Monroe's meth lab. The home had once belonged to his uncle, but Brady has been paying the utility bills for the past fifteen years. As far as the county knows it's been unoccupied all that time. A neighbor reported the fire before the sheriff's office had time to organize a raid. Other than smoke stains haloing the front windows and the charred timber beams of the exposed roof, the modest one-story bungalow looks untouched, but according to what she's heard on the radio, an entire wall of the kitchen has blown out into the backyard. Macy swears under her breath. Given the amount of fire damage, there might not be much evidence left for them to process.

Macy starts up the driveway. Someone has snapped a length of chain that once secured the gate. The broken pieces lie in the snow next to a sign telling those who cross to beware of dogs. There are other signs nailed to the trees. The homemade warnings are as riddled with misspellings as they are bullet holes. She takes a few steps and stops to look down in the snow. The dogs appear to be sleeping. She nudges the closest one with her foot. There's some movement. It's not been dead too long. It's not had time to freeze.

She hears Warren's voice but she doesn't look up to greet him. "They've both been shot," he says, clearing his throat.

"By us?"

"Nah, they were dead when the fire crew arrived." He points to the scars running along the flanks of the one closest to the path. "These dogs have been trained to fight. They would have attacked anyone who came too close to the house."

"So whoever did this didn't know the dogs well enough to get past them?"

"Who knows? Maybe Brady did all this before going home to shoot his wife."

"The timing isn't right. The fire was reported after the suicide. What have you found so far?"

He takes a deep breath. "So far it's your typical meth lab. We find at least one a day in this part of the state."

"This wasn't an accident."

"Probably not, but we'll know more after forensics takes a look."

"Did you find anything in Brady's trailer?"

"A black ski mask was on the seat of his truck."

"He was at the hospital last night?"

"I have no doubt it was him. He shot himself with Gareth's gun."

Macy glances down the road and counts three news vans. Camera crews are setting up on the opposite side of the road. "It's getting a little crowded."

"Brady shot a cop."

"Colin, right? How's he doing?"

"It looks like he's going to pull through. How is Jared? I understand you've known each other for some time. It's good that you were there for him."

Macy frowns. She'd arrived at the trailer park just in time to see Brady Monroe pull the trigger. "To tell you the truth, I'm a little worried about Jared. He didn't seem himself."

"Well, he's had a shock. It's to be expected."

Macy blinks back tears. During the ride to the hospital she'd held Jared's hand. It was hot like bread pulled from the oven.

Warren turns away and coughs into a clenched fist. "So, do you think Jared told us everything?"

"I think he repeated the conversation he had with Brady word for word."

"Why didn't you tell me you were investigating the sex trafficking case all along?"

"I wasn't sure if Leanne's murder had anything to do with it until this morning. Brady's conversation with Jared changes everything."

"Did you know Brady worked for Cross Border Trucking until he lost his commercial license seven years ago?"

Macy holds up her phone. "I just spoke to the guys in Helena. Brady's name did come up in the original case but we didn't have any documentation to prove his involvement." She points to the house. "I hope we'll find something more concrete to link the two cases this afternoon. Brady's last words aren't going to be enough."

"You're going to need to suit up if you want to go inside." He stands back, getting the measure of her. "I'm sure we can find something that will fit you."

The yellow jumpsuit is a men's large. They've bunched it up at the ankles and wrists and secured it with duct tape. The ventilation mask she wears covers most of her face. All she can smell is garlic and onions. She pulls it off and asks when the filter was last changed.

The man helping her suit up thinks for a moment. "Last Tuesday."

"How come it smells like someone else's face?"

His voice is weary. "Our team has done five raids since then."

Water drips down from the charred rafters and in places Macy can see straight through to the slate-gray sky. A cold wind blows through the house. The kitchen counters are crowded with melted plastic bottles and rubber tubing. Everything is tumbled over and disorganized. An over-turned dining chair is burned through to its metal frame. Ragged ends of blackened curtain fabric hang off the window frames. The damp floor beneath her feet is alive with syringes, blister packets of cold medicine, and plastic bottles. So far it's nothing she hasn't seen before.

Warren sounds like he's underwater when he speaks. "You can tell Brady was losing control."

Macy picks up a small glass pipe. There's residue caked inside the bulb. "Have you found any evidence that girls were being kept here?"

"Not yet, but given what Brady told Jared I'm sure we'll find something eventually. This whole business makes me sick." Warren stares out of what's left of the kitchen's back wall. Beyond the apple orchard the crystal peaks of the Whitefish Mountains are clearly visible. "I wish Brady's wife would have come into the station to tell us what she knew instead of accusing him straight to his face."

Macy finds it all too predictable. "I guess she wanted the drama."

"Then she should have gone on a talk show like everyone else."

Macy follows Warren through the rest of the house. An old television sits in a corner of the living room. From the looks of it someone took a boot to it long ago. The floor is covered in soggy newspaper and the sofa has been used as a bed. Warren warns her against going in the bathroom, saying that the suits they're wearing have limits on what kind of protection they can provide.

"Anything in the cabinets that indicate there were females in the house?"

Warren shakes his head and they continue the tour.

There are two bedrooms. Damp cardboard boxes filled with flat-screen televisions and computers are stacked up to the ceiling.

Warren points out a shipping label. "No doubt everything was smuggled over the border from Canada. Seeing as Brady lost his license to drive trucks seven years ago and all this stuff is recent, he hasn't been working alone."

They pass through a dark corridor leading toward the front door and Warren yells at the officers to clear out the shelving units that line both sides.

He gives one of the units a good shake. "I'm pretty sure there's a basement under the house. We just need to find the entrance."

Macy heads for the door. The sense that she's drowning grows stronger the longer she stays inside the house. "I'm going outside to get some fresh air," she says, pulling off her mask.

Warren scowls at the camera crews parked along the road. "I hope you're ready for your close-up."

Macy locks her face in neutral and addresses the group of officers loitering outside the house, warning them not to talk to any reporters. Soon after, she slumps down in the front seat of her car and sips coffee from a thermos. Steam blows up around her face. Once upon a time someone dreamed of building a house on this small hill. From the car, Macy can see the charred rafters in the roof thrusting outward like snapped ribs. The trees in the front garden are overgrown, barren, and surrounded by rubbish. The rope that had once held a swing has long since snapped. The apple orchard is abandoned. The gnarled branches twist in on themselves like arthritic joints. The little house that was lifted straight from the pages of a children's book is gone.

Macy takes in the façade, shifting her view as and when the police officers standing out front change their positions. Even though Colin is predicted to pull through, their faces are set along grim lines. The same cannot be said for Brady Monroe's wife. Tina Monroe was pronounced dead at the scene. Macy would have liked to have a word with her but now that's not going to happen.

A couple of officers start shoveling away the snow that has built up along the base of the façade. At first all Macy sees are tops of the window frames but eventually two basement windows are fully visible.

Instead of phoning, Warren sends an officer out to get her. She watches him run down the path. He slips when he hits the road and slides on his boots across the ice to her door. A cheer erupts from the camera crews. It's the most exciting thing they've seen since Brady Monroe's suicide. They turn their cameras on Macy as she heads back into the house.

The team has cleared the bookshelves from the hallway, revealing a padlocked entrance. Macy arrives just as it starts to snow. The flakes drift down through the open ceiling and fall on their bright yellow suits. She should be cold but her skin feels as if it's on fire and her plastic goggles are steaming up. She puts a hand to the wall and steadies herself.

Someone comes up from behind with a pair of long-handled bolt cutters and they all back away to give him room. The door swings open easily. Beyond where the light catches the unfinished timber walls there is only darkness. Dust motes rise and catch in the beams of their flashlights.

Warren tells someone to run some lines so they can get some lights set up down in the basement. He looks up at Macy. "I would say, after you, but that doesn't seem appropriate given the circumstances."

Macy manages to smile but he doesn't see it. "No," she says, hanging back. "I'll go last if that's okay."

The basement covers an area the size of the house. The unfinished ceilings are low and everyone aside from Macy has to stoop. The windows are boarded up from the inside with plywood sheeting. There is no fire damage but water from the hoses has leaked through the floorboards above. It drips on them like rain. Macy tiptoes through a puddle, being careful to avoid stepping on anything important. She counts several syringes, a glass pipe, and a couple of spoons.

An old wooden apple press lies overturned in the center of the room. She nudges it with her foot and the barrel rocks back and forth. A utility sink is tucked away in a corner and a small closet houses a toilet. There's a bar of soap resting next to the sink's faucet. It's greasy and short strands of thick hair stick to the blackened foam. She pokes around a shallow cabinet with her gloved hands and finds an empty box of tampons and a hairbrush entangled with large amounts of hair. All around her flash-bulbs are popping as the forensic team sets to work. They've taken off the plywood boards and strung power cables in from the road. Lights are being installed in all the corners. Macy turns around and finds Warren standing behind her with an evidence bag. She hands him the hairbrush. "This should be a regular cornucopia of DNA."

Warren points out the row of mattresses sitting on the floor. "It looks like you were right. They may have kept the girls here. Given what Brady and his wife were saying I think we have to assume Leanne's murder is somehow linked to all this."

Macy doesn't have the usual wave of euphoria she often feels when she's made progress in a case. She feels nauseous. There are lengths of chain bolted to the walls. A rusty pair of handcuffs rests on the floor at her feet. She almost stumbles as she makes her way toward the stairs. "We need to let forensics get on with it. Let's go talk outside."

They sit in Macy's car with the heat cranked to high. Now that she's taken off the protective suit she's freezing. Outside, it continues to snow. A termite control company has delivered a large tent that will enclose the entire house. Macy frowns when she sees a fireman take a chain saw to the charred tree that once held the rope swing. Minutes later it crashes over the fence and lands in the apple orchard.

Warren looks miserable. "I knew Brady's uncle Phil. He and his wife Clementine were good people. They couldn't have their own children so they fostered. Raised all kinds of kids in this house."

Macy asks what happened to them.

"They passed away quite a few years ago. Clementine went first and Phil went second. As I recall, it was only a matter of weeks." He points to the orchard. "I've eaten apples from those trees. I've had dinner in that house. They'd die all over again if they found out what was going on here."

"It's a beautiful spot. Maybe someone will put things right again."

Warren grimaces as he clasps and unclasps his fist. "That's a nice thought but I'm not sure I believe in happy endings anymore."

Macy points to his hand. "How did you hurt your hand, Warren?"

Warren leans back against the door and inspects the bruising on his knuckles. "I lost my temper and punched a kid who was high on meth. He won't remember, but I will."

"I suppose it happens to all of us at some point."

"No, it doesn't happen to me." He tilts his head toward the house. "The fact is I'm tired of seeing the same shit every day, and I don't see how I make much of a difference anymore."

"So what are you going to do? Polish off your Bible and go back to being a deacon?"

"Nah, I suspect that would require more faith in humankind than I can muster."

Macy puts a hand on Warren's forearm. "Don't worry, you'll get it back. Anything on Brady Monroe's fingerprints?"

He swallows hard before he speaks. "They don't match the partial we found out at Grace's house."

"I didn't think they would. Brady Monroe was about to kill himself. Given that he told Jared about the girls, I think he would have confessed to Leanne's murder when he had the chance." She takes another sip of coffee. "I wonder how many girls came through here. The basement looks as if it has been shut off for some time."

"Hard to say. Don't like to think on it too much."

"Whoever is behind this, they're local. They didn't waste their time getting over here. They're tidying up loose ends." Her phone rings and she looks at the caller ID. It's Ray. She answers and then holds the phone against her chest. "Warren, I have to take this. We'll talk later back at the station."

Macy has to wait for Ray to stop laughing.

"I saw you on the news. Yellow suits you."

Macy looks in the rearview mirror. There's a bright red outline on her face where the mask pushed snug against her skin. "That's enough, Ray. It's been a long day."

"Ah, come on, Macy. You've got to admit it's kind of funny."

Macy chooses not to engage. "I'm pretty certain they kept girls locked up in the basement of the house."

Ray quits laughing. "How certain?"

"Fairly certain." Macy tells them what they found so far, making a point of mentioning the handcuffs, the tampons, and the hairbrush. "I can't imagine how much DNA they'll find on that brush. It had a thicket of hair in it."

"What do we know about Brady Monroe?"

Macy pulls out onto the road, waving to the officers standing on the front porch when she turns around in the driveway. "He shot himself with Gareth Long's gun so we know he was at the hospital last night. There was a black ski mask in his truck."

"Any connection with Arnold Lamm?"

"Until seven years ago he was an employee. His prints don't match the partial we found at Grace's house but it's clear that he hasn't been working alone. Before he put a gun to his head Brady Monroe said that Leanne Adams was killed because of something she did. There was a sum of money involved but nothing specific. He also suggested that her killer liked to do things to young girls. He described him as a sick bastard."

"You need to find out who Brady has been doing business with."

"That goes without saying." She bites her lip. "Any chance you might come up here?"

Ray sighs. "That would be tricky. If I come up, everyone in the state will be looking at what's going on in Collier."

"True enough, but I thought it might be good for you to see the house for yourself."

There's a slight hesitation before he answers. "I think I'll just stick to updates over the phone for now. If things heat up, I'll make the trip."

Macy takes a left, heading south on Route 93. It's not yet three and it's already growing dark. She needs to get something to eat before heading over to Toby Larson's used car dealership.

"Macy," he says, softening his tone. "Are you okay?"

"You know me, Ray. I'm always fine."

"Well, if you're not, you sure put on one hell of an act."

"I'm going to go now, Ray," she says, hanging up before he has a chance to say anything else.

A billboard advertising Larson's Used Cars hangs frozen in the air above Collier. At least twenty feet tall in his cowboy boots, a deeply tanned Toby Larson wears no more than the boots, a cowboy hat, a smile, and a carefully placed price tag. Macy can't help but think that he looks cold. Toby steps outside to greet her and he still wears a cowboy hat and a smile, but is otherwise, thankfully, fully clothed.

He takes Macy's hand and delivers a generous smile. "Hello, Ms. Greeley. It's a pleasure to meet you."

Macy tucks a loose strand of hair behind her ear and lets him guide her into the showroom. Across from the cars on display a blond-haired woman sits at a desk behind a glass partition.

"Is that your wife, Pamela Larson?"

Pamela looks up from her desk and Toby gives her a wave. "Yes, that's my Pamela."

"I didn't realize she worked here."

"She doesn't really work all that much. I think she just comes in to keep an eye on me."

"It saves me having to track her down."

His tan fades. "Why do you want to speak to Pamela?"

Macy gestures toward an office with his name on the door. "We should probably continue this conversation somewhere private."

Toby's office is decorated with brown leather chairs and dark wood paneling. A stag's head and several fish mounted onto frames hang on the wall above his desk. The leather creaks when Macy sits down. Her feet are so swollen she's tempted to ask Toby for something to prop them on.

Toby opens the door to a small refrigerator. "What can I get you, Ms. Greeley? You look like a fan of diet soda."

"I'm not going to lie."

Toby sits across from her and pours her drink into a glass, complete with ice cubes and a slice of lemon. Toby is smartly dressed in nicely tailored slacks and wears a cashmere sweater over a shirt and tie. His gray hair is combed back from his face, further sharpening his features.

Macy's eyes linger on the stag. "Do you hunt, Mr. Larson?"

"I've hunted all my life. Fished as well."

Macy slips a notebook out of her bag and jots a few lines while Toby fidgets in his chair.

"Where were you on Tuesday morning between the hours of ten and noon?"

"I took the morning off. Monday evening was the annual Chamber of Commerce dinner. I overdid it as usual."

"Can anyone vouch for your whereabouts?"

"Only my two Labradors."

"When was the last time you were in touch with Leanne Adams?"

"I've not heard from Leanne in eleven years."

"I need to ask you some questions about your relationship with her."

"I'm not sure there's much left to tell."

"Grace Adams was born around the time you and Leanne were seeing each other. Have you ever given the idea that you might be her father much thought?"

Toby raises an eyebrow. "Wow, you get straight to it. I thought you guys liked to start off gentle."

"Are you going to answer the question?"

He holds his hands together, only fingertips touching. "When I asked

Leanne that same question, she told me I wasn't good enough to be Grace's father. According to her, the worthy gentleman was a trucker from Wisconsin."

"It doesn't sound like there was a lot of love between you."

"We drank a lot. There were times it was volatile."

"Did it upset you that Leanne was seeing other men?"

"Neither one of us were faithful. Hell, I was married. I couldn't exactly complain."

"But at some point you both committed to the relationship. You decided to leave Collier together. It must have been a blow when Leanne took off on her own."

"I was angry, but eleven years is a long time. I've moved on."

"What happened the night she left?"

"I packed my bags as planned and said good-bye to Pamela." Toby peers over Macy's head toward the offices on the other side of the showroom. "I expected my wife to welcome my departure, but it seems that I made a gross miscalculation. I failed to factor in her pride. She hid my car keys. We live pretty far out of town so I was stuck. Leanne finally called me at around midnight. She was in tears. She'd only tell me that she'd done something stupid and had to get out of town fast."

"Did she tell you that she'd left Grace behind?"

"She didn't say a word. That really upset me. It was one thing to treat me with such callous disregard but Grace was only seven at the time. I don't know how anyone could do such a thing."

"Did you go looking for Leanne?"

"I went out to the truck stop first thing in the morning. Her car was gone. I pounded on the door of her trailer but nobody answered. I honestly thought she took Grace with her. I didn't know that poor child was locked inside."

"How well did you know Arnold Lamm?"

"We were friendly but never close. He doesn't hunt, but we've been known to go fishing together, Chamber of Commerce meetings, that type of thing."

"Any business dealings?"

"Occasionally I'd rent out vans to his company when they were transporting smaller loads. I always seem to have a few on the lot. Easy money."

"Do you have records?"

"It's been a while but I'm sure they're in a filing cabinet somewhere. I'll have my secretary have a look."

"I'd appreciate it if you could start looking now."

Toby picks up the phone on his desk. "Was Arnold involved in this sex trafficking ring you've uncovered?"

"I really can't comment."

Toby raises an eyebrow. "That means he probably was." He puts down the phone and stands. "My secretary isn't at her desk. If you can wait a few minutes, I'll have a poke around and see what I can find."

Macy picks up her bag and coat. "In that case, I'm going to take a stroll across the showroom and have a chat with your wife."

"Better you than me."

Macy stops at the door. "Would you be willing to submit a DNA sample? We'd also like to take your fingerprints."

"Am I really a suspect?"

"At this point, I can't rule you out. You don't have an alibi for the morning Leanne was killed and you have a history with the victim. It's enough to get a court order."

"There's no need. I've nothing to hide."

"Someone will be here in the next hour. Meanwhile, if you could find those files?"

Macy taps on the window to Pamela Larson's office. Pamela's eyes slide in her direction. She frowns before stubbing out her cigarette in the ashtray and inviting her in.

Macy introduces herself. "I'm sorry to intrude but I'd like to have a quick word with you?"

"I suppose it's your job to stick your nose into other people's business."

"Only when their business is especially interesting."

Pamela starts to gather some papers off her desk. "I have an appointment to get to."

"Mrs. Larson, you can speak to me now and be a little late for your appointment or come down to the sheriff's office and miss it altogether. Your choice."

Pamela looks at her watch. "You have five minutes."

"Oh, I think you'll find I have more than that," Macy says, pulling out the empty chair and sitting down. "On the morning Leanne was murdered several witnesses are willing to testify you were at your health club."

Pamela lights another cigarette and eyes Macy through a cloud of smoke. "I had no idea I was a suspect. It's such a relief to know I've been exonerated without having to lift a finger."

"Oh, you're not off the hook yet. You could have paid someone to murder Leanne. You have both money and motivation."

Pamela taps some ash into an ashtray and tilts her head. "But how was I to know Leanne was coming back to Collier?"

"That's what I'm going to find out."

"I'm sure I'll be the first to know if you do."

"I understand you and Leanne were classmates in high school."

"We were actually best friends in high school, although it's difficult to believe that was ever the case."

"Why did you fall out?"

"We fell out over a man."

"Toby?"

"No, not Toby. Not that time, anyway. This was a college boy we both had our eye on." She frowns. "I lost that battle."

Macy glances around the office. There's an expensive-looking bouquet of roses in the vase on the desk. She reaches out and touches a petal. It is soft against her fingertips. These weren't stolen from a bucket in the entryway of a mini-market.

"You may have lost that battle but I'd say you won the war."

Pamela sits back in her chair but says nothing.

"How well did you know Arnold Lamm?"

"Fairly well. He was the college boy Leanne and I fell out over. At the time he and Elizabeth were already engaged." She pauses. "Does that shock you?"

"I have to admit that it does. I take it Elizabeth found out."

"Oh, I made sure of that. Elizabeth forgave Arnold but never spoke to Leanne again."

There's a soft knock at the door and they both look up. Toby stands holding a few sheets of paper.

"I hope you don't mind. I made photocopies of the invoices. I'd like to keep hold of the originals."

Pamela stubs out her cigarette. "Detective Greeley, it's been nice chatting with you but I really have to go now."

Toby looks at his watch. "Pamela, you said you'd cover the phones the rest of the day. Justine has just gone off to visit her father in Billings."

Pamela puts her coat back on the hook. "You really need to hire a temporary secretary."

"It's only for one day. She'll be back the day after tomorrow."

"I hope your husband doesn't treat you like this."

"I wouldn't know. I don't have one."

Pamela eyes her approvingly. "You know what? I think I've just raised my estimation of you."

Macy traces her eyes over the invoices. "Are you sure this is all?"

"There may be more but Justine's filing system has evolved over the years into something rather cryptic."

Pamela settles back into her chair. "We think she does it on purpose. It's made it impossible to fire her."

15

Grace peeks out the front window of the small apartment she now shares with her aunt and watches Macy's patrol car pull into a parking space right outside the front door.

Grace looks over her shoulder and calls to her aunt. "Macy is here. Are you ready to go?"

Elizabeth pokes her head around the corner. She's still wearing a dressing gown. "I'm running late. Invite her in and give her some coffee."

The bell rings and Grace swings open the door and stares. Dustin stands in front of her, holding his hat in his hands. Grace almost shuts the door in his face but stops. Macy is not more than ten feet away. She is sitting in her car speaking on her phone. She looks up and waves at Grace before turning her attention back to the conversation she's having.

Grace barely lifts her eyes to look at Dustin.

"Aren't you going to invite me in?" he asks.

Grace checks Macy again. She's still on the phone. Grace backs away from the door and lets Dustin in.

"Is your aunt ready to go?"

Grace stutters. "She'll be here any minute."

"Are you okay?" he asks, reaching for her.

Grace stands perfectly still and waits for Dustin to stop holding her. Her arms are pinned to her sides and his body is pressed up against hers. Her face is flushed from heat and rising anger. He's held on long enough. She tells him very quietly to let go.

He rubs her back with his hands and speaks in a whisper. "I thought you'd forgiven me. Why haven't you called?"

Grace pulls away. "You know why."

He holds her at arms' length and looks around the room. "What's going on?"

"You need to leave."

"Why? What have I done?"

"I saw what you did in my bedroom."

"I don't know what you're talking about."

"You said you'd changed."

"I have."

"You wrote on my wall."

"Grace, I've never set foot in your bedroom."

"It was a passage from the poem you gave me. Who else would have done it?"

"I swear I didn't do it."

"Then who did?"

"I don't know."

"All the letters you wrote to me are gone. My sketchbook is missing."

Dustin puts his hand over his mouth. "Someone took my letters?"

In the back of the apartment a door opens and shuts. For a brief second Grace hears the low drone of the television set coming from her aunt's bedroom.

"You have to go."

"I swear on my life, Grace. I didn't do this. What I wrote to you was private. I would never hurt you. I love you."

Grace looks down at the floor. "I don't know if I can trust you anymore."

Dustin stands in front of her with his head bent. "I'll get your sketch-book back, I promise."

"Just how are you going to do that?"

He looks away. "I don't know yet."

Grace hears footsteps and moves into the kitchenette. She opens the door to the refrigerator just as her aunt enters the room. The cold air feels good on her face.

"Oh, hello, Dustin. How long have you been here?"

"I just arrived. Are you sure you're up to going back to the house?"

"I have to be, don't I? Grace and I might be living here in town for a while. We need a few things." She pauses. "Grace, what are you looking for in the refrigerator? You can't be hungry again. We just ate."

Grace squeezes her eyes shut and tries to keep her voice even. "I'm warm."

"Then take off that ridiculous hat. I don't know why you insist on wearing that ugly thing all the time."

Grace shuts the refrigerator door and pulls Jared's hat from her head. She doesn't look at her aunt when she speaks. "When are we leaving?"

Elizabeth checks the time. "Any minute. Martha Nielson said she'd come along and give us a hand as well."

Grace's home on Summit Road looks as if it's aged years in the days since she's been away. In front there's a bowl of clear ground where the snow has been trampled down by footsteps. At the sides the snow level rises up undisturbed, reaching the lower sills of the ground-floor windows. The big oak door hangs open. Macy and Warren are on the threshold speaking to Elizabeth and Martha Nielson. Dustin Ash stands just behind them. Grace stands back, keeping an eye on things. Dustin's eyes dart away when she catches him staring. The front door swings shut and Grace walks toward the garage.

There are three patrol cars parked in the driveway and a couple officers lean against one of the vehicles chatting to one another. One of them tips his hat as Grace walks by and she feels blood rush to her face as she stumbles over saying a simple hello. The driveway has been cleared but there's still a thin layer of ice. She inspects the surface and wonders how difficult it will be to traverse. She's not used to driving in winter. During the summer she drove for days on end while her uncle Arnold dozed in the passenger seat. They'd set up the tent and her uncle would spend his days fishing while Grace sat in the shade filling her sketchbooks.

There's a well-worn path going around the back of the garage. Grace has heard that people have been coming to see where her mother was killed. She imagines them sitting among the trees at night watching out for Leanne's ghost. Yellow crime-scene tape is draped across the door to the garage like bunting. Grace pulls it away and the brittle plastic snaps in the cold. Using the remote control on the key ring, she opens the door. It groans but gives, swinging in a wide arc. The bay is wide enough for three cars but there's only her uncle's truck, a drift boat, and his workspace. She trails her gloved hand across the bed of the truck as she walks. Custom built—her uncle Arnold used to go over the specifications again and again. When he had friends over playing darts and drinking beer he'd always gotten around to bragging about it.

"Of course, it's a V8," he'd slur drunkenly. "It's a Ford F-250 extended cab. Custom built, for God's sake." He'd stagger around, bottle in one hand and pointing out the truck's features with the other. "Mint condition."

One particular summer evening, her uncle Arnold went even further.

"Mint condition," he said, lopsided grin stuck to his face. "Just like my Gracie here. She's mint." He narrowed his eyes at his friends and jabbed a finger toward his niece. "And she's gonna stay that way."

Grace gets to the front of the truck and plugs in the block heater. It's going to take at least two hours before the engine is warm enough to try starting it up. She glances at the side door that leads into the kitchen and thinks of how one small decision can change everything. If she'd stayed at the house instead of going off to sulk, Walter Nielson would have left her alone and Dustin wouldn't have come to her rescue. After that evening things between her and Dustin changed. It started with a secret. After he calmed her down and dried her eyes, he made her promise never to tell anyone about what happened. *I'll deal with Walter,* he said. *I'll make sure he never touches you again.*

Grace pulls open the door to her uncle's truck and climbs up into the cab. The cold plastic seats buckle and snap. It's spotless inside and out. That was one of Arnold's rules. Whenever they got back from a trip they'd clean his truck until it looked like new. There wouldn't be a smear, a smudge, or a speck of dirt to be found anywhere. He scrubbed the wheel wells and tire treads. She even saw him vacuuming out the filters. They spent hours in the garage together. He showed her how to adjust the spark plugs, change the oil, and check all the fluids. The truck had over two hundred thousand miles on it but it still looked brand-new. There wasn't a single scratch in the dark green paint. Using the remote control attached to the visor, Grace shuts the garage door and sits in darkness.

Dustin started showing up at the back gate a couple of weeks after her transplant operation, only calling out to her when he was sure her aunt was gone from the house, running errands. She listened to him say she was pretty. She listened to him call her baby. He said he wanted to kiss her, that she could be his girl. Throughout that long last night she replayed his words in her head as she lay in bed, weaving a story around him, a fairy tale around them. On the morning her mother died, he threw pebbles at her bedroom window. He carried long-stemmed red roses, which he held to his heart. Grace dressed quickly in her nightgown and kimono before running downstairs to let him in the gate. The air outside had been sharper than expected.

"Aren't you a pretty thing?" he said, his eyes wolf-like, his mouth leering.

Grace stopped, her feet freezing on cold pavement. She didn't like his tone. There was a familiar ring to it that didn't sit well with her. But then he smiled kindly and the threat was gone.

His voice was soft. "You just take your time. I'll wait all day if that's what it takes."

An expanse of overgrown grass stretched out in front of her. She took a tentative step forward, her eyes going wide from the shock of the cold dampness. Her second step was more cautious than the first. She was slowing down instead of speeding up. Expecting his anger, she received only encouragement.

"Come here," he said. "You promised me a kiss. I've been waiting four years to kiss you again."

But Grace grew more ill at ease with each footfall. She was getting closer and closer to that mouth of his. Realizing she could go no further, she stopped a few feet from the gate.

He held a hand palm upward, stretching it toward her through the iron bars. "Grace, this is our chance to make things right."

"No," she said, backing away. She wanted to say more. She wanted to tell him that nothing could ever make things right between them, but the words got tangled up inside her head. She could only repeat the word "no." She was surprised when she heard herself shouting it over and over again.

He snatched at the air between them with his hands. "Where are you going?"

Grace, already stumbling backward, tripped over her mother's kimono and fell to the ground. Once on the porch she backed into the house, not once taking her eyes off him. She now saw just how close she'd let him get. She'd led him on. This time it was her fault.

"Grace, come back. I just want the chance to start over." He shook the bars. "Please, Grace, I love you."

"I'm sorry," she said. Given how much she'd promised him in the past week, it seemed such a weak answer. *I loved you yesterday but not today.*

The side door leading from the garage to the kitchen opens, and Macy flicks on the light switch. Overhead the lamps blink into brightness in a quick march across the ceiling. Grace rolls down the window and asks Macy if they'd started packing up the things in her room.

Macy comes to the passenger side and gets in. "Don't worry. We followed your instructions to the letter. I'm sure you'll have everything you need now."

"Is my aunt still angry with me?"

"She's not angry, she's just upset that you argued."

Grace runs her hands over the steering wheel. "It's the first time I've ever talked back to her."

"Hopefully, it won't be the last."

"She knows my uncle promised that I could have the truck when I turned eighteen. It's not my problem that he didn't really mean it."

"Why do you say that?"

"I was never expected to live this long."

"You can't think like that."

She wipes tears from her eyes. "I'm tired of being told how to think."

"Welcome to my world." Macy runs her eyes over the interior of the truck. "Why were you so desperate to have the truck now? It will be a while before you'll be able to drive it."

"Yeah, I know. I just felt like getting my way for once."

"I get that."

Grace looks at Macy. "I never want to go inside this house again."

"I can't say I blame you. I was kind of surprised you were willing to come up here at all." Macy pauses. "Have you given any more thought to the message we found written on the wall?"

Grace puts her hands on the steering wheel. "No, ma'am."

"In the last couple of months have you received any odd telephone calls? Did you notice anyone in particular hanging around the hospital?"

"Are you talking about when I had my operation?"

"Yes, around that time your name was in the newspapers. There was a writer who did a couple of feature articles on the heart transplant. Someone may have gotten a crush on you."

"I didn't want to talk to anyone, but my aunt was trying to raise money for my medical care. The insurance didn't cover everything."

"How much did you manage to raise?"

"A lot more than we expected. A couple of people were very generous."

"Do you remember their names?"

"They gave anonymously."

"So no phone calls and no strange visitors?"

"Nothing that I can recall, but I was pretty out of it in the first week after the operation so I have no idea who came to see me."

Macy places her hands on her swollen belly. "What about the reporter? What was he like?"

"He seemed nice, but I didn't like his photographer."

"Why's that?"

"He called me a spoiled brat because I didn't want to have my picture taken."

"No wonder you look so upset in all the photos. Did he do or say anything else that you found strange?"

"Well, it may have been nothing, but he seemed to know a lot about my mom. I didn't like that."

"How old was he?"

"At least fifty."

"So they could have known each other."

"I suppose so."

Macy glances over at the door. "I need to go back inside. Are you okay out here on your own?"

"There are three patrol cars parked outside in the driveway. I think I'll be fine."

"All right then."

Grace waits for a few minutes and Macy doesn't reappear. She turns and climbs over the seat into the rear of the cab. There's a lever on the side of the wide bench seat. She pulls it and the seat pops upward. Underneath, a black metal box is bolted to the floor. She removes a ring of keys from her coat and finds the one she's looking for. The lid comes off easily. Inside, there's a 9mm semiautomatic, several clips of ammunition, and a few tightly bound rolls of fifty-dollar bills secured with a rubber band. She picks up the gun and holds it in her hands. She'd been with her uncle when he bought it. A man she'd never seen before drove up in an old Buick and after popping the trunk, he sifted through a heavy pile, listing the name of every firearm until he found what her uncle wanted, a 9mm semiautomatic. Her uncle often took it on fishing trips, sometimes lining up beer cans for target practice.

"Nothing wrong with learning how to protect yourself," he'd say, forcing her to take hold of the weapon. "There are some strange men out there."

Grace was fourteen at the time and already knew plenty about strange men. It was the same summer Dustin left town without saying good-bye. Grace couldn't understand why she felt so lost without him. She was old enough to know she should hate him and was upset to find that she missed him instead.

She puts the gun back in the box and picks up a bundle of money. She turns back the corners on the first few bills, checking to make sure they're all fifties before slipping the roll into her coat pocket.

Grace thinks about her mother's last words. *You'll have to be careful,* she said, her eyes drifting shut. *They're still looking for the money.*

Grace stretches out on the backseat. She doesn't know how much money they're looking for but she imagines it must be a great deal if it's worth killing someone over. Her mother seemed obsessed with money. Every night she'd spread out her tips on the kitchen table and count it all out. Occasionally, she found a foreign coin, usually Canadian. Leanne would frown and put it to one side. *What kind of cheapskate gives the waitress money she can't spend?* Leanne stored everything in a metal coffee tin that she hid in her bedroom. One evening she caught Grace pulling it from its hiding place.

She'd screamed at Grace. *Don't you ever touch it again. I swear I'll know if you do.*

It seemed like a lot of money. None of it was Canadian.

16

Ray's call wakes Macy from a deep sleep. She fumbles around the sheets looking for her phone. "We need to meet," he says, telling her that he has new information on the case but would rather not come all the way to Collier.

Macy suggests the diner in Walleye Junction and they agree to have breakfast there in an hour. She yawns into her palm and focuses in on the time. It's only six in the morning. She mutters a few expletives and staggers out of bed. She's been living out of a suitcase all week and is unsure if she has anything clean to wear.

For several miles she follows at a safe distance behind a gritting truck, content to take it slow so she has time to collect her thoughts. Her appearance bothers her. She feels so uncoordinated. She's always been able to enter a room believing she was taking ownership of it. Now she feels the need to skirt around the edges as if apologizing for her bulk. She sits up a little taller and reminds herself once more that she's pregnant, not diseased.

It's early Saturday morning and the parking lot is nearly empty. She chooses a spot close to the door and steps out into the freezing cold. Other than the diner all the businesses along the main thoroughfare appear to be closed. Macy concentrates on her balance. It's icy and the last thing she wants to do is fall. Given her size, she's afraid she'll never be able to get up.

She's reaching for the door handle when she hears footsteps approach from behind. She looks up and there's Ray smiling down at her and the next thing she knows she's smiling too. She hadn't meant to. She'd meant to sit across from him and scowl over their plates of food but now she's nearly in tears. She swallows hard and keeps her expression in check. Instead of touching they say an awkward good morning, shying away from any eye contact whatsoever. By the time she's breathing properly again, he's already moving toward the tables. He opts for a booth in a far corner, well out of range of the front windows.

The waitress who'd served Macy earlier in the week is nowhere to be seen. A young woman named Fern takes their orders and disappears after she serves them coffee. Macy stays busy emptying her bag of the notes she'd thought to bring along. She takes a sip of coffee and stares at the growing pile of paper. Bringing them was pointless. Ray will know that she's memorized everything pertinent to the case.

The waitress comes back with their orange juice and Macy watches Ray as he makes polite conversation. He's gained weight and the gray around his temples seems more pronounced. He turns toward her and their eyes meet for a second. She's so struck by how tired he looks that she can't help herself.

"You look miserable," she says.

"That's because I am."

Macy's mind goes into overdrive. She tells herself that it's an admission that means nothing. He could be talking about work. He could be talking about his health. He could be talking about his marriage. She tries to lighten the mood. "Being in close proximity to Collier seems to have that effect on people."

"In that case, it's a good thing I only came this far." His hand moves forward a fraction and stops. His expression remains inscrutable. "How are you holding up? All things considered, you look amazingly well."

Macy feels her cheeks redden. "I seem to thrive in Collier."

"That's good because things are about to get crazy in Collier." He pushes a file toward Macy and leans back in his chair. "I'm afraid the circus is coming to town."

"Circus?"

"Do you remember that little girl who was murdered in Helena last year?"

"What's going on?"

"Molly Parks was only eleven years old. Within the past two years there have been two other cases of girls who were molested but not murdered. One was twelve and the other was nine. All the same perpetrator but at different locations: Helena, Shelby, Dayton, and now he's here in Collier."

Macy taps the paper in front of her. "How are they tied in with this case?"

"That partial print on the back gate was inconclusive but the DNA from that hair we found in Grace's room was a perfect match with what we have in these three cases."

"Leanne's killer is a wanted pedophile?"

"And a sex trafficker."

"You've linked him to the meth house?"

"Yes, we found his prints and DNA in the basement." Ray points at the paperwork. "Here are the photos of the girls from this case."

Macy flips through the images, snapping them down on the table next to her, placing them in a neat row. She pulls out a file she brought with her and finds a photo of Grace and puts it next to the others. They bear a remarkable resemblance to each other—black hair, pale skin, and waiflike. She's struck by the fact that they all look as if they're slightly undernourished.

"It's not a coincidence," says Ray, leaning in and lowering his voice. "This guy was targeting Grace."

"But Grace is too old."

"Maybe he wanted to grow up."

"What about the Brady Monroe connection? These girls weren't smuggled over the border."

"Maybe one of Monroe's business partners is a pedophile. Brady Monroe told that paramedic that someone did things to young girls that he wouldn't do."

Macy's mouth drops open. "This guy has come back for Grace."

"What do you mean?"

"What if he was obsessed with Grace when she was younger but with her uncle around he couldn't get close to her?" She pulls out a transcript of what was written on Grace's wall and sets it next to the photos. "And now he wants something that he thinks only Grace can deliver. This stuff he wrote on her wall. *Nothing whatever pertaining to godliness and real holiness can be accomplished without* **GRACE**. *One who loves a pure heart and who speaks with* **GRACE** *will have the king for a friend. It is by* **GRACE** *you have been saved. For sin shall no longer be your master, because you are not under the law, but under* **GRACE**."

Ray picks up Grace's photo and turns it around so it's facing Macy. "What if it went further than that? What if this guy abused Grace when she was a child? It would explain her silence. He knows how to control her."

Macy catches sight of the waitress coming toward them with a tray of food. She quickly gathers up the photos of the girls and tucks them away in the file. "You think she's hiding her relationship with him."

"It's possible."

Macy mulls it over as she picks at her scrambled eggs. Outside, the sky begins to lighten. They'll both have to go soon. She looks up and Ray is watching her.

"Have you managed to gain Grace's trust?" he asks.

"In fits and starts. She's skittish." She thinks of Jared. "There's that paramedic."

"The one with Brady Monroe."

"Yes, but he was also first on the scene when Leanne was murdered." She clears her throat.

"Heck of a week."

"Grace has taken a shine to him. It might come in handy."

"I'll try to keep the Molly Parks connection out of the press as long as possible. We've already got sex trafficking and murder. If people know there's a pedophile on the loose there will be chaos."

"I'd appreciate that."

"Has Elizabeth Lamm been cooperating?"

"To tell you the truth, she's not saying much that's been helpful. She's a very proud woman. She's also dying."

"Cancer?"

"Yeah, Warren told me. They're waiting for some test results but the prognosis isn't good."

"If she doesn't have long to live I doubt she'll ever admit to any knowledge of her husband's involvement in sex trafficking. Any other leads?"

"Pamela Larson is still on my list of possibilities. She didn't kill Leanne but I wouldn't put it past her to offer financial incentives."

"But how would she have known Leanne was coming back to Collier?"

"That's a question that's been bothering me all along. How would anyone have known?"

"Leanne hadn't made contact?"

"If she did, no one is admitting to it. I'm working on getting access to phone records."

"When are you going up to Canada?"

"That's taking some sorting out. The registered owner of the car Leanne drove is currently in prison. They're tracking down his girlfriend but it hasn't been as straightforward as I hoped."

"And what about known associates of Brady Monroe?"

"We have a few possibilities. We're doing background checks."

"Anyone stand out?"

"Brian Camberwell is an independent contractor who occasionally drove for Arnold, which explains how his name didn't come up in the original investigation. He has a history of violence but has never been

charged. Apparently, he was ice fishing near Calgary on the day of Leanne's murder. We're making inquiries but keeping it quiet for the time
being." She pauses. "Just so you know, he also likes to beat up his wife."

"We'll need more than that."

"His wife happens to be Pamela Larson's daughter."

Ray puffs out his cheeks. "Collier is a small town."

"Too small."

"Any other employees at Cross Border Trucking stand out?"

"Walter Nielson worked for Arnold for years and was a close family
friend. He was murdered about four years ago. It might be related. Scott
Pearce is another name that has been thrown around. He wasn't part of
Arnold Lamm's inner circle but he's serving time for armed robbery.
Neither of them could have killed Leanne but they might have been
involved in the trafficking."

"Hate to break it to you, but Scott Pearce was released early."

"Why wasn't I informed?"

"I'm telling you now."

"How long has he been out?"

"Two weeks. He's registered at a halfway house in Helena. I'll handle
keeping tabs on him from my end."

"You should bring him in for questioning."

"From what we've found at the meth house I'd say the sex trafficking
operation was disbanded years ago. If Scott Pearce was involved, arresting him is going to have to wait until we have something that ties him to
it. Our first priority is going after whoever murdered Molly Parks and
has been abusing these girls. I don't want to spook the guy by showing
our hand too early." He points to the next name on the list of known associates. "Why is Toby Larson's name here?"

"He was close to Leanne and he's rumored to be Grace's father."

"What does he have to say about that?"

"He asked Leanne years ago. She told him he wasn't good enough to
be Grace's father." She leans back. "I can't rule him out as a suspect in
her murder. Leanne broke his heart when she left town. He seems quite

resigned to what happened, but for all we know he's held it against her for the past eleven years."

"It seems very unlikely. Now that we've found the house where the girls were kept it's more likely Leanne's murder is connected to the trafficking ring."

"Toby Larson went fishing with Arnold and on occasion loaned his company vans off his used car lot." Macy picks up a piece of toast and points it at Ray. "You have to keep in mind that we found no physical evidence on Leanne Adams. Her killer could be anyone. Meanwhile, Molly's killer left us a trail of DNA and fingerprints. He was at the back gate, in Grace's room, and in the basement at the meth house. Brady Monroe's ski mask was found sitting on the seat of his car and instead of dumping it, he kept the gun he stole off of Gareth. I'm seeing very different levels of control."

"You said Brady Monroe wasn't working alone."

"That's what I'm thinking. It would explain what we found up at the house on Summit Road. One of them goes up to Grace's room and creates a shrine while someone else cleans out the office. Brady Monroe was deteriorating fast, which is probably why he messed up so badly at the hospital. I don't see how he would have managed a break-in, the message left on the wall, and a thorough search of Arnold Lamm's office all on his own. He may have killed Leanne Adams though. Grace thought it was the same type of ski mask. The crime scene was a mess. The killer may not have been careful but he certainly was lucky."

"How is Sam Fuller? Have you managed to question him?"

"He's developed an infection in his lungs. I had Warren speak to him about what happened. He didn't add anything to what we knew already."

"I checked out that photographer who worked with Grace for the feature article. He's been in Mexico for the past week and a half. According to his boss he's not really an asshole, just a frustrated artist."

"Must have been a bit of a letdown having to work for the *Collier Gazette*. Any connection to Leanne Adams?"

"Nothing that we can find, and he hasn't got a record. Maybe they had an affair. It wouldn't have been out of character for her to sleep with the guy."

An army truck full of young soldiers pulls up outside and both of them watch the recruits spill out onto the parking lot. They're probably from the training base that's located on the southern end of the Flathead Valley. One of them pulls a face at Macy when he catches her staring at him. She smiles and looks away.

"How are your daughters? I hope Taylor is doing better."

He purses his lips. "She's back in the hospital."

"Is she not eating again?"

"No, she's self-harming this time."

"Christ, when did that start?"

"It's early days. We're still trying to figure it out." Ray rakes his hands through his hair and grimaces. "Jessica knows about us."

Macy puts down her fork very gently and wipes her mouth with her napkin. She's not seen Ray's wife Jessica for nearly two years. They'd been friendly but were never friends.

He looks away. "She wants you to be transferred to another office."

"That's not going to happen."

"I told her that."

"How'd she find out?"

Ray spins a pencil around the tabletop with his finger. "I never threw away our photos. I never erased our e-mails. Maybe I should have, but I didn't. Jessica found them."

"That wasn't very smart."

"No. No, it wasn't." He glances down at her belly and Macy can tell he's trying not to cry when he asks. "You need to tell me the truth, Macy. Is the baby mine?"

17

Jared's head is so sore he can't lift it from the pillow. Keeping his eyes shut is the only thing that feels right. He sleeps some more, waking up when his dogs jump into bed with him. They're growling low and barking in short bursts. He takes hold of the closest one and scratches its ears. Its hair smells of wood smoke. The phone has been ringing intermittently and someone has been coming to the door on a regular basis. He's not answered either. He waits quietly until he hears the resigned crunch of wheels pass out of the driveway. Jared doesn't know if these visits are daily, hourly, or weekly. He's lost track of time. He hasn't bathed. He's not eaten. At the hospital they'd prescribed tranquilizers and sent him home. He thinks it's been two days. He digs his head into the pillow and scratches the coarse hairs on his cheeks.

Jared lights a cigarette and checks his pack. He only has three left and then he'll be forced to leave the house. Very gently he stubs out his half-smoked cigarette and leaves it in the ashtray. He thinks he can slink unnoticed into Trina's store. If there's anyone in town who will understand, it's Trina. She'll leave him in peace and fill up his basket with cigarettes and whiskey and hand him his usual breakfast burrito.

He figures he can be back home in half an hour if he avoids all conversation.

He leans out from the bed and checks the time. It's nearly two. He scrolls through the messages on his cell phone. There's still nothing from Hayley. Her silence is getting to him. Brian is keeping a close eye on her, but he's got to work, he's got to sleep, he's got to take a shit.

Fucking Hayley.

Wrapped in blankets, Jared heads for the living room, pushing his dogs to the side when they refuse to make room for him on the sofa. Comforted by their presence, he's taken to letting them stay inside the house all the time. Long wisps of brown and white dog hair cling to his blankets like lake flies on window screens. His dogs barely lift their heads before scratching out another nest and hunkering back down into the recesses of the sofa. He picks up the television remote from the coffee table and switches on the news. He grows more anxious with each new disclosure.

"This is Connie Evans reporting live at the scene of what police are describing as a house of horrors."

The reporter stands on a road in front of what appears to be a house but it's tented over. In the background he can see a forensic unit gathered on the front lawn.

"The investigation is ongoing but details are slowly emerging. It appears that with the help of others, Brady Monroe ran both a methamphetamine lab and sex trafficking operation out of this modest home just north of Collier. The police are linking this house to the grim discovery of four dead Eastern European women in a roadside picnic area eleven years ago."

They run old news footage from when the bodies were found. A younger version of Macy walks through a parking lot and ducks under a yellow ribbon of crime-scene tape. In the foreground Ray Davidson, now the chief of state police, fields questions from reporters. Following a brief summary the news report returns to Connie Evans and the house of horrors.

"Authorities are unwilling to comment on how this house is tied into

the recent murder of Leanne Adams but public outrage is growing with each new disclosure."

Grabbing a down-to-the-dregs bottle of whiskey off the coffee table, Jared heads for the bathroom. His gray face stares back at him from the mirror but all he sees is Brady Monroe. Jared is not ungrateful. He knows damn well the only real difference between him and Brady is a decent dental plan. A couple of pills in hand, he opens the whiskey. It doesn't taste good but he drinks it anyway, popping the pills in his mouth and washing them down together. The capsules free fall before sinking into the lining of his stomach where they burn like cinders. Seconds later it's all coming back up again. He leans against the toilet and closes his eyes but all he can see is Hayley curled up and barely conscious on his bathroom floor. Rocking back and forth, he tries hard not to cry.

Someone bangs on his front door and he sits perfectly still, hoping they'll give up like the others have. He hears a key turning in the lock and staggers to his feet. He grips the side of the sink and waits.

Macy's voice fills the house. "Don't shoot. I have pizza."

The front door shuts and Jared waits for his dogs to start barking but nothing happens. He yells through the half-open door. "Who gave you keys to my house?"

Macy's face appears right in front of him. "They were exactly where I hid them four years ago."

Jared draws the door shut. "Where's that?"

"I'm not telling. They might come in handy again."

"I'm just getting in the shower," he says, pulling off his sweatshirt and throwing it into the laundry bin. He rubs his beard and decides not to shave. "What day is it, anyway?"

"It's Saturday, the third of December. Time to face the world."

Jared comes in the living room and the television is still tuned in to the local news. Macy has her feet propped up on the coffee table and a box of pizza sits on her lap. It's already half finished. The dogs are lying next to her on the floor, seemingly unfazed by her presence.

"Hey, are you going to save me some?"

"This one is mine. Yours is on the kitchen counter."

Jared doesn't say much while he's eating so Macy does most of the talking, filling him in on everything he's missed in the two days he's been in bed. He points to a photo of Grace, which once again fills the television screen.

"It's her birthday today."

"Whose?"

"Grace's. I told her I'd get her a cake."

"You hardly know her."

"I thought it would make her happy."

"You've not changed at all, have you?"

"What do you mean?"

"You have this need to make everyone around you feel loved even if you don't have the feelings to back it up." Macy closes the empty pizza box and puts it aside. "When we were together you were so affectionate and caring. You'd listen. You'd hold my hand. I thought I'd woken up in an alternative universe."

"And why was that a problem?"

"It was a problem because your heart wasn't really in it. Every time I left your house it felt like I slipped off a cliff or something. I wouldn't get a phone call for weeks and then you'd be asking to see me and telling me how much you were missing me."

"You never said anything."

"Actually, I did, but it kept happening so I gave up. I either had to accept it or go nuts." She wipes her mouth with a paper towel and takes a sip of her drink.

"I'm sorry."

"Do you remember when we split up?"

"It wasn't my finest hour."

"You went all textbook asshole on me. It was like nothing intimate had ever passed between us. You arranged to meet at a busy restaurant in Helena. You chose a table right in the middle of the room. You actually moved the chairs so there was a safe distance between us."

"You had a gun in your purse."

"You were right to be cautious."

"You must have known what was coming."

"Of course I knew. You'd been AWOL for nearly a month."

"I was such an asshole."

"I'm not going to say otherwise."

"But you should have said something then."

"Oh, come on. You weren't even brave enough to dump me. I had to prompt you. Besides, I was so angry I could barely speak."

"Now's your chance."

"It's too late."

"It's never too late."

She raises her voice. "What do you think I was doing when you weren't around?"

"To tell you the truth, I didn't give it much thought."

"Well," she says, narrowing her eyes, "I was fine. I saw other guys. I kept busy. Do you remember that law enforcement convention I went to in Vegas?"

Jared nods.

"I almost got married that week."

"What?"

"You know you're going to blow it with Lexxie, don't you?"

"You almost married someone else while we were dating?"

"Do you think she's sitting around waiting while you're out with Hayley?"

Jared can't believe what he's hearing. "Lexxie isn't anything like you."

"You keep telling yourself that."

"Please don't tell me you just came here to harass me?"

Macy struggles to get up from the sofa. "I came because it's time for you to get your ass out of bed."

Jared waves a piece of pizza in the air between them. "Admit it. You still love me."

She laughs and tells him he wishes that were true, but seconds later her smile is gone. "When are you seeing Grace?"

"After what you've told me, maybe I shouldn't."

"She needs someone she can trust. She may confide in you."

"You think she knows more than she's letting on."

"I'm not sure, but something is going on."

"Why isn't she saying anything?"

"I think she's scared." When Macy glances up at the television, pictures of the four dead girls fill the screen. "And I don't think this is the first time Grace has come across these guys."

Jared closes his eyes. "Sometimes I think I should call up my parents once a day and thank them for giving me a happy childhood."

"I know what you mean." Macy picks up her phone and reads a text message. "They've found where Leanne has been living for the past few years. Do you feel like going on a road trip up to Canada tomorrow morning?"

"Where in Canada?"

"Some place called Finley."

"It's just over the border. I've seen the exit signs but I've never stopped there."

"So what do you think? I could use the company and it would be good for you to get out of here."

"They've given me three weeks off work so I've got nothing better to do."

"If I had three weeks off, I wouldn't stop at Finley. I'd keep driving."

The Sugar Plum Fairies is the only bakery in Old Town. Inside, everything from the trim, to the picture frames, to the delicate writing on the name tags is pink. The three women who've run the place since it opened more than a dozen years earlier are as round as they are tall. Their well-pressed aprons and white uniforms are filled to bursting. Hairnets stretch tight over strawberry-blond hair that is scraped back into buns. They all wear white shoes with thick soles. They all have cherubic cheeks and eyes of cornflower blue. Except for their ages and names they could be triplets. How this could be so is a mystery because the three women aren't even related.

Jared enters the bakery and the Sugar Plum Fairies approach the counter like they're approaching the bench in a court of law.

"Oh, Jared," says Beth, wiping her hands on a kitchen towel draped from the tie of her apron. "We heard what happened. It must have been awful."

"Awful," echoes Lynn.

"You poor thing," adds Jessica.

Beth lowers her voice. "We were just talking about it."

Lynn leans in. "It's all anyone is talking about."

"That and what happened to Leanne Adams." Jessica shivers, rubbing away the goose bumps on her arms along with the baking flour.

Beth raises her voice. "After watching the news we're afraid to go out. They're saying her killer is wanted for sex trafficking."

Lynn frowns. "The world today."

"It's a scary place," finishes Jessica.

Silence follows. Jared peers over them into the kitchen. The rows of cupcakes laid out on a metal slab catch his eye.

Beth hands Jared one of the cupcakes and changes the subject. "How's your mother?"

Feeling on safer ground, Jared thanks her before dropping his gaze to the display case. Behind glass, ready-made cakes are lined up in neat rows. "She's fine, but my dad is kind of bored. Misses his workshop."

Beth laughs and the other women laugh with her. "More like he misses his buddies at Murphy's Tavern."

At the thought of his father, Jared manages a fleeting smile. "I imagine you're right."

The least gossipy of the three shuffles up closer to the counter. Lynn has been a friend of Jared's mom since time began. "What can we do for you today?"

"I need to buy a birthday cake."

"Boy or girl," chimes in Jessica, the baby of the bakers. She's returned to her stool next to a metal table full of cupcakes. She's got flour on her cheeks and a cone of pink icing in her hands. It comes out in a pink swirl onto one cupcake after another. Her face in a concentrated twist, she dips up and down like a well-oiled machine.

Jared feels his cheeks redden. He knows what's coming. "Girl."

"Girl," they all sing in unison.

"Is it for Lexxie?" asks Jessica, looking to her friends. "I didn't know it was her birthday."

"It isn't."

"So, it's for someone else," says Beth, winking at the others. "Sounds complicated."

"Let Jared be," interrupts Lynn.

Jared grows more uncomfortable. "She's just a friend."

Beth looks disappointed and Jessica goes back to decorating her cupcakes.

Lynn gestures toward what's on offer. "Had you ordered ahead we'd have more of a choice but as it is, this is all that's left to take away. Does she like chocolate?"

"No idea. She's a bit quirky. Always dressing in old-fashioned clothes."

Beth cocks her head to the side. "You're not sweet on Grace Adams?"

Jessica's ears prick up. She messes up the cupcake she's working on. "Did you say Grace Adams?"

Lynn speaks in a low voice even though there are no other customers in the shop. "The cake is for Grace Adams?"

Jared loses patience. "Yeah, is that a problem?"

The women fall silent. Somewhere in the back a timer goes off and Jessica hurries away toward the ovens. "Don't you dare say anything else until I get back."

Beth wipes her hands on a towel. "Don't mean to pry but why are you buying a cake for Grace Adams?"

"Look, it ain't no big deal. I don't know her too well but the poor girl seems a bit friendless. I thought it would be a nice gesture."

Lynn taps the glass. "You know what her momma was like."

"That's hardly Grace's fault."

Beth purses her lips. "That's true enough, but in my experience the apple never falls far from the tree."

Jared wants to argue, but a part of him is remembering how Grace looked lying nearly naked out in the snow. "She's just a sick kid."

Jessica pipes up. "But she is pretty, isn't she?" She carries in a baking tray and joins the others at the counter. She looks as plump and warm as the buns she's taken out of the oven. "Not pretty in the conventional sense though. She's got that look about her like you see in those high-fashion magazines, and then there's those old clothes she wears."

Lynn picks at a loose thread on her name tag. "Vintage is what they call it nowadays. Back when I was young we just called it hand-me-downs. I swear to God I thought I saw her wearing my momma's old coat. You know the gray one with pale blue buttons?"

The girls nod.

"She was wearing it at church."

"Well, Grace is petite just like your momma was," says Jessica.

"Nothing like her mother, Leanne," adds Beth.

"Not a breath of Leanne in her." Lynn looks up at Jared. "You might not remember her but Leanne was a big woman."

At the moment Jared can only picture the emaciated woman he'd almost stumbled over in the woods, but Lynn, Beth, and Jessica have other memories.

Jessica cups her hands out far in front of her breasts. "She was huge."

Beth slaps her friend's hands down. "Stop being crude."

"I was just saying."

Lynn lowers her voice. "You know she and Toby Larson had an affair.

It upset Pamela something fierce. It's not very Christian of me but it was nice seeing Pamela taken down a peg or two."

Jessica giggles. "Amen to that."

Beth leans in and speaks in a hushed voice. "You know, when people first heard it was Leanne that was murdered, rumors started flying. People were saying that maybe Pamela did it, but it's not really her style. I don't see her getting her hands dirty."

Lynn's voice is cutting. "You're right, Pamela would have paid to have someone do it for her."

Jared parks his pickup truck in front of Grace's apartment building. There's a patrol car stationed outside. He waves at the officer through the open window. He and Ted Bishop went to high school together.

"How's it going?" asks Jared.

Ted tilts his head in the direction of a low wall separating the parking lot from the gray snarl of traffic moving along the road. Like a tightrope walker Grace balances along the top of the wall with her arms spread wide. In her red coat, hat, and scarf she could be an exotic bird.

Ted points at Grace. "That is one weird chick."

"Been here all day?"

"Nah, just a few hours. How you holding up?"

"Better than Colin. Any word?"

"He's awake and talking, thank God." Ted slams the steering wheel with the flat of his hand. "Whoever was on dispatch should be fired. Colin had no business walking in on a domestic on his own. They still haven't figured out who called an ambulance instead of backup."

"Don't worry, they will."

Ted leans out the window farther. "Are you going to be here long? I'd kill for a coffee. I'll be gone ten minutes, tops."

"Sure thing, but it's your balls on the line if Macy shows up."

"I still need them so you'd best keep a close eye on that girl."

Grace skates across the icy parking lot in her snow boots, only stopping when she notices Jared's truck. She puts a hand to her eyes, blocking what's left of the day's sun. Her face is slow to smile.

"Hey, Grace," he says, leaning out the window, a half-smoked cigarette hanging from his lips. He feels a degree of warmth that surprises him. "Look at you. You seem all grown up today."

She glides across the final few feet. "Eighteen at last."

Breathless and blushing right outside his window, she plucks his cigarette from his lips, taking a quick puff before passing it back. The movement is so intimate he can only stare.

She looks him full in the face. "My aunt doesn't know I smoke sometimes."

Remembering Carson's warning, Jared feels his skin thicken. His life is complicated enough without getting involved with a girl like Grace. And then just as quickly Grace giggles and she's a child again. He unwinds his heart a little, reminding himself that this is a girl who needs a friend.

"I brought you a cake just like I promised." He lifts up the box so Grace can see it.

Grace leans in, admiring the pink ribbon wrapped around the outside. "I'm not sure you should have bothered."

"Don't say things like that."

Grace shuffles backward a few feet and does a twirl. Her red coat spins outward like a cone.

"Hey, Grace, you okay?"

She stops mid-twirl and tilts her head. "Better now, thank you."

"Your aunt home?" He turns to the apartment building. Before he hadn't worried about being alone with her, but now he's not so sure.

Grace rests against the door, coy again. "Yeah, she's home." She watches him for a few seconds. "You want to come in?"

"Only if you're sure it's okay."

"Come on." She giggles, pulling him by the arm through his truck window. "I want some cake."

Jared hands Grace the box and gets out of the truck. A car horn sounds and he sees Ted Bishop turning into the parking lot. He waves and follows Grace inside the apartment.

Grace's aunt is noticeably absent. Grace bustles about the kitchen and waves a hand toward a dark hallway when he asks. Her aunt is taking a nap. Jared unpacks the cake from the box and it sits large and pink on the kitchen table between them. It's too grand for the small apartment.

Grace's eyes light up. "It's beautiful. I don't have any candles though."

Jared reaches in his jacket pocket. "I thought of that."

In two quick strides she pulls him close into a hug and thanks him, then turns away and he knows she's crying. Keeping her gaze downward, she moves about the kitchen. She's wearing an old-fashioned navy dress with a high, slim waist. She's wound her hair up in braids and pinned it loosely so stray strands fall about her face. Leaning over a drawer she resurfaces with a large carving knife and a strange expression. Then she laughs and her whole personality shifts again.

"Kind of a big knife for cutting a cake."

"The others are in the dishwasher. I'm going to wake my aunt. I know she'll want some." She disappears down the hallway, leaving Jared alone.

There's a knock at the door and Jared calls out, asking Grace if he should answer it. Receiving no reply, he steps forward and opens the door.

Pamela Larson's voice is clipped tighter than a box hedge. "What in hell are you doing here?"

"Jesus Christ, keep your voice down."

Pamela looks beyond him, catching sight of the birthday cake. "Don't tell me you bought Grace Adams a birthday cake?"

"That's none of your business. What do you want?"

She holds up a check. "I want to see Elizabeth."

"She's sleeping." Jared looks at her properly for the first time. He can tell she's been crying. She's pulled her hair back in a haphazard knot and kohl is smudged above and below each eye. "What's your problem anyway?"

"My daughter just tried to kill herself and you're asking what my problem is? Seriously, Jared, you've got the emotional IQ of a doormat."

His voice softens. Picking a fight with Pamela won't get him any closer to seeing Hayley. "How is she?"

"Not great. She thinks you never want to see her again." She looks back toward her parked car. It's a big Cadillac and steam from the exhaust is billowing up behind it. A young man sits behind the wheel, waiting. "We heard about what happened out at Brady Monroe's place. It must have been awful. I can't imagine how Brady could have fallen so far."

"You knew him?"

"Jared, this is Collier. Everyone knows everyone." Pamela twirls her wedding ring. It's loose on her finger. "How well acquainted are you with Grace Adams, anyway?"

"Don't tell me you came here to gossip."

She holds up the check again. "No, I came here for Elizabeth. She's set up a fund for the Monroe children. I thought I should do my part."

Jared regards her with hooded eyes. "That's generous of you."

The young man waiting behind the wheel honks the horn and Pamela waves before turning toward Jared. "What should I say to Hayley?"

"Tell her not to worry. Tell her I want to see her."

She steps off the porch. "I'll let her know."

Jared turns away from the closed door and finds Grace standing in front of him with a worried look on her face. She speaks so softly Jared has difficulty hearing her.

"Who was that? I thought I heard voices."

"Pamela Larson."

She takes a quick glance out the window. "What did she want?"

Jared places the check on the counter. "She wanted to drop off a check for your aunt. Something about a fund your aunt has set up for Brady Monroe's children."

"It's just like her to organize something like this when she should be resting." Grace sinks into the nearest chair and holds a cushion to her face.

Jared looks past her toward her aunt's bedroom. "Is she joining us?"

"She says she'll be out soon but we shouldn't wait for her." Grace puts the pillow down and looks up at the ceiling. "She won't tell me anything, but I know she's not been well."

Jared takes Grace's hands and notices how cold her fingers are. He gestures toward the table. "It's your birthday and that's one hell of a big cake. I can't eat it all on my own." He pulls her up by the hand and guides her along, planting her in front of the birthday cake while he lights the candles.

Before dipping her head to blow them out, her eyes briefly meet his. "I never expected to live this long."

They sit on the sofa eating softball-sized slices. Grace insisted, saying that it wasn't as if there'd be other guests. Jared looks around the apartment properly for the first time. The shag pile rug is the color of spawning salmon and every wall surface is covered in wood paneling.

"Whose place is this, anyway?"

"Some woman who went to my aunt's church used to live here. It's pretty awful but it beats going home."

"Do you think you'll ever live up on Summit Road again?"

"My aunt wants to, but I don't."

"What will you do?"

"I'm not sure. I get scared if I think too much about it. I feel so cooped up in here all day."

"If you like, maybe I can take you somewhere."

Grace tilts her head toward the patrol car outside. "Macy would never allow it."

"I'll talk to her. I don't see why you can't have a few hours of freedom." Jared reaches for his coat. Even though he's tired he's meeting Lexxie for dinner. They need to talk. "I'm sorry. I better get going."

She puts a hand on Jared's arm. "I know what it's like to see someone die like that."

Jared holds his car keys in his hands and waits for his nerves to settle.

"It's the worst thing you can possibly see and everyone around you expects you to get over it like that." She snaps her fingers together and turns away. "I don't think I'll ever get over it."

Grace walks into the kitchen and quietly places the plates in the sink before leaning on the counter and pressing her palms to her eyes. She stays like that while Jared lingers near the door. He can't reassure her. He feels exactly the same way.

"Grace," he says, reaching for the door handle. "I'll call you tomorrow."

"You'll talk to Macy?"

"And you think about where you want to go."

18

Macy sits behind the wheel of her patrol car and concentrates on the little hatchback in front of her. Its hazard lights have been blinking at her for most of the trip. Twice Jared has had to pull over and coax the hatchback's engine back to life. It's taken almost an hour to travel twenty miles, but they are finally nearing the Canadian border. It wasn't supposed to be this way. Originally, Jared was going to ride with her, but when he found out how much the state was going to charge Sofia Jankowski to have her car delivered he insisted on driving it himself.

It took a while but the Canadian authorities tracked down the car owner and his girlfriend. Tommy Moss was serving time in prison while his girlfriend Sofia was living in her own purgatory. With Tommy in jail, she'd settled in Finley and was raising their two children on little more than a monthly check from the province and a prayer. According to officers sent to interview her, Sofia had been renting a room to Leanne Adams for the past two years. Further checking revealed that Sofia Jankowski, now a citizen of Canada, had first entered the country eleven years earlier when she was only sixteen years old. Macy is hoping her age and the timing of her arrival aren't a coincidence.

Macy changes the radio station, skipping through what's on offer until she finds some news. Since the story broke, the media has concentrated all its attention on three little girls. Two of the girls are alive and one is dead. The dead girl is named Molly Parks and her photo is everywhere. Now that there's been a connection made with Leanne's murder, the newspapers and television news run a constant stream of news about Molly Parks. It's only a matter of time before someone makes the connection to Grace.

The talk radio programs have had people calling in from all over the state. They've formed groups on the Internet and have threatened to travel to Collier to hold protests in the Town Square. At the last estimate there were only a few of them standing out in the freezing cold, holding placards and shouting their demands every time a microphone is shoved in their faces. The more popular response has been to buy more guns and lock up their children.

One radio talk show comes on after another and it's all the same. *If the law can't deal with this we will,* says one caller. *If we leave it to the courts he'll just get off on some technicality,* says another. A mother cries into her telephone, *We've got a right to protect our babies.*

Macy leans forward and shuts off the radio before picking up the phone and dialing her mother's number. "Hi, Mom," she says, slowing her patrol car further when the hatchback threatens to stall again.

"Hi, sweetheart. You sound tired. Is everything okay?"

"Stop worrying, everything's fine. I just needed to hear your voice. How did the shopping trip go?"

Her mother lists all the stores she visited with her friends to buy everything Macy could ever need for a baby.

"You bought a high chair already? I won't need that for months."

"You're lucky we stopped at the high chair."

Macy spots a sign indicating that the exit for Finley is five miles farther on. "Listen, Mom, I've got to go, but I'm coming down next week so we'll have plenty of time to catch up."

"I know I say this every time we talk but I want you to be careful."

"Don't worry, the most dangerous thing I've done all week is eat fried chicken."

"Please don't joke about this. I'm serious."

"And so am I. I'm fine, Mom. I promise."

Boasting a population of 171, a faded sign welcomes Jared and Macy to the BEAUTIFUL TOWN OF FINLEY, but Macy's first impressions fail to inspire anything other than despair. Finley is nothing more than a scar scraped across a high, barren plain. Farther along the road a vandal has summed it up nicely by removing letters from a request to *Please Drive Slowly*. It now reads *Please D i e Slowly*.

The diner where she and Jared stop for coffee has the best view, and that is of the on-ramp for the highway. The coffee tastes as if it has spent the past week cooling and reheating. Macy swirls it around in her mug but try as she might she can't bring herself to have a second sip. The waitress returns and Macy asks for some hot water and a tea bag.

She asks Jared how he's holding up and he closes his eyes. "Yeah, I suppose I'm functioning." He gives her a lopsided grin. "I know Finley is no garden spot but this is a nice excuse to get out of Collier."

"Have you spoken to anyone about what happened?"

"I really don't want to talk about it."

"It can help, given enough time."

"That's what everyone is saying."

"Have you talked to Lexxie?"

He shows her his phone. "Lexxie has been calling me ten times a day."

"She knows she's losing you."

"Well, she's not making things any better for herself."

"We both know this doesn't have anything to do with Lexxie. The woman you want to speak to most is Hayley, and until you're free to be with her you're going to be a miserable fuck."

Jared watches her over his cup of coffee. "It sounds like you're speaking from experience."

"I'm speaking as your friend. Hard as it is, you need to move on."

"Speaking of which, we should get going. What time did you say this woman was expecting us?"

Sofia Jankowski's home is one of a handful spread out on a grid of scrubby windswept lots. She stands at the front door and watches as Jared and Macy pull up in their cars. Across the street, stray dogs gather in a children's playground and root around in the churned-over snow. As soon as Macy and Jared step out onto the sidewalk, they start barking.

"They run in packs," Sofia says with a strong Polish accent. "My kids, they don't play outside anymore."

There is a toddler on her hip, and an older son stands protectively by her side. Although they are not thin, they look hungry and their lives bear the same used-up quality as the hand-me-downs they wear. Sofia's tired eyes follow Macy and Jared everywhere. She says she works as a hairdresser, commuting to White Sulfur Springs a few days a week, but Macy knows she is not much more than a shampoo girl. She also knows her boyfriend, Tommy Moss, isn't up for parole for another year. She wants to ask Sofia how she manages on her own but she already knows the answer. Sofia isn't managing.

While the kids watch television, Sofia and Macy sit at the cramped kitchen table. Instead of pulling out a chair, Jared paces what little linoleum there is, his eyes darting around, catching sight of everything that will never be fixed: a broken curtain rail, a ceiling lamp's juryrigged wiring, and the refrigerator door secured with duct tape. He steps out, saying he needs to buy cigarettes at the store, but Macy knows this is a lie. A few miles north of the border he stopped at a discount outlet. There are boxes of contraband cigarettes stacked up in the back end of the patrol car like Christmas gifts.

Sofia sips her soft drink straight from the can. "Leanne shouldn't have taken the car. I'm lucky I don't lose my job." She thanks Macy for getting it back to her so quickly, apologizing once again for the trouble

Jared had keeping it running. "Twice I beg for rides off men I hardly know." She makes a face like she's just swallowed something unpleasant. "There are many assholes out there."

"How come you didn't report the car as stolen?"

"Leanne watched my kids. I prayed for her to come back. Without help I do not know how I will manage." She hands a thick brown envelope to Macy.

Macy turns it over in her hands. "What's inside?"

"Photos, papers. Things I found in her room." She picks at the frayed edge of a place mat. "I need money so I took what she owed me for rent. All her other stuff is in there." She juts her chin out toward a battered nylon case that sits bloated and heavy in the hallway.

"How did you meet Leanne?"

Instead of answering, Sofia stares into the darkened living room where the silhouette of her eldest child sways only inches from the brightly lit television. "Sometimes I want to give up. I don't know if I can do this on my own."

Macy doesn't know how to respond. The same doubts have been keeping her awake for months. She slides a box of tissues across the table to Sofia and remains silent but Macy wants to say something, to agree. *I feel the same way. I don't know if I can do this on my own either.* But saying it aloud isn't a risk Macy is willing to take. Saying it aloud might make it true.

Sofia smiles sadly. "Leanne was difficult but I miss her now. I get so lonely."

Macy thinks of the vandalized road sign. *Please die slowly.* In a town like Finley it is far better to get dying over as quickly as possible. "So how long had you known Leanne?"

"I'm not so sure. A long time. I can't remember how we met. Maybe through Tommy."

"Did you realize she was ill? The medical examiner said it was hepatitis C. She was dying of liver failure."

"Yeah, I knew. She lost so much weight. You see how she looked like."

Macy's memories of Leanne are limited to the black-and-white photos provided by the coroner. They weren't flattering. "You were quite young when you immigrated to Canada. It must have been difficult for you without any family around."

Sofia glances over into the living room, checking on her kids again. "It didn't exactly turn out as planned."

"Did you originally intend to go to the U.S.?"

She shrugs. "I wanted to but it didn't work out."

"Sofia," she says, meeting the young woman's eyes. "I think I know what really happened to you when you arrived in this country. I'm hoping that you're willing to talk about it."

Sofia runs her fingers along the edge of the table. "I'm worried I'll be deported if the truth comes out."

"The truth is going to come out anyway."

Sofia looks away and her eyes flutter. "I still have nightmares."

"How many girls flew over with you?"

"There were four of us. We all knew each other back in Poland but we weren't close."

"What can you tell me about the trip?"

Sofia presses a tissue to her eyes. "I was so stupid. I just wanted to get to Chicago where I have family. Back in Poland they made it sound so easy. We flew into Montreal on tourist visas and a nice Polish lady met us at the airport. After she took our money, she drove us to a warehouse a few miles from the airport."

"What went wrong?"

"Everything. As soon as we were inside that truck, the drivers locked the doors and said they wanted more money."

Macy waits quietly. She already knows what happened next. It's not the first time she's heard stories like Sofia's.

"We didn't have any so they took turns with us. There was a bed behind the driver's seat. Whoever wasn't driving would pick one of us to come up front. I was lucky because I wasn't the prettiest. Poor Anya spent a lot of time in that bed."

"What happened when you got to the U.S.?"

"It was dark when we arrived so I have no idea where we were. They locked us in a basement. We had to sleep on mattresses on the floor. If we didn't do as we were told they chained us to the wall."

"Did you see any other men?"

"There was one, but he was older. I think he was the boss. The drivers seemed to do whatever he told them."

"How long were you kept there?"

"I think it was two days before they moved us again."

"Was it the same truck?"

"It was a different truck but this time I didn't see the driver. We thought we'd be on the road a long time but we only drove a short distance and stopped for a day. It was hot but at least they gave us water. We took turns sitting next to the air vent."

"How long was it before Leanne rescued you?"

Sofia doesn't lift her eyes from the table. "Leanne didn't get us out of that truck."

"Then who did?"

Sofia picks up a folded newspaper from the kitchen counter and points at Grace's photo. "Grace. We all thought we were going to die and this little girl opens the door and sets us free."

Macy spends a few seconds thinking about what she's just been told. It's not what she expected. "But Grace was only seven at the time."

"She was just a little thing. I don't know how she managed to break the lock."

"What happened after Grace let you out?"

"She took us to her trailer and we waited for her mother. We were all frightened of Leanne but Grace stood up to her. Leanne wanted to kick us out but Grace talked her mother into driving us to someplace safe."

"How did you end up in Canada?"

"We drove all night, taking back roads. We only realized we were in Canada when Leanne's car broke down outside of Calgary."

"What about the other girls? Have you had any contact with them?"

"We went our separate ways."

"And Leanne?"

"I always thought she went home, but I ran into her a couple of years ago. She was living in a shelter in White Sulfur Springs so I took her in." She points to the photo of Grace again. "I didn't do it for Leanne, though. I did it for Grace."

"Did she say why she didn't go back to Collier?"

"She said there were people who wanted to kill her because of what happened. She'd get upset when she talked about how Grace was living with her sister."

"Do you know why she left Grace behind?"

"I don't think she meant to. She planned on going back right away but then her car broke down. Things kind of went downhill from there."

"We have reason to believe Leanne left the States with a great deal of money."

"As far as I know she never had any money. She talked about sending for Grace but then wouldn't because she couldn't afford the medical bills. She said Grace's uncle paid for everything."

"Do you know where the money she sent Grace on her birthdays came from?"

"I never asked. I think she was ashamed of how she earned it. When she couldn't pay rent she'd tell me she had a lot of money back in Collier. Once she offered me half if I went and got it for her. To tell you the truth, I always thought she was lying."

"She wasn't any more specific?"

"No. I helped her out, but she never really trusted me. I don't think she trusted anyone."

"When we spoke yesterday you said you had a recent phone bill?"

"Yes, it's just here," she says, reaching for an envelope. "Leanne made two calls and received one."

"This bill is from the past month?"

"Yes, it's only just arrived."

Macy runs her eyes over the numbers and recognizes the Flathead

Valley area code. The first phone call Leanne made lasted for a little over ten minutes. A few minutes later she called another number. Three days before Leanne was murdered someone called Leanne from that same number.

Macy holds up the phone bill. "Do you mind if I take this? I'll send you a copy."

"It's not like I can afford to pay it anyway."

Macy looks at the amount that's due. "Don't worry, I'll take care of it."

"You don't have to."

"Honestly, this is the best lead we've had so far. It's the least I can do."

"I only noticed because I think it was the first time someone called Leanne."

Sofia's son tugs at his mother's arm and whispers something in her ear before pulling her toward the living room. Sofia kisses the top of his head and looks up at Macy. "I'm just going to put a DVD on for him. I'll be right back."

While she waits, Macy lays out a series of photos lifted from the DMV records of some of the truck drivers that worked for Cross Border Trucking. In the next room, she hears Sofia speaking to her son in Polish. Even though Macy doesn't understand a word she knows they're negotiating which film he can watch.

Sofia comes back and stares at the photos Macy has laid out on the table. "How much longer? I've got to feed my boys lunch soon."

"I promise we're almost done. I just need you to look at these photos and tell me if you recognize anyone."

Sofia reaches over and picks up a photo of Brady Monroe. "He was one of the drivers who took us across the border. This one I know from the news as well. He shot himself, yes?"

"What about the other driver?"

Sofia inspects each image in turn, studying the faces until she finds the one she's looking for. "Him," she says, swearing in Polish. "I know him anywhere. He's the bastard who raped me. His name was Walter, I think."

"Walter Nielson."

"Are you going to arrest him?"

"I can't. He was murdered four years ago." Macy slides another photo out of her files and taps it with her index finger. "What about this man? Have you seen him before?"

"That's the older man from the house."

"Are you absolutely sure?"

"Yes, that's him. Who is he?"

"That's Grace's uncle, Arnold Lamm."

Sofia pushes the photo away. "I don't understand how Leanne could have left Grace with such a man. I would have let my children die before I let him near them."

Jared doesn't bother knocking on the back door. Loaded down with shopping bags from the grocery store, he bustles into the kitchen and starts unpacking the contents without any explanation. Sofia's face collapses and when she starts crying, it takes a long while to calm her down again. Jared gives her a big bear of a hug and from her chair Macy quietly winces. It's the type of hug she's always hated—claustrophobic and unyielding—but there is a twinge of something she can't quite put her finger on—a type of jealousy. In those few minutes she wants what Sofia has. She wants someone to care.

Macy clears her throat. "Sofia, do you mind if I have a look at Leanne's room?"

"Yes, of course. I show you."

"Just point me in the right direction. You can stay here with Jared and help him unpack."

Sofia wipes her eyes. "It's at the end of the hall just past the bathroom."

All Macy finds in Leanne's room are empty drawers and dust. She spreads the contents of the envelope Sofia gave her on the bed and starts picking through what's left of Leanne's life. There isn't much to go on. There are no tax returns, insurance forms, or bank statements and most of the pages have been ripped out of her address book. Elizabeth Lamm's phone number and address are jotted down in neat handwriting and there are a few numbers listed for White Sulfur Springs, including the homeless shelter. Less than a hundred Canadian dollars are neatly secured with a paper clip. Wrinkled receipts and nonsensical notations on bits of paper make up the rest. There's an old newspaper clipping folded up inside a small coin purse. It's an article that was published in the *Collier Gazette* after the bodies were found dumped in the roadside picnic area. In the margins a child's hand has written down a license plate number.

The first phone call Leanne placed matches the number listed for Elizabeth Lamm. The call was made only three weeks before Leanne died. She checks the other phone number with the Collier area code against the entries that are left in Leanne's phone book and finds nothing so she picks up her cell phone and dials. It goes straight to voicemail.

"Hello, you're through to Larson's Used Cars in downtown Collier. Your call is important to us. Please leave your name and number and we'll get right back to you."

Macy switches off her phone and holds it to her chin. She doesn't like being lied to. On the same day Leanne spoke to Elizabeth, she also called Toby Larson's car dealership. They spoke for thirteen minutes. Less than three weeks later there's an incoming call from the same number at the dealership. Macy notes the date is three days prior to Leanne's murder.

She closes the bedroom door and dials Warren's number. "Hi, Warren," she says.

"Are you still up in Finley?"

"Yeah, my hunch was right. Sofia did cross over the border to Collier eleven years ago. She's identified the drivers as Walter Nielson and Brady Monroe."

"Did she say anything about the night Leanne took her back to Canada?"

"It wasn't Leanne who rescued the girls from the truck, it was Grace."

"Really?"

"Yep, surprised me as well. I didn't think she had it in her."

"Anything else?"

"She's identified Arnold Lamm. He was in that basement with them. She said that he appeared to be in charge of things."

"I'd say it's been worth the trip."

"I also have a copy of Sofia's phone bill. Leanne called someone at 153 Summit Road. It could have been Grace she spoke to but I doubt it. More likely it was Elizabeth. The call lasted around ten minutes and was placed about three weeks before Leanne was murdered."

"I wish Elizabeth hadn't kept that to herself."

"Shortly after Leanne talked to Elizabeth she called Larson's used car dealership. The call lasted thirteen minutes."

"So Toby lied too."

"It gets better. Leanne received a call from Larson's Used Cars three days before Leanne was murdered."

"Are you sure?"

"It's all here in black and white."

Warren sighs. "I'll bring Toby Larson in for questioning. What about Elizabeth?"

Macy looks at her watch. "I'll deal with Elizabeth tomorrow. My gut feeling is that Leanne called because she wanted access to Grace and Elizabeth told her to stay away."

"That sounds about right."

"Let's see what Toby has to say before we bring Elizabeth in for questioning."

"When are you back?"

Macy cracks open the door and listens. The distinct sound of hammering comes from the kitchen. "We might be a while still."

"Okay, I'll keep you posted."

Jared drives the patrol car back to Collier and Macy sits beside him reading the article she found among Leanne's belongings. Her immediate thought is to call Ray, but she tucks the newspaper article back in the envelope and takes a deep breath instead.

"Can you imagine the sum total of your life fitting inside one suitcase?"

"Seems like Leanne was a very lonely woman."

"I've read the reports from Child Protective Services. I can't feel sorry for her."

"I wouldn't know about that. I don't think anyone hangs out in a place like Finley by choice."

"It's Sofia I feel sorry for. The woman seems lost."

"There's a lot of that going around." He glances over at Macy. "You okay?"

"By my standards your little love triangle almost looks healthy."

"And here I am thinking you've got it all figured out."

"No, I don't."

He gives her a long look and asks about her situation.

"No fairy-tale endings, I'm afraid."

"You're having the baby on your own?"

"I'm afraid I'm as fucked up as you are."

"What about the father?"

"We're no longer together."

"Does he know?"

"He pretended he didn't but that's all changed. We finally had the talk."

"And I thought I had an unhealthy relationship with the truth. So you still see him?"

"Kind of difficult not to. He's my boss." The image of Ray's face squashed up against the Plexiglas at the Helena ice rink has been in her mind all day.

"The baby's father is the captain of the state police."

"Yep."

"Isn't he married?"

"Like you're one to judge."

"It just doesn't seem like something you would get mixed up in."

"He was separated when we started seeing each other." Macy slumps down in the seat and closes her eyes. "I was stupid. I should have waited until he was divorced."

"How long were you going out before they got back together?"

"Nearly two years."

"What an asshole."

"I don't blame Ray."

"Why the hell not?"

"His oldest daughter has a lot of issues. Anorexia, self-harm, you name it. It was awful for Ray. He blamed himself. One thing led to another and he and Jessica got back together." Macy turns away and looks out at the view. The sun is just about to slip down behind the ridgeline. She found out she was pregnant the day Ray and Jessica renewed their wedding vows. That same afternoon Macy's car skidded on a sharp bend and plowed through a railing at high speed.

"I'm sorry. I shouldn't have asked."

"It's okay. It's good to talk about it. If I bottle it up, I get angry." She takes a quick look at her cell phone. There hasn't been any word from Ray all day. "There's still hope for you though. Hayley could leave her husband."

"Probably not. Brian would get custody of the kids."

"That doesn't seem likely."

"About ten years ago Brian got busted for dealing drugs and Hayley took the fall. She was using back then but everyone in town knew it was Brian who was the dealer."

"So she's got a record."

"And Brian's got a punching bag."

"What are you going to do?"

"I'm not sure there's much I can do. I know I have to end it with Lexxie, but that's the easy part."

"Not so easy for Lexxie."

"She's gotta know what's coming."

"You keep telling yourself that."

Macy's phone rings. "Hello, Warren," she says, turning toward the window. She listens for a few seconds and frowns. "Of course he's going to deny taking the calls, but someone there spoke to Leanne and he's the one who doesn't have an alibi."

"For a guilty man he's being unusually cooperative. We're going through his work diary and seeing if the times you gave us match when he was in the office."

"Lean on him a bit more and see what happens."

"What about Pamela? She works there too."

"Sure, bring her in. Just let me know how it goes," she says, hanging up.

As soon as she returns to her hotel room Macy strips off her clothing and climbs into bed. Propped up against the pillows she scrolls through the hundreds of unsent text messages on her phone. They're all meant for Ray. Since their breakup, they've tracked the stages of her grief, their tone altering with her mood—denial to rage to despondency before coming full circle back to denial again. Bargaining hasn't been possible. Acceptance is out of the question. Before drifting off to sleep, she writes another message to Ray, but this time she hits the Send button.

I don't know if I can do this on my own.

19

Macy calls Warren into her office. "It seems I owe Toby Larson an apology."

Warren shuts the door and takes the seat opposite her. "I wouldn't worry too much about Toby's feelings. After all these years being married to Pamela, he's pretty thick-skinned."

"I still feel bad when I get it wrong."

"What did you find out?"

"It turns out Sofia Jankowski answered the incoming call that was placed from Larson's Used Cars. She remembers it well because it's the only phone call Leanne received in the two years she lived there." Macy levels her gaze at Warren. "It was a woman who called. Sofia didn't get a name but she did describe her as being very rude."

"That sounds like Pamela Larson."

"We need to bring her back in for questioning. At the very least we'll charge her with obstruction."

"We know she didn't kill Leanne, so what do you think she's done?"

"She may have let the killer know when Leanne was coming to visit Grace."

Warren whistles. "Do you really think she's that cold-blooded? That would make her an accessary to murder."

"I agree that it seems a bit extreme given her issues with Leanne date back eleven years, but the facts speak for themselves. After speaking to her sister, Leanne called Toby's number, but Pamela answered instead. Pamela used the conversation to gain Leanne's trust. Three days before she was murdered, Pamela called Leanne and let her know the best time to come see Grace. She set Leanne up."

Warren starts to get up. "It will be interesting to see who else Pamela's been speaking to. I'll see about getting a warrant to check her phone records."

Macy tips her head toward the door. "I think Grace and her aunt should be waiting out in the reception area. Do you mind sending Grace in?"

"Not at all."

Macy sits across from Grace and watches as she reads over the newspaper clipping that was found among Leanne's belongings. She notices that Grace's eyes keep drifting to the license plate number written in the margins.

Macy points to the margin. "Grace, I need to know if that is your handwriting."

"My mother told me never to tell."

"That's because your mother was trying to protect you."

"It's my fault she had to leave town."

"You were seven years old at the time. Nothing that happened was your fault. I need you to tell me what these numbers mean. So far we've been unable to match them to any vehicle's registration." She rolls her chair around the desk so she and Grace can sit facing each other, their knees almost touching, and spends the next half hour telling Grace about the trip she made up to Canada to interview the woman her mother was living with the last few years. "Sofia's last name is Jankowski, and according to records she arrived in Canada around eleven years ago."

"What's that got to do with me?"

"It has everything to do with you. Sofia told me what you did for her and her friends."

"I swear I didn't do anything."

"Grace, there's no reason to lie anymore. You're safe now. Sofia says it was you that rescued her from the container on the back of that truck. She even told me that's why she was willing to look after your mom these past couple of years."

"It was the same truck as before. I couldn't let it happen again."

"What happened the first time you saw the truck?"

She stares up at the map on the wall above Macy's desk. Someone has marked the location of Finley with a thumbtack. If you drew a straight line from Collier it's not very far at all.

Macy tries to meet her eyes but Grace won't let her. "Did you see the girls that we found dead at the rest stop?"

"No, I never saw them. I heard them though. I thought it was my mother calling for help so I went looking for her. I worried about her all the time."

"But it wasn't your mom."

"No, ma'am. The girls were locked up in the container of a truck that was parked away from the others. The one that could speak English was named Katya."

"What did she say?"

"She said they were scared and wanted water. I tried to bring them some but a man came out of the diner and chased me into the bushes along the back fence. A coyote bolted and I think he must have figured he'd been chasing it all along because he let me go after that."

"Did you tell your mother?"

"I tried. I went home but Mom was passed out, and later when I checked, the truck was gone."

"And then you read about it in the papers?"

"No, first I saw it on the news, but I figured it was them." She points to the article. "It even said they found tire tracks from an eighteen-wheeler. My mom told me I wasn't to go near the trucks again."

"So your mother knew about it and did nothing?"

"She said she'd call the police, but she never did. A few weeks later the truck was parked in the same spot so I broke into the garage and stole some bolt cutters. My mother wasn't too pleased to find four girls hiding out in our trailer."

"No, I imagine she was pretty pissed off."

"She understood the trouble we were in. She couldn't come back for me. She couldn't be with Toby. I ruined everything."

Macy brushes the hair out of Grace's eyes. "But you saved those girls' lives. God knows what would have happened to them if you hadn't come along. I know Sofia is very grateful for what you did."

"I may have made a mistake when I wrote down the number," she says, holding it up and looking at it again. "I didn't have any paper so I had to memorize it."

"But you definitely got it from the truck Katya was in?"

"Yes, ma'am. I remember trying really hard to get it right."

"Don't worry. We'll figure it out. Do you remember anything else about the truck?"

"It looked like all the other ones. The only difference was where it was parked."

"You said the driver chased you. Do you remember what he looked like?"

"I only remember that he looked angry."

"Grace, you were incredibly brave. You should be very proud of what you did for those girls."

"I still get upset about Katya."

"Then try to think about Sofia instead."

Grace looks up at Macy. "Do you think the man who chased me is the same man who killed my mother?"

"That's what we're hoping to find out."

. . .

Elizabeth knocks at the door of Macy's office and waits.

Macy waves her in and offers her a seat. "I apologize. I would have come by to see you and Grace at home but it wasn't possible."

"That's fine. I'm happy to help."

"I need to ask you again whether you've had any contact with Leanne." Macy slides a piece of paper across the desk. "I have a copy of your sister's phone bill. Three weeks ago Leanne called the house on Summit Road and spoke to someone for more than ten minutes. I'm guessing it was you that took the call. In your original statement you claimed to have had no contact with Leanne. I'm assuming that you'd like to change your story."

"I should have told you about it, but I was worried Grace would find out that I spoke to her mother."

"What did your sister want?"

"She wanted to see Grace and I told her she wasn't to come near our home."

"Did she say anything else?"

"She said I couldn't stop her."

"I imagine that didn't go down well."

"We argued. Every last grievance found its voice in the ten minutes we were on the phone. I hadn't realized I'd been screaming until later." Elizabeth reaches up and touches her neck. "Can you believe my throat was sore?"

"I imagine it felt good to get all that off your chest."

Elizabeth manages the slightest of smiles, but there are tears in her eyes. She pulls off her glasses and blinks as she cleans them with a tissue. "I should have told Grace. It was wrong of me to lie."

"Now, is that all? Are you sure there isn't something else you want to tell me?"

Elizabeth opens her cornflower blue eyes wide. "I'm afraid there's a lot more."

"Take your time."

"I thought I'd put a bed in Arnold's office. Grace needed somewhere downstairs where she could rest while she was recuperating, but first I had to clean it out to make space. I'd been avoiding it. There is so much stuff in there. I took hours going through the various boxes and files. A receipt for a meal out at a restaurant would send me back twenty years. I'd remember what I wore, what we ate, how Arnold laughed, how handsome he looked in a suit." Elizabeth puts a closed fist to her chest and keeps it there. "I found some photos of Grace."

"What kind of photos?"

"They were horrible. I can't get the images out of my head. They were in an envelope taped to the bottom of a drawer. At first I didn't know what I was looking at but then it was too late to make everything right again. All those wonderful memories of Arnold flew right from my head."

"In these photos, how old was Grace?"

"I'd say around fourteen. It's hard to tell." She clasps a hand to her mouth but her words find their way through the thick mesh of fingers. "My poor baby was naked."

Very gently Macy rests a hand on Elizabeth's forearm. "Please tell me you still have them?"

Elizabeth stares straight ahead. "I couldn't deal with what it might mean so I put them back where I found them. I just wanted to pretend for a while that they didn't exist. I can't believe I was so stupid."

20

Grace's aunt leans back on the sofa and tosses her unfinished cross-word puzzle to the side. "Where's he taking you?"

"The mall and then maybe dinner." Grace is hoping for dinner but it wasn't really part of the deal she'd struck during the phone call with Jared. She casts around for her house keys, eventually finding them on the kitchen counter.

Her aunt reaches for the television remote. "I spoke to Detective Greeley earlier today and she assured me you'd be well cared for. I'm expecting you to be home no later than eight."

"I'm eighteen years old now. I think I can stay out past eight."

Elizabeth turns on the television and switches the channel to the local news. They're talking about the weather, but at the bottom of the screen an update runs about Molly Parks and the two other little girls, same as they have been for the past couple of days.

Her aunt points to the screen. "I don't think you realize how worried I am about you going out."

Grace wishes her aunt wasn't right. She leans over and kisses her on the forehead. "I promise I'll be careful."

Grace heads outside wearing a red coat and matching galoshes. The hem of a floral dress pokes out from beneath. Her shoulder bag is bulky and bangs against her hip.

Jared rolls down the window and she skips over to the truck, taking a drag off his cigarette like she'd done before.

"I'm late," she says, smiling.

"And you're smoking again." He snatches the cigarette from her lips and flicks it into the slush.

"You're not exactly taking care of yourself, so why should I?"

"I'm old and ugly. It doesn't matter much."

"You're not that old."

"I'm too old for you." He gestures toward the house. "How are you guys settling in?"

"I hate it here."

"What does your aunt think of you coming for a ride with me?"

Grace looks over her shoulder and squints into the front window where her aunt stands cross-armed and watching. "She's worried."

"I don't want her getting the wrong impression."

Grace runs around the other side of the truck and opens the door. "Then bring me back in one piece."

Jared waves at Elizabeth. "Where does she think I'm taking you?"

"The mall."

"But we're not going to the mall, are we?"

"The mall in Collier has to be the most pathetic place on earth."

He puts his truck in gear. "So where to then?"

"You know that truck stop south of town on Route 93?"

"Yeah, I know it. Of all the places in the world, why would you want to go there?"

"It's where my mom and I used to live."

"My question still stands."

"I thought if I went to see the trailer where we lived, it might make it easier to move on."

"Fair enough." He glances over at her. "I want you to tell me if it gets to be too much. Will you promise to do that?"

"I promise."

Grace keeps her eyes low to the horizon as they drive. She can tell Jared is ill at ease. He takes furtive glances out the windows and in the rearview mirror, looking everywhere but at her. Once they're out on Route 93 his gaze shifts to the front and pretty much stays there. She watches him out of the corner of her eye and memorizes the landscape of his face: the nose that looks like it's never been broken, the forehead that protrudes a fraction too far, and the sharply angled jawline that's always locked in a clench.

She touches his arm to get his attention. "Do you really think you're too old for me?"

"Grace, I was very clear on the phone. I'm your friend and nothing more. If you can't accept that, I'll turn around here and take you back home."

She teases him for overreacting and instantly regrets it.

He speeds up to pass a slow-moving truck and when he speaks again his voice is clipped. "I'm not going to be sorry for taking you out here, am I?"

"No."

"When did you live out there?"

She kicks her stocking feet up onto the dashboard. The socks are red and pink with little toe separators so they're like gloves for feet. "On and off until I was seven."

"That's no place for a kid."

In front of them, the road is pockmarked with holes and a black patchwork of short-term fixes. Wood smoke hangs in the air, hazing over the hillside views. The old snow has shrunken back. The landscape is spiked with the stalks of dead vegetation.

They pass a turnout that marks the farthest stop of the Collier town bus. As a young girl she'd sat on the bench in the wood enclosure, notching the soft wood with messages. More often than not her mother would forget to fetch her from the bus stop and Grace would have to walk home. When trucks barreled alongside, the ground would shake. She stayed out of sight, off in the shadow of the trees, her legs getting all scratched up by brambles.

The truck stop is only a little farther along the road. There are no trees here, just fallow fields. Everything is windswept with dust and stained with smoke. Desperation hangs about the low-slung buildings and deep shadowing porches. Trucks line up in the gravel lot like tombstones and a row of Harley-Davidsons sit tightly packed together outside of the diner. A neon sign flashes the current prices of diesel and special offers: *All You Can Eat Buffet $6.99, Full-er-up Breakfast with free refills on coffee $3.99 and Ladies Night is Pretty Much Every Night—So Come on In.*

Jared pulls into the icy lot and parks well clear of the trucks. "Are you sure about this?"

Instead of answering, Grace slips on her boots and jumps out of the car.

"It's this way," she says, steering a course directly toward the maze of big rigs. In the gray afternoon light, her red coat stands out like a beacon.

In the narrow spaces between the trucks it smells of oil and burning brakes. There's a long vertical slit of light at the far end and the space grows more confined as they move toward it. Jared stops short when she turns around. She tilts her head up at him, their bodies perfectly aligned.

"You don't have to come with me," she says.

Jared looks up at the containers that tower above them like buildings. "You've got no business being out here on your own."

Grace turns away. Out in the open little eddies of wind blow dust up into the air and her hair swirls around her face. She brushes it out of her eyes with her gloved hands and points to a trio of mobile homes cowed down together in untouched snow. Rolled randomly like dice onto the small pocket of land, they are separated from the parking lot by a low metal fence.

Jared looks back at the wall of trucks. They're all alone out here. "I never knew this place existed," he says, raising his voice above the sound of the wind.

Grace makes her way through the deep snow, heading toward the farthest of the three trailers. At one end, the roof is caving in. The metal siding is rusted through in places, and tattered ends of curtains blow out from broken windows. There is a small set of steps leading up to the entrance. Grace pulls on the handle and the screen door falls from its hinges. She jumps back and watches it crash onto the ground. She looks at her gloved hand. A thin line of rust stains the palm.

"You okay?" asks Jared, his breath warm on her neck.

Grace says yes and pulls away.

Jared's voice follows her, but she loses some of his words in the wind.

"Yeah," she answers, peering through the small window cut into the front door. The dirty Plexiglas distorts the view. "It was just me and my mom."

The door is locked. Even though she shakes it hard the handle doesn't yield. So many memories pile on top of her that she feels she may buckle under the weight of them. The damp sweat of summer nights. Her mother's manic laughter. The sour smell of morning. Surly-eyed men staggering from her mother's room. Her mother's first cigarette.

She turns to face Jared, relieved to find him there. He looks over his shoulder, back toward the trucks and the diner. The scent of fried food is heavy in the air. She sees what he sees: gray smoke rising from the chimneys stacked above the kitchen, large waste bins spilling garbage out from their tops onto the gray slush.

"Maybe they have a key back at the diner," he says.

Instead of answering, Grace scrambles off the steps and scrapes about under the mobile home's foundation. She finds the front door key lodged beneath a brick. She holds it out in front of her for Jared to see, but he doesn't look pleased.

The place looks like it's spent time in a twister. All the kitchen drawers and their contents spill across the dimly lit room. Odds and ends of cutlery, old phone books, and bits of clothing are scattered on the floor.

The cabinets are open and broken crockery, smashed drinking glasses, and foodstuffs spill outward. A moldy patchwork quilt half covers a small sofa that has collapsed in the middle where someone has set fire to it. The wall behind the sofa is blackened.

Grace wades through the wreckage toward her mother's room, and Jared shuts kitchen cabinet doors as he follows along behind. A short procession accompanied by steady percussion. The bedroom ceiling is half caved in so Grace has to stoop. A rust stain spreads across the bare mattress, mirroring the stain on the low-lying ceiling above their heads. In the windows, the strips of hard plastic blinds blow inward, rattling against the cracked glass.

With her eyes focused in on a low section of veneered wood paneling, she trips across damp bedding, her clumsy boots getting caught in the folds. Squatting low, she runs her fingertips across the walls, leaving parallel trails in the thick dust. There is a ridge where two of the panels meet. It is raised just a fraction and her hands stop moving when she finds it. She digs her fingernails beneath the veneered wood and pulls. A short length of panel pops off and dust blows outward. The cavity behind the wall is cold and damp. The draft blowing through it echoes the gusts of wind building outside. Her hands reach through a web of dusty insulation. She finds what she's looking for low down toward the bottom. Her fingers fold around the unfamiliar shape. It's a package about the size of a brick. She puts it aside and grabs hold of the coffee tin.

"What is it?" asks Jared.

Grace struggles to her feet. Her legs feel thick. Only a tornado could make them move. "It's my mother's."

Jared gives her a sympathetic tilt of the head but he doesn't step forward like she wants him to. He just points at the tin. "Is that what you came for?"

Grace mumbles something he doesn't catch before forcing her legs to walk to the door. She stops inches away and waits patiently for him to let her pass. His warm breath skims off the top of her head.

He's not done talking so he doesn't move. "You okay?"

217

Grace shrugs, unsure of what to do next. It's more difficult being here than she had thought it would be. "I need a Coke or something."

Touching her for the first time that day, Jared takes her arm and leads her back to the front door. "I think I better take you home. I don't like this place."

Grace is losing her nerve. Something inside her tells her it's now or never. "I'd rather order something at the diner."

Jared looks at her for a few seconds and she can tell he's thinking things over. His gaze shifts to the diner and then back to her. "You best put that tin you found in your bag."

Grace turns away and struggles to open her bag. Tears cloud her vision and her hands shake from more than just the cold. She slips the tin inside so it's resting next to the bottle of lighter fluid she's brought with her.

They head across the parking lot, walking side by side, but moving like two magnets, twisted so they won't touch. She steps closer and he shifts his course so the distance between them never alters. Her bag feels heavy and she's not sure how she'll manage. Within the canvas tote, the tin and bottle of lighter fluid bang against her leg.

The wooden boards that lead to the front door of the diner creak underfoot. The air inside is saturated with greasy talk. It takes a moment for them to adjust to the steady thump of country music and raised voices. Booths run up and down the length of the building and a long counter stretches out in front of them. Jared coughs and eyes settle on them from underneath baseball caps. A waitress working from behind the bar tilts her head toward the booths. Grace looks at the woman, waiting for recognition that never comes.

The waitress has a voice that's been working hard all its life. "I think you'll find some seating down at the far end. I'll be with you in a sec."

Jared follows Grace along the length of the building, passing booths that house diners like prisoners in cells. They're about halfway along when a man jumps to his feet and blocks Jared's path, separating him from Grace. He is reed-thin and hopped up on something. He shoulder

218

checks Jared and heads off in the direction of the exit. The other men at his table laugh and Jared takes in their dilated eyes and nervous banter.

Grace grabs his hand. "Come on."

The men make little walking motions with their fingers and laugh some more. Behind them the waitress comes tripping along with a tray of drinks and plunks it down on their table.

"Real mature," she says.

Jared and Grace find an empty booth at the far end of the diner. The emergency exit sign looms over them. Jared keeps looking at it, sitting forward in his seat like he's getting ready to lunge for the handle.

Grace shrugs out of her coat and places her bag next to her on the seat. "You worry a lot."

Jared slouches back into the cracked red cushions, trying to look relaxed, but failing. Unlike her he hasn't bothered to take off his coat.

He pulls out his packet of smokes and taps it on the tabletop. "So what's in the tin?"

Grace doesn't answer. She instead looks up and smiles pleasantly.

The waitress is standing next to their table, her eyes flitting back and forth between Jared and Grace. She pulls her pen out from behind her ear and turns her eyes to Jared. "I know you. I never forget a face."

Grace thinks *yes you do* but says nothing.

"I'm normally in uniform when I'm here."

The waitress shifts her weight from one foot to the other like she has to go to the toilet. She looks back toward the bar, checking things out before her eyes settle back on him. She speaks in a whisper.

"You're not a cop, are you?"

"Only a lowly paramedic."

"It's Jared, isn't it?"

He nods and she makes some small talk, but Grace can tell she wants to ask why they're hanging out there together. Grace waits until the waitress is out of earshot before speaking again.

"I think Tempi likes you."

"You know her?"

"Sometimes she'd keep an eye on me when my mom was out. When it was quiet I'd sit at the counter and do my homework."

"She doesn't remember you?"

"That's probably because I'm not a man."

"She's a bit old for me."

"Don't let her hear you saying that."

Grace is halfway through her Coke when she pulls the coffee tin out of her bag and wipes it down using napkins from the dispenser. The lettering has rusted away in places but otherwise it's the same.

Jared leans forward. "So open it."

Grace's eyes glaze over with a thin skin of tears. "Not sure I can."

Jared pushes the tin closer to her using the tip of his index finger. "Come on. You dragged me all the way out here."

Grace pushes it back toward Jared and asks him to open it for her. She leans back in her chair. "Just tell me what's inside."

Jared lifts the lid. There are a few pieces of cheap jewelry, some unpaid IOUs, and at least ten tightly rolled bundles of money. He picks up a small leather-bound diary and flicks through the yellowing pages. It's full of dates and notations that make no sense. He puts everything back before replacing the lid. "Do you want to tell me what all this means?"

"When my mom left I wanted to believe that something happened to her. That she'd have never abandoned me like that. That she'd never leave me alone in a place like this."

"Well, given how much money is in here, I'd say she fully intended on coming back."

"Yeah. Who'd leave that behind?" Grace glances beyond Jared, her eyes on the entrance. She pulls on her coat and puts the coffee tin back in her bag. "I've got to use the bathroom."

She walks back to the counter, oblivious of the half-lidded eyes tracking her progress. Instead of following the signs to the bathrooms, she heads out the front door, hopeful that Jared's back is still turned. The temperature has dropped further and the parking lot is icing over. What little light there is is flat so there are no shadows. Skirting past

the diesel pumps, she ignores the men filling up their tanks. The doors
to the portable toilets continue to flap about chaotically in the wind.
She hears someone retching behind the only door that's firmly shut. She
crosses the parking lot, passing within the shadow of the trucks.

The sky is darkening in the distance as the light fades and a snowstorm closes in on Collier. With her red coat wrapped around her, Grace
stands in front of her former home. She lets her bag slide from her
shoulder and the deep snow muffles the sound of its fall. Leaving it behind, she takes only the lighter fluid and a box of matches. This time
the doorknob gives way with a twist of her wrist. Grace wades through
the rubbish in the main room and takes hold of the blanket that is
draped on the sofa where she once slept. Holly Hobbie is printed on
one side, a patchwork quilt on the other. It stinks of damp and mildew.
Holly's white face is tinged gray like she's shadowed with two days of
beard growth.

Back in the bedroom, it's too dark to see properly. She walks to the
opening in the paneling and reaches in again. The bundle weighs less
than a sack of flour and she's just able to stuff it into the deep pockets of
her coat. The bottle of lighter fluid snaps open easily but she spills some
of it on her hands. The smell reminds her of family barbecues but it's
always her aunt and uncle who are there with her. Her mother is nowhere to be seen. She splashes the liquid over the bed and floor, making
her way through the small mobile home, tripping on unseen things in
the dim light as she goes.

With the wind coming up behind her through the open door, the
matches only flare up before blowing out. She pulls the door shut and
stands just inside. The next match sizzles and lights. The smell of sulfur
hits her nose. She lights more and lets them fly. Some burst into flame
and others go quiet. She sets the box alight and tosses it onto the sofa.
Bright-colored flames leap upward in the darkness. Above the kitchen
sink the ceiling catches on fire and around her the walls blister and
melt.

She'd been excited when she told her mother about the girls she freed from the container on the back of the truck. *We have to help them, Mommy.* But her mother slapped her hard and screamed in her face. *What have you done? You've ruined everything. What have you done?*

Grace is on her knees when the door bumps into her back. She feels a hand grab her roughly on the arm as she's twisted back, around and out.

Jared drags her down the short set of steps. The wind and smoke swirl around them in a spiraling panic. He yells at her to get up, but her legs won't work properly. He stumbles across the yard with her in his arms.

They fall and land in a heap on top of her bag. The coffee tin digs into her ribs and her face is buried in the snow. A bout of coughing forces her to her knees. Jared pounds her back and kneels next to her. He's telling her that *I've got you* and that *you're safe now* but she can't speak. Her tongue feels too large for her mouth and her throat is sore. Looking over Jared's shoulder she catches sight of the burning trailer and on top of her crying and coughing she begins to laugh high and loud.

Jared pulls her up to standing and grabs her bag. He tells her that they've got to go before someone sees them, and when she doesn't move fast enough he carries her across the dark, icy lot—past the flapping restroom doors, past the city of trucks, past the icy diesel pumps, and past the long row of Harleys.

They hear voices and hide in the shadows between the parked cars. He holds her close, crushing her against his chest. He whispers for her to be quiet and loosens his grip. Grace rests the side of her head against him and feels his heart beat beneath all those layers of fabric. They wait for a group of men to board their bikes and ride away. The men brag about this and that as they smoke cigarettes and stagger around drunk. Grace spots the tall reedy one that shoulder-checked Jared. He's kicking in the side of a car with his steel-toed boots and laughing but there's no joy in the sound. One in their number points to the back of the lot where black smoke billows up high and disappears in the storm clouds, but they can't be bothered to raise the alarm. They rev their engines and drive away. Through tears, Grace watches their lights streak like comet tails on the darkened highway.

Jared bends low and asks Grace if she's okay. His face is cast in shadow, his voice quieter than it was before.

She holds on tighter.

He peels her arms away. "I need to get you home."

She says something too soft for him to hear.

"What was that?" he says, bending low once more.

Grace doesn't hesitate. She reaches up and kisses him on the mouth. There's the briefest taste of tobacco and he's gone, backing away from her with a pained expression on his face.

"No, Grace. I told you before. We can only ever be friends."

Within easy reach of the headlights the flurries fall thick and bright, but they barely have time to settle on the windshield before they're flicked away by the wipers. Beyond the blinding white flakes the view is endless black. To go out on a night like this would be like falling off a cliff. Nobody would find your body until spring. The wipers start to stick to the glass and Jared cranks up the defroster. The low hum of the fan, the rattle of the truck, and the soft melody of the song playing on the radio fill the cab but Grace finds no comfort in the words or the hum or the rattle.

She moves her lips the bare minimum to get the words out. The acrid stench of smoke coats her like a second skin. "I don't blame you if you don't want anything more to do with me."

"Come on, Grace. I'm not like that."

"I don't believe you."

"I've never given you any reason not to trust me."

Grace turns away and blinks into the falling snow. The interior lights illuminate her profile. Her narrow chest heaves up and down with each breath. She wants Jared to hold her in his arms like he did back at the truck stop, but she knows he isn't going to come near her ever again. Her face is a scrunched-up mess of nerves when she turns toward him.

"You have to promise."

"Promise what?"

"Promise that you'll be a proper friend to me. That you'll always be there for me."

Jared lets out an anxious sigh. "Of course I promise, but I can only do my best. I'm not perfect, Grace. You'll have to take me as I come."

21

Unused to the noise of traffic right outside the windows, Grace hasn't been sleeping well. She burrows her head deeper into her pillow. The previous evening her aunt presented Grace with a schedule for her mother's funeral.

"There will be a short service at the crematorium at four, and after that Martha Nielson has offered to have us over for an early supper. It will be just a few people. We've decided to keep it simple." Her aunt had gone on to tell Grace about her doctor's appointment in the morning, mentioning it in an offhand way that was at odds with her tremulous voice. "I think it's a good idea for you to come with me since I've had some tests done."

From the bedroom Grace can smell freshly made coffee and eggs cooking on the stove. She hears her aunt's footsteps, the hum of the television news, and the sound of the refrigerator door being opened and shut. She rolls over onto her back and pulls the quilt upward so it's covering her neck. Almost hidden, she holds it there and waits for the panic to pass. It feels like a low-pressure ridge is settling between her throat and her heart. It's not the service at the crematorium or having supper at Martha Nielson's house that worries her. It's the doctor's appointment that's kept her up half the night.

Elizabeth comes into the bedroom. Dressed in a dark woolen skirt and jacket, she looks like she's going to church. She says her usual *good morning* and sits down on the edge of the bed. They've been tiptoeing around each other since the day they argued about Arnold's truck. Elizabeth shakes Grace's leg and tells her to come get some breakfast before it's cold.

Grace takes her aunt's hand and squeezes it. "What if we just hide out here all day?" she says, hopeful to the last.

Elizabeth gives her niece a tidy little smile. "It's a nice thought but I have this feeling life will come knocking on our door whether we like it or not."

Elizabeth is tired so she lets Grace drive to the hospital for the appointment with the oncologist, but she fidgets in her seat and insists on instructing Grace as to which roads to avoid so they won't get caught up in the traffic around Old Town.

"Dr. Fischer has a hearing problem," says Elizabeth as she indicates to Grace to take a right at the next intersection. "He refuses to wear a hearing aid. He ends up shouting all the time because he can't judge how loud his own voice is anymore."

Her aunt doesn't exaggerate. In his office Grace jumps up in her seat each time the doctor opens his mouth, and next to her she sees her aunt doing the same thing. An enormous man, Dr. Fischer dominates his side of the desk. Grace looks upward into his elongated face and dark eyes, waiting for something resembling good news to come out of his sausage-sized lips, but he says all the wrong things: inoperable, prognosis isn't good, chemotherapy.

He finishes going through the test results and snaps the file shut. "Elizabeth," he booms. "You're going to have to fight hard if you want to beat this."

"But you've just said it's inoperable? I don't understand."

Dr. Fischer brushes away his previous prognosis with a smile and a fresh flurry of bellowing. "Those are all just statistics, Elizabeth. You can beat this. You're better than this."

Elizabeth isn't convinced. The cancer has spread beyond her stomach and is inching its way into her other vital organs. "I'm tired. I can't spend the rest of my life fighting against something that's going to kill me anyway." She gathers her things, signaling her niece to do the same. "I'll take pain medication but nothing beyond that. I watched my mother suffer through two rounds of chemo. It didn't make her live any longer."

They are waiting for the elevator when Grace realizes she's forgotten her gloves in Dr. Fischer's office. He's still at his desk. She asks him the one question she still wants answered.

Six months if we're lucky echoes down the corridors.

The doctor tries to persuade her to speak to her aunt but Grace isn't convinced he knows what's best.

Grace finds Elizabeth outside the elevator door doubled over, her face contorted with pain. "Promise me, Grace. You won't let me die here."

In the living room of the tidy little bungalow on Spruce Street, Martha Nielson has built a shrine dedicated to her dead husband, Walter. There are pictures of him everywhere. In the presence of so many of his keepsakes it feels as if they should be mourning Walter rather than Leanne. Grace examines his photographs closely. She remembers him well—how the swell of his belly had pinned her to the ground and the way his swollen lips had smothered her cries.

There's a voice at her shoulder. "He'd have been fifty-nine last Saturday," says Martha, clutching on to Grace's arm. "The kids came over and we had some cake."

Grace rests a hand on the edge of the display. Birthday cards sit as bookends to an urn. Amazed that such a big man could be contained in such a small way, she asks Martha if the urn contains her husband's ashes.

Martha runs her fingertips down the side of the pewter vase. "Yes, he's still here with me. I couldn't bear to have him buried alone."

Grace's mother had been nothing more than skin and bone. Grace imagines the crematorium delivering what's left of her in a thimble. *We're very sorry, Grace, but this is all there was.*

Martha gazes out the window overlooking the snowbound front yard. In the bleak early evening light the entire world is powdered gray. "Have you thought about what you'll do with your mother's ashes?"

Aside from her aunt's closest girlfriends, there'd been no one else in attendance at the crematorium service. Grace had stood next to her aunt dry-eyed and silent. She'd expected the theatrical blast of a roaring furnace but there was nothing aside from the quiet brush of heavy drapes closing. She'd expected her aunt to remain composed but Elizabeth had broken down in sobs, her small frame fluttering in a way the drapes could not. Afterward she'd adjusted the collar on Grace's coat and cried some more.

Martha Nielson holds tighter to Grace's arm and asks about the ashes again.

"I don't know," says Grace, staring at the Jeep pulling up outside the house. She turns in time to see Martha's eyes crinkle around the edges into a smile.

"Oh, look who's here," says Martha, raising her voice and moving toward the front door, pulling Grace along with her. "Did you know Dustin was one of Walter's best friends?"

Grace makes her excuses and heads for the kitchen. The counter is covered with plates of food and bowls of salad. A large ham sits sliced and ready to serve. She pulls the phone from its cradle and dials Jared's number, but there's no answer. Macy picks up on the first try.

Grace can barely speak. "Macy."

"Grace, is that you?"

"Can you come get me?"

"What's wrong? Has something happened?"

"Please come."

"Where are you?"

Grace can hear Dustin's voice in the living room. He's not more than ten feet away. "At 23 Spruce," she says, hanging up.

Grace ducks into the pantry and sits with her back braced up against the door so no one can get in.

Ten minutes later her aunt knocks. When she speaks she keeps her voice low. "Grace, sweetheart. I know you're in there."

Waiting for Macy, Grace has been doing a full inventory of Martha Nielson's pantry. There are rows and rows of preserves: pickled cucumber, wild huckleberry jam, runner beans, elderberry conserve, sun-dried tomatoes, applesauce, buffalo berry jam to name but a few. All the labels are handwritten with a thin black pen. All the lids have bows. Grace pictures Martha in her apron, steam rising up from pots, working her fingers raw. Her kids are grown up and her husband is dead. There's nothing left for Martha to do but make jam. Grace leans forward inspecting the labels closely. There are untouched rows dating back to the year Walter died. Grace plucks a dust-free jar of huckleberry jam off the shelf and secretes it away in her purse.

Unperturbed by Grace's silence, her aunt continues speaking. "When you were little you used to hide in there when you were scared. Do you remember?"

"I just want to stay in here a bit longer. I'm feeling overwhelmed." She's more scared now than she ever was as a child. She expects her aunt to tell her to stop being rude but that doesn't happen.

"Just know that I love you. I'll be here when you're ready to come out."

She leans back and pulls a thin cord. The light snaps on and off like a flashbulb.

From her hiding place in the pantry Grace hears a dance of sensible heels break out in the kitchen as the ladies move plates of food from the counter to the dining room table for the meal. They're all whispering.

Grace imagines the knowing glances they throw toward her hiding place every time they walk past. Occasionally the deep baritone of a man's voice cuts through the chatter but he's shooed away when he tries to interfere. Soon the voices are muffled. They rise and fall with the saying of grace and they rise and fall with the telling of stories. Grace doesn't need to hear anything. She already knows all of them by heart. No one mentions her mother, not even in passing, but Grace hears her own name spoken more than once.

Why don't you try? Yes, that's a good idea, why don't you try? There's a scrape of a chair, footsteps, and the rise and fall of a voice she knows too well.

With only a thin wooden door separating them, Dustin Ash leans in close and talks at a whisper. "Grace," he says. "Your aunt is dying. Who's going to take care of you when she's gone?"

"I can take care of myself."

"By hiding in cupboards?"

"Go away."

"You need to stop this nonsense. I won't hurt you."

Grace tries not to cry. "Tell me who killed my mother?"

"I can't do that."

"Why not?"

"Grace, I need you to listen carefully. The man who killed your mother has something of ours and we need to get it back."

"My sketchbook?"

"He has the photos, Grace. He found them in your uncle's office. He wants the money your mother took. Do you have it?"

"I wouldn't tell you if I did."

"If I give him the money he'll leave town and never come back."

"Why should I trust you?"

"I'm the only one you should trust."

"I'll tell my aunt, she'll help me."

"Will she? I don't think so. She lies to you, Grace. Did she tell you your mother called her last month? I know they spoke."

Grace bangs her head on the door. "Please go."

He lowers his voice further. "Think about what I'm offering. I can look after you."

"Like you looked after Molly Parks and those other girls? Don't try to deny it. I know it was you."

She hears him take a deep breath before he speaks.

"I'm a lost soul without you."

"You need to go get lost again."

"If I go away there will be other little girls and they'd be on your conscience. We can make a fresh start, Grace. Just you and I. No one ever has to know what's happened in the past. All this time you wanted me to come back. I know what's in the sketchbook. He returned it to me. It's all there in black and white. You drew my picture. You practiced writing your new name—*Grace Angelica Ash*."

Grace has to put her hand over her mouth to stop a cry from escaping.

"I love you, Grace. That's all that ever really mattered."

"Tell me his name."

"I'm sorry, I can't do that."

"I'll do what you ask if you tell me."

"I can't."

"You can."

"He's threatened to sell the photos if we don't cooperate. Let me do this for you, Grace. It will be my way of making things right."

Grace slowly slides up the door and stands. The metal handle feels cold against her palm. She can hear him breathing. It's as regular as clockwork. He isn't going anywhere. He promises to never hurt her again. He promises to look after her. He tells her that he is the only man who can truly love her. She changes her mind several times before she's brave enough to face him.

She opens the door and blinks into the bright overhead lights but Dustin is gone. She doubles over and puts her hands to her face. Laughter escapes in nervous bursts. Stiff from sitting on the cold floor, she moves with difficulty. She brushes off the dust coating the back of her skirt. Outside in the dining room the lunchtime chatter continues. Aside from one voice, the remaining people are as familiar as a hymn. She listens. She wants to be sure he's gone.

"Oh, there you are." Elizabeth stands in the doorway with her arms stretched wide. "Dustin managed to get you out after all."

Grace can't look her aunt in the eye. "Is he here still?"

Elizabeth hesitates. "He had to rush off. That nice detective has just arrived though."

"Macy?"

"Yes, but I think you should call her Detective Greeley. I'm sure it's what she expects from all of us."

"It's okay, Elizabeth." Macy comes up from behind Elizabeth and steps into the kitchen. "Grace can call me whatever she likes."

"I was worried you wouldn't come."

"I got here as soon as I could. Are you ready to go?"

"I just need to get my coat."

Grace feels strange sitting in the front seat of the sheriff's patrol car. Macy checks her messages while she drives, and puts on the sirens to avoid sitting in traffic.

They stop at an intersection and she glances over at Grace. "Do you want to tell me what's going on?"

Grace takes hold of the handle above the door as Macy flies around the corner. "I was upset but I'm fine now."

"You shouldn't be."

"Pardon?"

"Given everything that's happened, you shouldn't be *fine*."

"I don't understand."

"It's okay to be upset. To cry. To scream. To pull out your hair. To hit someone."

"It's never done any good so I've learned not to bother."

"Oh, I don't know about that. Jared told me about the trailer."

"Am I in trouble?"

"Not this time, but don't pull anything like that again."

"He's angry with me."

"No, Grace. He's worried. There's a difference."

"Did he tell you I tried to kiss him?"

"No, it seems he left out the best part."

"I'm so embarrassed. I thought he liked me."

"Don't be. These misunderstandings are more common than you think." Macy looks in her rearview mirror. "Are you ready to talk about what happened back there at Martha Nielson's house?"

Grace shreds the tissue on her lap. "I'm working on it."

"Don't bottle it up for too long. It will just make you feel worse." She pulls the car into the parking lot of the diner and finds a spot near the doors. "How do you feel about having some dinner? Your aunt told me that you didn't eat anything."

It's after the dinner rush so there aren't many customers. Macy chooses a booth near the windows before going to find the bathroom. "I'll be right back. Order a diet soda and hamburger for me if the waitress comes by."

Grace is still sitting in the same position when Macy returns. An unopened menu is laid out in front of her.

Grace stares out at the traffic passing on Main Street and tears roll down her flushed cheeks. "When I was fourteen I thought I was all grown up but I was just some stupid little girl."

"We all go through that phase," says Macy, sliding into the booth across from her. "It's just that some of us get a little more bruised than others."

"Nobody seems to have noticed how much I looked like Molly Parks when I was younger."

"Give them enough time and they will."

Grace rubs her eyes.

Macy keeps her voice low. "My theory is that the same man who hurt Molly and the other two girls may have done something terrible to you as well."

Grace pulls her coat around her. "I trusted him."

"That's usually how it starts."

"He took me to that house they've been showing on the news. I thought I was ready." She looks down at her hands. "I actually thought I loved him."

"You probably did."

"I was expecting a cottage in the woods but it was nothing like that." It was nothing like she'd imagined it would be. A single bulb hung from the low basement ceiling. The mattress was filthy and even though it was midsummer, it was cold.

"Was anyone else at the house?"

"I didn't see anyone. It was disgusting inside. I kept on thinking that it was going to get better, that he had some nice surprise planned for me. Instead he took me downstairs to the basement. He went around turning on lights and I just followed him, not knowing what to do. I was more scared of the house than I was of him. He had me sit on a mattress that was laid out on the floor and told me to get undressed. He was so casual about it. I felt so childish when I admitted I was scared."

"What did he do?"

"He did the same thing he always did when I was upset, he talked to me. He sat down next to me on that mattress and looked me right in the eye. He told me how much he loved me but that people wouldn't understand so we needed to keep it secret for the time being. He reminded me of how many times he'd been there for me in the past and that I could always trust him."

"I take it you believed him."

"Every single word. Even now I still believe him when he says he loves me. In the last four years I haven't learned a damn thing." Grace looks around the diner. There's only one other table occupied and it's on the far side of the room. "He suggested it would be easier if I kept my eyes closed. After I let him undress me I sat there waiting. When I opened my eyes he was holding a camera."

"He took your picture?"

"He took lots of pictures. I couldn't stop crying. I didn't understand. When he tried to kiss me I begged him to stop. I swear I got down on my knees and prayed." Grace looks at her hands. She hadn't realized that Macy was holding them.

"What happened?"

"I guess I was luckier than Molly Parks. He kept on saying how sorry he was. He promised he'd never try something like that again. A week later he left Collier and I didn't see him again for four years."

"You hadn't heard from him in all that time?"

"Not a word."

"Did he visit you the day your mother died?"

"He started coming round a week earlier. At first he just left letters for me at the back gate. He even wrote me a poem."

"So the morning your mother died you got dressed up for him?"

"I was going to let him into the house but I changed my mind."

"Is that why he killed your mother?"

"I swear it wasn't him. Besides, he was more sad than angry. He said he wanted to be friends like before."

"Did you believe him?"

"Yeah, I guess I did at first, but then I saw what was done to my bedroom wall. It was from a poem he'd written me. I hated him after that."

"So you knew who did it and you didn't say anything?"

She looks up. "Whoever killed my mother is trying to set him up. He's never been in my bedroom."

"You still should have told me."

"He told me my uncle had the photos all this time. My uncle knew what happened to me and he never said a word."

"These were the photos from the basement?"

"And now my mother's killer has them."

Macy leans back and watches the young woman across from her unravel. "Is there anything else you want to tell me? Like his name, for instance."

"He has my sketchbook. I don't want anyone to see it."

"Grace, I need his name."

"You're angry with me. I knew you wouldn't understand."

"I'm not angry, but I need to do my job. As much as I'd like to spare your feelings I also need to stop this guy before he hurts another child."

"Everyone in Collier is going to find out."

"Why do you care so much what these people think? You don't owe them anything."

Grace grabs her bag and slides out of the booth. "You really have no idea what it's like living in this town. You'll go back to Helena but I'll be stuck here. I promise you these people will remind me of what happened every single day."

Macy follows her outside but stops short when she sees how close Grace is standing to the road. Traffic is heavy and a fire engine barrels down the center lane, followed by several patrol cars. It's almost impossible to hear anything over the lament of sirens. Dark smoke rises up into the air from buildings near the town square.

Macy eases her way down the icy steps. "Grace, no one who really understands what happened to you would ever think you're stupid."

Grace turns to face Macy but keeps her heels hanging over the edge of the curb like she's a diver preparing to do a backflip from a springboard.

Macy extends a hand. There's a deep pain in her side that wasn't there before. "Please, Grace," she says, taking a cautious step forward. "Come back inside."

Grace shifts her gaze toward the town square and watches as a news helicopter descends on Collier.

"Grace, I can't protect you from this man if you don't tell me his name."

Grace's eyes flit up and down the road, searching for a break in the traffic. Farther north in the direction of the central bridge the light has gone red. "I don't believe you."

"Give me a chance and I'll prove it."

Grace addresses the oncoming cars, raising her voice so Macy can hear her. "I don't want anyone to see the photos or the sketchbook."

"I promise I'll take care of it. I just need a name, Grace." Macy raises a hand and touches Grace's shoulder. "I can't help you if you don't give me a name."

Grace takes a deep breath before reaching up and squeezing Macy's fingers. "Dustin Ash," she says before jumping off the curb and disappearing behind a fast-moving truck.

Macy's screams are lost in a barrage of horns. She walks up and down the sidewalk, peeking between the cars, which slow down but never quite stop. She doesn't see Grace anywhere. Traffic starts to move faster again and she too quickens her pace, heading south along Main Street. She stops when she gets to the next intersection. Across the street music blasts out of Murphy's Tavern every time someone opens the front door. There are crowds of people outside but she recognizes none of them.

Macy slowly walks back to the restaurant with her hands clasped firmly at her sides. Sharp cramps sweep across her abdomen. On the wooden walkway she bends forward and waits for it to pass.

"Damn it," she says, pulling out her phone and dialing. "Warren, I've lost Grace Adams outside the diner in Old Town. Send some cars out looking for her. She can't have gotten very far."

22

ayley is late. Jared gazes out at the summer cabins strung along the quiet lanes winding through Olsen's Landing. In the moonlight the red metal siding is the color of mud. A half mile to the north the central bridge spans the river at its widest point. Through the trees he can see the headlights of cars passing along it in a steady stream. He's tucked his truck up next to his family's cabin where it can't be seen. As a child the summers he spent on the river were the best of his life. He and his brother would sleep on the fold-out sofa in the loft and his parents shared the one bedroom. All their friends came to hang out along the shoreline for fishing, picnics, and barbecues. Nobody went home hungry and nobody went home early.

Jared scrolls through the messages on his phone. There's nothing from Hayley, but Lexxie has been trying to get in touch for two days, and he hasn't returned the calls. They'd gone out to dinner on the evening of Grace's birthday and ended up arguing on Lexxie's doorstep. *You need to talk to me,* she said, not worrying if the neighbors heard her shouting at him. *What you're doing is crazy. Hayley can't give you what you want. I can.* Lexxie was right about one thing. What he's doing is crazy.

Jared snaps the phone shut and waits. Pamela's message had been very specific about the time and place Hayley wanted to meet him. He looks at his watch and lights up a cigarette. It's after six and Hayley is overdue by nearly an hour. Since Brian took away her cell phone Jared doesn't have any other way of contacting her. Jared has bought her a new one. It sits on the seat next to him. He's already added his contact details. More than anything he needs to know she's safe. A few minutes later headlights trail across the spruce pines and cabin walls. Relieved she's finally arrived, Jared gets out of the cab and takes a few steps forward, stopping when he realizes the engine sounds too big. He hugs the wall and watches as the vehicle slows down to a crawl before the narrow lane takes a sharp turn. Brian Camberwell's profile is clearly visible in the glow of the dashboard lights.

Jared slips on the ice as he scrambles back to his truck. His knees knock hard against the frozen surface and he just manages to get his hands out in front of him before he falls into the side of his truck. He grabs the door handle and pulls himself up but drops the keys when he's getting them out of his pocket. He feels light-headed digging around in the snow on his hands and knees trying to find them.

Jared keeps his speed down and his headlights off as he makes his way up the narrow lanes. Every few seconds his eyes flick up to his rearview mirror looking for Brian's headlights but no one is following him. The truck's suspension bounces along the ruts until he passes Trina's grocery store and the road becomes smooth again. He switches on his headlights and drives directly to Hayley's street. He is relieved to see her car in the driveway. He checks his mirror again but there's still no sign of Brian. For the moment he knows he's safe. Jared pulls over to the side and keeps the engine running. The lights are all on in the front rooms of Hayley's house and he can see her silhouette moving about the kitchen. He calls her and she picks up on the first ring.

He keeps his voice low. "Is everything okay? I went out to Olsen's Landing to meet you and Brian was there."

Jared watches Hayley pace the floor of her kitchen. "I never agreed to that. We're supposed to meet later outside my sister's apartment."

"That's not what your mother told me!"

"I'm so sick of her games."

"Is she trying to get me killed?"

"No, I think she's just trying to piss you off."

"Why was Brian out there anyway?"

He hears Hayley's breath catch. "Who knows? A half hour ago he got pissed off at something and stormed out of the house. I don't even think he knew where he was going."

Jared rubs his face. Even though it's cold in the cab of his truck, he's sweating. "What brought that on?"

"Near as I can tell it was something he saw on the news."

"You've got to talk to your mother. This isn't the first time she's pulled this kind of shit with me."

"It may be a while before I get a chance. The police arrested her about an hour ago. She's been charged with obstruction of justice."

"Jesus, what did she do?"

"I'm not sure. It sounds serious though."

Jared goes quiet for a few seconds. He watches Hayley's silhouette lean against the counter and dip its head. "Are you okay?"

Her voice drops to a whisper. "I miss you. Where are you now?"

"Outside."

She comes closer to the kitchen window and presses her palm flat against the glass. "You're so close."

He swings his car out onto the road. "I'm too close. I need to go."

"Can you pick me up outside Janice's apartment in an hour?"

"I'm not sure that's a good idea. Murphy's Tavern is right next door. I drove by earlier and it looked like half of Collier was out front."

"Just park in the back of the lot. I'll come find you."

It's early evening and Collier is buzzing with noise and traffic. The pavements outside Janice's apartment building are crowded with smokers spilling out of the front entrance to Murphy's Tavern. Jared finds a space at the far end of the parking lot. It will be another hour before Hayley shows up. He goes inside. The tavern is busy and the wait is three deep at the bar. Jared stands at the entrance, scanning the crowd. A five-piece bluegrass band is playing on a small stage. The guy collecting the cover charge recognizes Jared and waves him through.

"Hey, Jared, you okay? Heard you've had a rough week."

Jared has to shout to be heard. "They say bad luck comes in threes."

"So does that mean you're done now?"

"God, I hope so."

A bartender Jared knows tilts his head in the direction of the town square before plunking a beer down in front of his friend. "I'm surprised you're not working. I heard there's a building on fire near the town's square."

"I've been given a few weeks off so it's not something I need to worry about."

"To be honest," he says, looking over at the stage, "bluegrass is not really my thing, but this band is good for business."

Jared slides onto an empty barstool. "Too bad they're not good for music."

Everyone at the bar is talking about Leanne's murder and they soon pull Jared into their conversations, offering him drinks he doesn't accept and pumping him for details he doesn't give. Grace's name keeps coming up. There's a rumor going around that she had an affair with a married high school teacher.

Jared tries to be patient. "If you knew her at all, you'd realize she's the last person to have an affair with a married man."

The bartender slides another beer toward Jared and winks. "Some people reckon she's the only virgin left in the Flathead Valley."

Jared doesn't laugh with everyone else. He leans against the bar and works his way through his beer, focusing more on what's going on in his own head than the conversation around him. At one point he hears someone whisper his name. *Jared's had a rough week, let him be.*

When he slips away, nobody notices.

The parking lot is icy and heavily rutted. Jared has to work hard to keep his balance. He checks his phone and finds three missed calls from Macy and a text asking him to meet her at the sheriff's office. He's about to ring her back when something catches his eye. A shadow moves between parked cars and his eyes follow it, filling in the gaps and making it into a man.

"Hey," he yells, slipping his phone into his pocket. "Anyone out there?"

Jared takes a step back and moves to the right, walking slowly and keeping his eyes on the dark recesses between the vehicles. The lights from the tavern's back door don't reach this far. Everything fades from gray to black. Aside from the glint off windshields and metallic paint it's almost total darkness. He hears things though. A footfall. The brush of fabric. A strangled cough. Jared moves forward, straining his eyes. His truck is within easy reach. He thinks of the gun he keeps in the glove compartment and asks again.

"Is anyone there?"

There's a light tap on his shoulder and he spins around, almost striking out at the person behind him. He stops when he sees Hayley's face. He starts to put his arms around her but thinks again when he remembers where they are. Her smile is fragile. She dips her forehead to his chest and holds it there.

Jared is so relieved to see her he doesn't think twice. He takes her hand and they climb into the cab of his truck. Hayley doesn't speak. She doesn't even whisper a simple hello. Before Jared can settle in behind the wheel, her hands are everywhere. She rises up multi-limbed like some Hindu goddess, taking hold of him with her mouth, her legs, her arms, her fingers, her toes. One second she's kissing him and the next she's wrapped up inside him, snatching every bit he has on offer. She tastes of peppermint and tobacco and her cheeks feel flushed under his touch. Jared closes his mouth over hers and pulls her in closer still, holding her face tight in his hands, trying to contain her.

He's making promises every time his lips are free. Losing his breath, his mind. The windows mist over and the lights from passing cars trail around the interior of the cab. He watches her fear ebb away, sees her smile return. He pulls off her coat, hat, and scarf and it all crumples beneath them. He snakes his hands under her sweater, feeling the grooves between her ribs, undoing the clasp of her bra. She's raking her hands up and down his chest, peeling away his layers, undoing his belt and pulling him down on top of her. Jared is inside her and he's telling her things he can't take back.

He kisses her hard on the mouth and wishes they were at home and that she was completely his. Making dinner in his kitchen, getting her kids ready for bed, maybe making one of their own. Wrapped up and half undressed, they talk about when this will be easy. He kisses her bandaged wrists and plays with her fingers, smoothing each one out from knuckle to nail. He makes more promises, knowing that he'll have to keep every last one. It's the first time he's ever seen Hayley cry. Their heads rest against a door and they're in the parking lot of Murphy's Tavern and it's never been this good before. It's like coming home.

23

No one is answering the phone at Grace's apartment. Macy swings her car out onto Main Street and puts the sirens on. It only takes a couple of minutes to drive the short distance to Grace's door. A patrol car is parked outside. She pulls up alongside and exchanges a few words with Ted Bishop, the officer on duty. He hasn't seen Grace, but as far as he knows Elizabeth Lamm is still home. Macy has to ring the bell several times before she gets a response. Elizabeth comes to the door wearing a dressing gown and slippers.

"I was just going to bed." She looks over Macy's shoulder. "Where is my niece?"

"I was hoping she was here." Macy clears her throat. "She got upset and ran off."

Elizabeth gestures for Macy to come inside. "Grace has had a difficult day."

Macy stands just inside the doorway with her hat in her hands and watches as Elizabeth walks into the kitchen. Macy is finding it difficult to hide how angry she is.

"Grace has had a difficult life."

"It is true that she's had more than her fair share of problems."

"Did you know that Dustin Ash tried to rape your niece when she was fourteen and that he returned to Collier intent on rekindling their relationship?"

Elizabeth puts a hand over her mouth.

"He took those photos you found in Arnold's office."

"I swear I had no idea."

"Maybe you just pretended it wasn't happening."

"What do you mean? I would never do that. Not with Grace."

"Elizabeth, the man you were married to for thirty-three years ran a sex trafficking operation. You knew something was going on but chose to ignore it. I need to know who Arnold was working with. Whoever murdered Leanne is still out there and Grace won't be safe until we catch him."

"It wasn't Dustin?"

"We have reason to believe it was someone else."

"I'm not sure who was involved. As a rule Arnold and I never spoke about it."

"I want names, Elizabeth. You must have had your suspicions."

"Sometimes, I overheard them talking. Much of it didn't make sense but I know Brady Monroe and Walter Nielson did a lot of the runs over to Canada. I was always convinced that Scott Pearce and Dustin Ash were involved."

"What did Dustin Ash do?"

"He used to be an accountant, so I imagine he took care of the money."

There's a long silence on Warren's side of the desk when Macy tells him that Dustin Ash murdered Molly Parks and tried to rape Grace when she was fourteen.

Warren sounds frustrated. "But she said she didn't recognize her mother's killer."

"Grace is adamant Dustin isn't the killer."

"Why should we believe her?"

"She has no reason to lie."

"She might have been worried her past with Dustin would have come out. She let the man back into her life. Who knows? Maybe she's in love with him."

"If that were the case, she wouldn't have called me to come get her when Dustin showed up at Martha Nielson's house. Grace hid in the pantry for nearly an hour. Apparently, she and Dustin had a very long conversation through a closed door."

Warren crosses his arms. "And during this little confessional with Dustin did she think of asking him who killed her mother?"

"He wouldn't tell her."

"They never make it easy for us, do they?"

Macy tries her best to keep her face neutral. The stomach cramps she felt earlier have returned. "It gets worse. Leanne's killer has the photos of Grace that were taken from Arnold's office."

"And who's to say it wasn't Dustin who took them? If he's the man who killed Molly Parks, we have physical evidence that he was in Grace's house."

"Fair enough, he may have lied to Grace about being in her bedroom. She told me the messages written on the wall were from a poem he'd written her."

"So much for restoring my faith in mankind." Warren leans back in his chair and closes his eyes. "I think he's living out in one of the cabins at Olsen's Landing, acting as a caretaker or something. I'll need to do some checking."

"Warren, we can't leave it until tomorrow. Someone might tip him off. We need to do this tonight."

Warren reaches for the phone. "You hang tight. I'll get it organized."

Macy excuses herself and goes straight to the office they cleared out for her. Closing the door behind her, she doubles over in pain. Grabbing the back of her chair, she takes deep breaths until the cramping sensations pass. Her phone rings and she has difficulty keeping her voice steady. The officer who's keeping an eye on Grace's apartment reports that Grace returned home a few minutes earlier.

"That's a relief," she says, opening the door to her office to let Jared in. "Whatever happens, make sure she stays there."

Macy starts in on Jared without saying hello. "Where have you been?" she says, sitting down heavily in the chair behind the desk. "I've been trying to reach you for the past half hour."

"Look, I've got better things to do than to stand here and listen to you yell at me."

"And here I was thinking you gave a shit."

"You know damn well that my problem is that I give too much of a shit."

Macy waits a few seconds before speaking. "I'm sorry, I'm upset. I shouldn't take it out on you."

"You want to tell me what's going on?"

"Do you know Dustin Ash?"

"Yeah, sure. He's not been around much in the past few years but seems a decent enough guy."

"He tried to rape Grace when she was fourteen."

"Isn't he a family friend?"

"They're usually the ones to look out for. After he left town four years ago he murdered Molly Parks and abused two other little girls. We'll need to get DNA from him for confirmation but I know I'm right. When he returned to Collier a couple months ago he told Grace he'd found God and wanted to make a new start with her. She'd forgiven him because he convinced her it was just that one time that he lost control. It was only when the news carried stories about Molly Parks and the other two little girls that Grace realized she'd been lied to."

"I don't get it. Was Dustin trying to have a proper relationship with Grace?"

"By making things right with Grace he believes he'll be forgiven for his past sins and won't be tempted again."

"Why would Grace ever let him near her?"

"She's lonely and vulnerable. A soft target. It's how they pick them."

"But Grace said no this time."

"That's right. She did."

"Why didn't she just tell someone what happened?"

"Shame. Fear. A warped sense of loyalties. Who knows?"

"Will he be arrested tonight?"

"We should be heading out in a few minutes." She looks up at him. "I'm sorry I lost my temper. The fact is I like having you around. I've missed you."

"Macy, are you saying what I think you're saying?"

"Jared, don't flatter yourself. I've missed you as a friend. That's as far as it goes."

Jared comes around to Macy's side of the desk. "You know I'm going to have to hug you."

"If you think you can pry my big ass from this chair, you're welcome to try."

A half hour later Jared drives Macy's patrol car to Olsen's Landing. Next to him Macy roots around in the glove compartment until she finds a candy bar. She rips off the wrapper and offers half to Jared.

"No thanks. You okay?"

She takes a bite and talks with her mouth full. "My boss is coming up to Collier tomorrow."

"You deserve better."

"We all do," she says, grabbing hold of the handle above the door when Jared swings around a corner.

In front of Trina's store, sheriff patrol cars sit parked out in the open with their lights flashing. Macy imagines they all arrived with their sirens on. "I bet half of Collier knows what we're up to by now."

She grimaces and takes hold of her stomach.

"What's wrong?"

"Just a bit of indigestion."

"You're sure?"

"Sure I'm sure." Moving as quickly as she's able, Macy exits the cab and heads over to a group of officers. They're all heavily armed and wear bulletproof vests.

Sheriff Warren Mayfield has a map of Collier spread out on the hood of a patrol car. "Just so you know I pulled Dustin's DMV photo and we got a positive ID from the little girl who lives down in Shelby. The judge signed this a few minutes ago." He takes an arrest warrant out of his breast pocket and hands it to Macy.

Macy looks it over before handing it back to Warren. "Much as I'd like to join you I think I better sit this one out."

"You're going to miss out on all the fun."

"I'll have to watch it on the news like everyone else."

Warren indicates the location of the entrance to Olsen's Landing at the rear of the parking lot. "This should be pretty straightforward. There's only one access point and we know he's home. I had a guy go along on foot to check. According to Trina, Dustin Ash is living here, in unit thirty-two. It sits right on the edge of the forested area. I suggest we go in on foot from the entrance, fanning out so we've covered all possible escape routes. I'll station some men along the access road below the central bridge in case he tries to make a run for it across this open field. There's no way he can cross the river." He runs his finger along the long arc of the Flathead. "In this section the ice is still too thin. It would be suicidal to try."

Macy points to the central bridge. "This is as good a vantage point as any. I think I'll park up here and keep an eye on things from a safe distance."

Twenty minutes later the two patrol units in front of Macy's car exit onto the access road below the central bridge but Macy continues driving straight, slowing to a crawl when she hits the span.

Jared points off to the left. "That's Olsen's Landing just beyond the field."

Macy pulls up onto the curb and they get out and stand at the railing. Ahead of them the full moon leans heavily on the trees, fenceposts, and overhead cables, casting solid black shadows across the brilliant white field. One hundred feet away a few of the summer cabins that sit nestled among the trees are just visible. Lights are showing in only one set of windows. The rest of the cabins look uninhabited. To the right, the Flathead River is a patchwork of ice floes. To the left is the tail end of Main Street and the beginnings of Route 93.

Macy holds up her phone to Jared and frowns. "They must have reached his cabin by now. Something isn't right."

Below them on the access road the two patrol cars sweep the meadow with their searchlights. There is no movement, but from the shadows cast down by the trees dark figures emerge. Voices call out to each other just as Macy's phone rings in her hand.

"Hey, Warren, please tell me we have good news."

Warren sounds out of breath. "Dustin's Jeep is here but he's gone. It might be that someone got to him before we did. There are signs of a struggle. I've set up a perimeter along the main road."

"He's the caretaker so he'll have access to the cabins. You'll need to search every one of them."

"It's going to be a long night."

24

Even though she's still wrapped up in her coat, Grace is shivering. She's been back at the apartment for half an hour and she can't seem to shake off the cold. Exhausted, she slouches down onto the sofa and lets her hopes sink further. There is nothing here she can call home. A few partitions away, her aunt stubbornly sleeps through what is left of her life, capitulating now that her house and husband have both been taken away from her.

On the coffee table Grace finds her aunt's list of things to do. She stares at the last entry. *Move to Helena.* Wanting to ease her aunt's load, Grace takes up the pen and crosses out this final task. She looks up at the sound of approaching footsteps. Caught in the dim light of a small table lamp, her aunt's pale face floats out of the darkened hallway. She emerges with a blanket draped around her shoulders. With her long silver hair hanging loose she looks like a young child who's aged beyond her years.

"Grace, where have you been?"

"I took a long walk," says Grace, steadying her nerves. "I can't stand being trapped inside all the time."

Elizabeth takes a seat in the reclining chair. "So, you had a nice time with Macy?"

"Yes, I did," says Grace, thankful that her aunt has left her glasses on her bedside table so she can't see how much Grace has been crying.

"Grace, please take my hands."

Elizabeth's hands are warm, dry, and smell of lavender soap. Her own hands are icy cold, but her aunt doesn't chastise her this time.

Her aunt speaks slowly. "Your mother called me about a month ago. She wanted to come see you and I told her it was out of the question."

Grace holds her aunt's hands a little tighter, but says nothing.

"For years I watched you cry every time you received a birthday card from your mother. She'd not once included a simple message. She'd not once told you she loved you. But what I did was wrong. I should have given you the right to decide for yourself."

"I wouldn't have seen her."

"Pardon."

"I think I would have chosen not to see her. I feel guilty about it but it's the truth. I would have liked to have the choice though."

"If I could change what I've done, I would."

"You were trying to protect me. You did it for the right reasons."

"I am sorry."

Grace glances at the clock. "You should go back to bed, it's been a long day."

"Are you sure?" Her aunt makes a move to get up. "We could talk for a while, if you like."

"I'm going to bed soon too."

Elizabeth kisses Grace on the forehead. "I love you."

"I love you too."

The heavy sound of footfalls echo from the apartment above and Grace tracks their progress across the ceiling. Ghostly laughter soon follows. She shifts her weight and her eyes, dropping them into her lap along with her expectations. It is time to leave Collier. She mulls over the idea like she might do with a puzzle. So many pieces slot right into place. Leaving Dustin and the gathering ghosts far behind is the only thing that makes any sense.

Grace throws some clothes into a bag along with the money she found in the trailer. In the kitchen she scribbles a quick note to her aunt and prepares some snacks for the road. The telephone rings and she stands frozen with the refrigerator wide open. She looks down the hallway toward her aunt's room but there is no telltale slit of light beneath the door. On the sixth ring, Grace picks it up.

It's a man's voice she doesn't recognize.

"Grace Adams?" he says.

Grace grips the phone tightly. "Yes, who is this?"

"Do you know where the old Harris Mill is?"

"I'm going to hang up if you don't tell me who this is."

"I want you to meet me there tomorrow morning at ten."

"I can't get away. The police are watching me all the time."

"That's not my problem. Dustin told me you had the money. If you want what I have you'll find a way."

Grace is left listening to a dial tone.

25

M acy takes Jared by the arm and pulls him back to the truck. "Come with me. I want to have a look in Dustin's cabin."

Jared studies the group of officers standing at the edge of the field for a moment longer. A wind kicks up and he shivers. He's only just noticed he's cold. He looks up and Macy gazes at him with an uncertain expression on her face. She puts her arms around her belly like she's protecting it, covering the eyes and ears of her unborn child.

Olsen's Landing is filled with patrol cars. Neither Jared nor Macy speaks as the car moves along the lanes. Jared points out his family's cabin when they pass by it and Macy doesn't bother to comment. They stop about fifty yards away from Dustin's place and stare out the windshield. Dustin's Jeep still sits outside, and inside the cabin the lights are on.

Jared puts the car in park before getting out to help Macy. He glances around the darkened woods. Flashlight beams flick through the trees. Voices call out. Radios crackle. Beyond the cabin he sees the flashing lights of the patrol cars stationed below the bridge. A helicopter circles overhead, its searchlight sweeping across the snowbound roofs.

The cabin's door has been forced. It hangs open, inviting them in.

Jared pushes it and the hinges creak. The lights are on and a fire burns in a woodstove in the corner of the living area. There are stacks of books lined up against one of the walls and music plays from hidden speakers. At first it seems so ordinary but then Jared starts to notice that things are out of place. The coffee table is overturned. A lamp has tumbled onto the sofa. Broken glass crackles underfoot. There's a puddle of blood on the floor near the front door. Pink footprints fan out in all directions.

"Did the police do this?"

Macy's eyes sweep across the room. "Apparently, it was like this when they arrived."

Macy wanders back to the bedroom with Jared hovering close behind. A cold breeze blows through the unlatched window. The curtains are torn and hang lopsided from the rail.

"He must have climbed out this way," she says.

Jared flicks on the wall switch and looks around. The bed is unmade and unopened packing boxes are stacked high up against one wall. The door to a small closet is open and inside a few items of clothing rest askew on hangers.

"He can't have gotten very far."

Macy picks up a yellow notepad and flips through the pages. "Do you remember what Brady Monroe said about Leanne taking off with a lot of money?"

"Yeah, seems to make sense that a lot of people would be after her."

"There is another possibility."

"What's that?"

"The money never left Collier. It was hidden in the trailer and Grace went back to get it."

"There was only a couple grand in the coffee tin."

"Yes, but you weren't with Grace when she started the fire. I wouldn't put it past her. She's proving to be rather resourceful. Sofia told me that Leanne claimed to have left a lot of money behind." Macy starts opening the dresser drawers one by one.

"What are you looking for?"

"I'll know it when I see it."

A couple minutes later Macy finds something beneath the bed that looks like a notebook and starts turning the pages. She tucks it into her bag without showing it to Jared.

"We can go now," she says, gesturing toward the door.

Jared leads the way. Helicopter blades drum just above the roof and searchlights trail across the windows and fill the cabin with light.

He turns and looks back at Macy. She's framed in the bedroom doorway.

"I don't think I can live in Collier any longer," he says.

"Don't kid yourself. You'll live wherever Hayley lives."

Jared puts his arm out behind him, holding Macy back. "Did you hear that? Was that the front door?"

Macy tries to move past him. "It's probably Warren."

"Wait here," he says, grabbing her by the arm.

"You're being ridiculous."

"Just wait."

Jared eases the front door open and steps out into the night. It's much quieter than it was earlier. They're searching cabins farther up the lane. "I don't see anyone."

Macy follows him out and switches on her flashlight. "When you stayed here as a child did you play hide-and-seek?"

"Of course. My brother and I were legendary. No one could ever find us."

"Where did you hide?"

"The boat house was always a good place. We'd climb up into the rafters and stay there for hours."

Macy points her flashlight toward the river. "After you."

"No way. We need to get out of here. There are too many guys with guns wandering around Olsen's Landing. It's not safe."

Macy lets him push her toward her car. "I'm trying to remember if you've always been this bossy."

The helicopter thunders overhead, sweeping its searchlight through the woods to the west of them. Seconds later a figure breaks through the trees about fifty feet farther down the lane and staggers toward the river.

"Oh shit," says Macy. "That's Dustin."

"I'll watch him."

Macy tries to grab hold of Jared's arm as he moves away from her. "Stay right where you are."

"It's all right. I'll hang back. Just call for help."

It's so dark under the trees that it's almost impossible to see where they're going. Jared can hear his heart beating inside his chest and the pounding of his feet sets off a low throbbing vibration in his ears. The road takes a hard right and ends at a parking lot. Out in the open the unblemished snow glows in the moonlight. Below them the bank drops sharply to the Flathead River. From above it looks as if the surface is frozen solid all the way across to the opposite shore.

Dustin stands at the top of the boat ramp clutching his side. The incline is steep and icy. He takes a tentative step and Jared reaches out to stop him. They both misjudge the surface. Their feet slip out from beneath them and together they tumble down the slope, building speed the closer they get to its base.

On his back, Jared spins flat like a starfish across the frozen river, coming to rest about twenty feet from the shoreline. He gets up on all fours. His head aches from where it struck hard against the ice. He looks around. Dustin is on his feet and walking unsteadily toward the opposite shore. Jared stands slowly but the ice shifts with the movements of the river. It's like walking on water. Even in the pale light he can see icy pools bubbling up everywhere.

He tracks Dustin's silhouette then all of a sudden it's gone. Jared cries out at the space where Dustin was standing before he fell through the ice. For a few seconds Jared stands perfectly still, fearful he'll do the same. Slowly he drops onto his belly and spreads his weight out evenly. Ahead of him Dustin's dark head bobs in and out of the water. He's clutching at the edge of the ice floe with his bare hands. The surface breaks off in chunks every time he tries to pull himself out.

Jared slides toward him on his stomach. The ice thins further and the river water rises upward and seeps into his clothing, adding to his weight. He blinks his eyes in the gray light and yells at Dustin to hold on. The shadow of Dustin's hand waves up out of the black water but when Jared grabs at it more ice gives way. Jared scrambles backward on all fours and a crack follows him, ripping the surface like a split seam. Dark water bleeds over the sides of a cut that grows in inches and then in feet. Jared looks up and sees Dustin gripping on to its edge, his wet hair plastered to his head. In the moonlight his features are as grainy as an old photograph but his pale eyes glow like white neon. Dustin tries to pull himself up onto the ice again but there's no strength left in his arms. He takes one last look at Jared and is swept away.

Jared puts his head to the side and gathers his strength. Farther off shore the black water swells and ice floes splinter and separate. He slides on his belly, backing away as quickly as he dares. The river pushes hard and he rocks up and down with the current. Behind him he can hear people shouting his name. Macy screams at someone to get a line out to him.

Jared twists his body around so he can see where he's going. Headlights from vehicles parked above the boat ramp reflect off the ice and he's blind for a few seconds. He puts his head down and scrambles forward to where a length of rope has been thrown. There's a loop tied into it but his hands are so numb he can't hold on. He struggles to put it over his neck and shoulders. His teeth chatter uncontrollably and he can't stop shaking. He clenches his jaw and paws at the knot with his hands, trying hard to heave himself toward the thicker ice. From the shore someone gives the signal to pull and he's dragged straight into a fracture in the surface.

The ice breaks beneath him just as the rope goes slack. Jared sinks fast in his heavy coat and clothes. He can't breathe. He struggles to swim to the surface as the current drags him downstream toward the rapids south of town.

The rope digs hard into his shoulder blades and ribs as it's pulled taut. Ahead of him he can see the surface lightening as he's drawn closer. He struggles to put his arms up and catch hold of the edge. Hands reach for him and he's pulled out of the water. He lands in a heap in someone's arms and gasps for breath.

26

Lexxie has been in Jared's house again. His dogs are in their pen. They've been fed. Their water bowls are full. From inside the garage he looks out at his driveway. He's tired but he's not missed anything. There are no other cars. It's after midnight and he's finally home. They'd wanted to keep him in the hospital overnight, but he had other ideas. He took the borrowed clothes, got dressed, and drove off in the ambulance he came in.

Jared sends his dogs into the house ahead of him. They pad about calmly. Nobody else is there but he can tell Lexxie has been everywhere. The place is once again wiped clean. In the dining room the table is set for two—two chairs, two plates, two wineglasses, and two candles that are burned down to the nub. There's roast chicken, mashed potatoes, and green beans. There's a bottle of wine and a bottle of water.

There's a note.

Jared sits down in a chair and reads. The meal in front of him represented his last chance to make things right. Lexxie is leaving him and Collier for good. She does not wish him well.

Jared scoops up some mashed potatoes and green beans and pulls the platter holding the chicken toward him. He opens the wine and pours a large glass. He eats it all, shoveling the food into his mouth and not tasting a thing.

Outside of Lexxie's house, there's a box of Jared's stuff sitting on the front step next to the morning paper, but she isn't answering the door. He looks through the side window of her garage and sees her car is there. He rings the bell again and waits. He's walking away when the door opens.

Her voice cracks when she speaks. "What have you got to say for yourself?"

Lexxie wears a flannel robe and her hair is pulled back into a loose knot. She looks as if she has a cold but Jared knows she's been crying.

"I'm sorry. I should have listened to your messages. I should have talked to you." He gestures to the ambulance he drove up in. "It's been a bad week."

Lexxie looks up at the sky. There've been news helicopters circling over Collier all night. "I'm moving to Helena. I've got a job offer at the hospital there. I was hoping you'd come with me. It would do you good to get out of Collier."

Jared finds it hard to disagree with her logic. "I'm kind of stuck here for the time being."

"You've always been stuck. I know that now. You've not changed one bit since the day I met you. You're still waiting around for your life to start."

Jared tries to defend himself but comes up short.

"What are you going to do, Jared? Trail around living off the scraps from Hayley's life? She's not going to leave Brian." She starts to shut the door on him but stops and turns to say one last thing. "Sometimes I feel like someone should just put you out of your misery."

At the sheriff's office, Jared and Macy sit opposite each other with coffee bought from the vending machine.

Macy yawns into her fist. "You okay?"

261

"Just sore all over." Jared closes his eyes. "I feel bad for Grace. People round here will never understand."

Macy reaches over and looks through the blinds, pinching them open with her fingertips. All the desks are full. The Collier sheriff's department will be doing paperwork forever. "I found one of her sketchbooks when we searched Dustin's cabin."

"Is that what you put in your bag?"

Macy blows out air like she's been holding it in for a while. "Dustin told Grace he'd never been in her bedroom. I don't know what to believe anymore."

"Does it matter?"

"Not really."

"What will you do with it?"

Macy leans back in her chair. "I'll log it as evidence."

"It could disappear. Nobody knows you have it."

"Compared to the missing photos, I'd say the sketchbook is the least of Grace's worries."

Jared's phone rings and he looks at the caller ID. It's Hayley. Instead of answering, he glances up at Macy. "The evidence from the other abuse cases. It's a definite match? Dustin murdered Molly Parks?"

"Yes, we have a match on fingerprints and one of the girls identified him from his DMV photo. We're still waiting for DNA. Not that it matters much anymore. Dustin's dead."

Jared almost reaches for his phone. All he can think of is returning Hayley's call.

Macy thumps her pen on the table like a tiny seesaw. "We're arresting Brian Camberwell."

His eyes snap up. "Are you serious?"

"Remember that number Grace wrote down in the column of that newspaper article? We couldn't find a match because it was an old registration number for one of Arnold Lamm's trailers. We found it in his files. Brian was the registered driver of the truck that transported the girls that died. Grace will have to testify, but if all goes according to plan, he's looking at life in a federal prison."

"Why didn't you say something before?"

"I didn't know until a few minutes ago."

"I saw Brian's truck out at Olsen's Landing early yesterday evening. I was supposed to meet Hayley there and I thought Brian had come looking for us, but he must have been there to see Dustin." He looks at his phone again. Hayley has left a message on his voicemail. Macy leans in when he plays it for her. Even from her side of the desk, she can hear Hayley pleading for her life. Hayley shouts her husband's name more than once.

Along with half the officers in the station, they take to the roads of Collier. Feeling useless, Jared sits in front with Macy. Her big baby bump is squeezed up into the steering wheel and her jaw is clenched tight. Sirens screaming and a string of squad cars on her trail, she edges through a narrow gap to cross Main Street before taking a hard right and heading straight into oncoming traffic. Macy doesn't blink. The approaching vehicles drive onto sidewalks and into center divides, parting from the road like teeth on a zipper.

Jared gestures toward Hayley's street and yells, "Take a left here."

He jumps out of the door before the car is fully stopped. Stumbling through the deep snow, he checks the driveway for Brian's truck before running through the open front door. He's unprepared for the brightness of the well-lit entrance. Every surface is cleanly polished to the point it shines. Little things catch his eye. Family photos, an overturned chair, a discarded shoe. The house is too quiet. He can't imagine how someone could draw breath within its walls. Standing as still as a river stone, Jared feels the cold rush of police officers flow around him.

An officer who goes by the name of Henry takes hold of him. "You stay put for now."

From outside comes the sound of more sirens. There's an army encamped on Hayley's street. In his head Jared pieces together what he's seeing: a child's backpack and a small suitcase with half its contents spilling onto the floor, a blue-eyed doll, a coloring book, a pink sweat-shirt. He tries to think. It's a weekday. The girls should still be in school.

Macy's small voice is shriller than the sirens out front. "Jared," she calls from the back of the house. "Get back here."

Jared finds Macy in the master bedroom, shouting down the phone. "Please tell me that someone called an ambulance?"

Beyond the unmade bed, an officer is on his knees. Jared catches sight of Hayley's bare leg. The positioning is odd. He moves forward and the officer makes room. Jared places his fingertips to Hayley's neck. There's a pulse and it's strong. He shouts her name and shakes her as hard as he dares, resting his forehead in the crook of her neck when he gets a response.

Her tears mix with the blood and snot dripping from her broken nose and lips. She tries to sit up and he pushes her back down. "I tried to stop him." Her eyes dart around the room. "He's taken them."

He probes her ribs with his fingertips. "The girls are fine."

Hayley grimaces and coughs, turning her head to the side. "Don't lie to me." She leans her head back, exposing her bruised throat.

Voices and footsteps fill the room. Carson and another paramedic named Paul shove the bed out of the way.

Carson's voice is calm. "What have we got here?"

Jared goes through a list, his voice breaking off when he sees the phone he'd given Hayley lying on the carpet next to the nightstand. He can't help but think that he's failed her one too many times.

Carson rips a dressing from its packaging. "We got this," he says, glancing over at Paul for confirmation. "Hayley is going to be fine."

Jared kisses Hayley on the forehead. "I'm going to go see about your girls." When he gets to the living room, he has to wait for Macy to finish her phone call with the girls' elementary school.

"Can you give us an exact time?" She writes down a few details on a piece of paper. She calls a colleague over. "Brian Camberwell picked up the girls twenty minutes ago. I need an APB put out on his truck."

The officer looks confused. "We already did that."

"Do it again." She looks up at Jared. "How's Hayley?"

Jared keeps it clinical. It's the only way he can respond without breaking down. "She's got several facial injuries. Fractures to her nose and swelling around her right eye. She's got a few cracked ribs and her right leg is broken but until we have X-rays we can't be sure how bad it is." Jared's voice trails off. There's a bootprint on Hayley's thigh. He can't get the size of it out of his head.

Macy takes Jared's arm and steers him deeper into the room. "We need recent photos of her daughters."

Standing in front of a bookcase they both reach for the same photo.

Macy speaks first. "Why do they have pictures of Grace Adams in their house?"

"That's not Grace," he says, feeling ill at ease when he remembers what Hayley told him about Dustin helping her with the girls. "That's Hayley's eldest daughter, Isobel."

"Why didn't you tell me they look so much alike?"

"I haven't seen Isobel in nearly a year. I had no idea there was a connection."

Macy picks up her phone. "Warren, I need you to speak to Pamela. I want you to tell her what's happened. If this doesn't get her talking I don't know what will."

27

Grace slides open the window and throws her bag into the small backyard before climbing out after it. She sinks up to her waist in the snow that has drifted there. Next door a dog barks in short little bursts. Grace pulls her hat down and runs across the back alley to the garages. Her truck is parked in the one closest to the end. She swings open the door and it bangs against the wall. In her mind it sounds like a sonic boom.

She backs her truck out and sits for a couple of seconds in the alleyway. Ahead of her the road curves to the right toward the front entrance to the complex. She has no idea whether the patrol officer out front will recognize her uncle's pickup truck. She takes a deep breath and drives. As she turns onto the street, she checks her rearview mirror one last time. The patrol car hasn't moved.

Grace heads south on a road that runs parallel to Main Street. She wants to hurry but she keeps her speed down. Two blocks on there's several patrol cars parked halfway down the block to the left. Grace pulls to the side just as an ambulance screams past. She catches sight of the driver but it isn't anyone she knows.

Just before a bridge that crosses the Flathead River, Grace turns right onto a frontage road and enters the industrial part of town. The gate to the old Harris Mill has been forced open. Grace pulls up close to it and gets out. Other than the wind it is quiet, and the air is so cold it burns her throat. Beyond the gate a single set of tire tracks runs through the snow in a straight line toward the distant buildings. Grace clutches the chain-link fence with her gloves. She doesn't see anyone. She looks over her shoulder, back toward the main part of town. A helicopter circles the area near Olsen's Landing.

Grace follows the tracks until she is out of sight of the main road. The old lumber mill stands three stories high and is nearly the size of a football field. She opens her bag and gets out the bundle of money she found in the trailer and holds it in her hands as she stares out the front window. She can't bring it with her. It's the one thing he wants. Once he has it he'll probably kill her. She grabs a flashlight from the glove compartment before stepping out into the cold. The main mill doors are secured with a chain but there's a big enough gap for her to squeeze through. The beam of her flashlight sweeps across the empty building. Most of the heavy machinery has either been sold or salvaged as scrap metal. The rest is draped with cobwebs so thick they look like cotton candy. There's a set of stairs leading up to a mezzanine. She kicks at the treads until she discovers a loose one about halfway up. There's a dark recess underneath. She reaches inside of the bag, pushing her uncle's gun out of the way to get at the bundle. She puts the money inside and kicks the tread back in place.

Outside, the wind has dropped and tiny snowflakes drift down from the sky. Something catches her eye and Grace turns toward the far side of the mill, which butts up against the Flathead River. A little girl walks in her direction. The child's head is bent down and her hands are thrust deep in her pockets. Thick black hair hangs across her face. She is dressed fashionably, but her blue coat is far too thin and instead of snow boots, she has sneakers on her feet. It's only when she gets closer that Grace realizes that this little girl is crying. Grace stands perfectly still, waiting for the moment the girl realizes she is not alone.

The girl stops walking but she does not raise her eyes.

"What are you doing here?" Grace whispers. She's seen the girl with her grandfather, Toby, a few times but it was always from a distance. She's never been this close before.

The girl doesn't respond. Her long black hair falls limp around her face. Grace wants to see this little girl's eyes. There's something about the chin and nose that remind her of herself. The girl continues to sob. She uses the sleeve of her jacket to wipe away the mucus and snot that collects on her upper lip.

Grace finds a tissue in her bag and comes close enough to wave it in front of the girl's face. "Take this."

The girl is obedient. She does as directed without talking back, but she still doesn't look up. She mumbles thanks and blows her nose like a boy would—a long elephantine blast. She wads up the used tissue and crams it in her jacket pocket. Grace hands her another when she sees the girl's shoulders start to tremble again.

Grace leans forward, trying to peer around the girl's veil of black hair. "Are you Hayley Camberwell's daughter?"

"My momma says I'm not supposed to talk to strangers."

Grace notes the fading light. A snowstorm is moving in. She doesn't understand why the child is out here on her own.

"Where's your mom?"

The girl wipes her eyes with the backs of her hands. "She's not well. She had to stay at home."

Grace pictures Toby Larson's aging features and sees nothing of herself, but his granddaughter could be her twin. Grace's heart feels unbalanced in her chest. Hayley Camberwell might be her half sister after all. Grace stares hard at the girl in front of her, trying to figure out whether she should believe they're related.

"Do you know my momma?" says the little girl, more than once.

"No, but I know your grandfather, Toby Larson." She holds out her hand. "So we're not really strangers."

The extended hand hangs suspended until Grace drops it, unacknowledged. They stay silent for a bit. The light dims further behind thickening clouds and the crows rise and fall in the trees that line the shores of the Flathead River.

The girl looks up at Grace with fierce eyes. "You're that girl from the news. My grandmother doesn't like you much."

"Well, I'm a little different and people don't always take to that. I'm Grace. What's your name?"

"Isobel."

Grace looks up at the darkening sky and decides that she has no choice but to get Isobel out of here. It isn't safe.

"I need to get you home," she says, taking hold of Isobel's arm and opening the door to her pickup truck.

Isobel shakes her head.

"It's going to be okay. We'll go find your mother."

Isobel pulls away. "I can't leave. I need to get back to my sisters. I promised them I wouldn't be long."

Grace glances around the empty mill yard. "Where are they?"

The girl points toward the back of the mill. "They're with my dad."

Grace bites her lip. She now knows who killed her mother. "Did he leave you on your own?"

"He got upset and stomped off like he always does. I thought I'd better go for help."

"Do you think he's still gone?"

The girl shrugs.

"Get in the truck. I'll take you to your sisters."

The light is grainy gray between the buildings that encroach upon the narrow lane that runs toward the back of the mill. Grace keeps the headlights off and creeps forward. They round the corner and Grace comes to a stop about fifty feet before a line of trees. Up ahead a truck sits off to the side, resting on the soft shoulder and facing away from them. The lights are on and the engine is running. Grace leans on the steering wheel, thinking hard. "Seems like your daddy's come back."

"You should know my daddy isn't a nice man."

They stay there watching the other truck. Grace can see the top of Isobel's father's head but nothing more. "I don't see your sisters."

Isobel peers over the dashboard, rocking back and forth and squinting her eyes until she's satisfied. "They're only little. No way you'd see them from here."

"What were you doing out here anyway?"

"He said we were going on a trip, but then he got real angry when my little sisters started crying for our momma."

"You're scared of your daddy, aren't you?"

"He says my mom wasn't well, but I could hear them fighting. I think he hurt her again."

Grace stares out the windshield for a while. She has no idea what she's doing.

She reaches into her bag. "Does your daddy have a gun?"

"Yes, ma'am." She narrows her eyes when she sees Grace's pistol. "Are you gonna shoot him?"

"Nah, I'm just going to talk to him."

Isobel turns toward Grace and lowers her voice. "Cause it's okay with me if you shoot him."

Grace frowns. The words Isobel has just spoken don't sit well on her sweet face. "I never knew my daddy."

"You're lucky."

Grace looks at the girl again. "I want you to run up to the road to get help. Flag down a trucker if you have to. Tell them to call the police." She closes her eyes and hopes she's right. "And don't worry, they're nicer than you think."

"Doubt that, my daddy drives trucks."

"Just you wait. Everything will be fine."

Grace takes off her gloves and puts them on the girl's hands. They flop over the tops of her slim fingers. She pulls Jared's cap out of her pocket and slips it over Isobel's head so it's covering her ears. Without another word, Isobel slides away, easing the door shut with a soft click.

Grace's lonely boots crack through a thin crust of snow and sink a few inches into the road. The silent landscape envelops Grace like a dream and her breath escapes bone dust white. A voice inside of her screams at her to turn back, but her breath steams ahead impatiently. She walks through wisps of cloud, thinking about the family she now has—nieces, half sisters, and a father. Looking for comfort, she slips her bare fingers around the cold handle of the gun thumping heavily against her hip. Fresh snow falls hard and icy like darts, stinging her cheeks and painting the air between herself and Brian Camberwell's truck with broad strokes of white.

At the back bumper she follows a tentative hello with an apology for being late, but she finds it difficult to raise her voice higher than a whisper. The man sitting at the wheel doesn't turn to acknowledge her presence. She says hello several more times, trying her best to sound casual. Those last few footsteps to the passenger door seem to take forever. She stands at the window and the top of her head barely skims the bottom of the glass.

She looks on, detached, as her bare knuckles knock on the cold metal door. There is no response. She takes hold of the freezing handle and eases up onto the chrome running board so she can look inside. Through the thin layer of condensation she can see two children slumped on the seat next to their father. He's sitting under the bright ceiling light, awash in an unkind glow. His forehead hangs heavy over his face and his jowls are as thick as earflaps. He mutters to himself, barely opening his mouth to speak. Grace strikes the glass with three short raps but he makes no move to invite her in. Left with no choice she backs along the side and tries the door handle. An equal measure of fear and relief comes with finding it unlocked. The intense heat of the interior hits her immediately. The children stir in their sleep and their father's gaze finds her at last. He has a gun in his lap.

"Where in the hell have you been?" His shouts awaken Isobel's sisters. Instead of crying the girls slide their young eyes from side to side, surveying the scene like seasoned pros.

Grace can't think what to say. She's lost her nerve. She stares at the little girls, trying to find something familiar in their features, but she's coming up short. *Maybe I'm wrong about Isobel,* she thinks.

The man slams his big head back into the seat and it bounces forward like a basketball. "I asked you a question, Isobel."

Grace swallows hard. She looks back toward her car. Isobel is long gone. She can barely see her front bumper through the heavily falling snow. *Isobel is safe,* she thinks. *At least that's something.*

Grace reaches for her gun, stopping short of her coat pocket when Brian's big head swings back at her like a wrecking ball. "I'm not Isobel," she stutters. "I'm sorry. I'm late. It wasn't easy getting away."

Brian Camberwell watches her, his head dipping a fraction so that he might get a better view. His eyes narrow when he realizes his mistake. "Well, if it isn't Dustin's little friend. I thought you'd lost your nerve."

Grace stares at the gun on his lap and remains silent.

Brian smirks. "I knew your mom. May she rot in hell." He presses his palms into his eyes before reaching for the fifth of Jack Daniels resting on the dashboard. It's half full and the label has been picked off at the edges. "You know, you're lucky. If it had been up to me, you'd be dead by now. Did you bring the money?"

"I've never told anyone," she says, finally recognizing Brian from all those years ago. He was the driver who chased her away from Katya's trailer out to the fence line where she'd hid in the shadows. "I never told anyone about those girls in the back of your truck."

"It doesn't matter. I'm fucked anyway." He twists off the bottle cap and repeats the word *fucked* again and again between swallows. "Do you know what that feels like?"

Grace wants to run but instead concentrates on the emptying bottle. She answers truthfully, "Yes, sir. I do."

"What do you fucking know? Bet you've never had a rough day in your life."

Grace decides it's best not to argue. "I have the money."

He leans back. "And I have the photos."

"I don't want them."

He lets out a low laugh that doesn't sit right with his mood. He ruffles the hair of the girl closest to him and she flinches. "What are you talking about?"

Grace's shoulders are blanketed in white. She's getting cold. "You've got a chance of getting away on your own but you'll never manage with your daughters."

He shuts his eyes and takes a deep breath like he might be going underwater. "Tell me something I don't know. I reckon half the state is looking for me by now."

"I promise I'll take them someplace safe." She hesitates. "They're only little. You need to do right by them."

Brian Camberwell lunges forward and grabs his two remaining daughters roughly by the arms and pulls them close to him. He kisses them fiercely on the tops of their heads. Tears puddle in the shallow grooves beneath his eyes. He lets go and the girls melt back into the seat, the eldest of the two inching closer to the open door every time her daddy turns away.

"It would have been okay if Isobel were here. I would have gone through with it."

Grace's eyes dart to the gun on Brian's lap. "Maybe you should take a walk and think things through for a bit." She's hoping he's drunk enough to consider the suggestion. "I can look after your girls while you're away."

"Do you think I'm stupid or something?"

"No, sir," she says, feeling her throat close.

"Then don't treat me like I am."

He takes another long drink, wrapping his big hand around the bottle, white-knuckle tight. Grace watches his Adam's apple bounce around his neck like a rogue wave. He grimaces and chokes back what might be a sob. Snow melts from Grace's hair and runs down her forehead. She pushes a damp strand from her face and he looks up at her.

"Why are you still here?"

Grace is unbalanced. Her toes almost slip on the damp ledge. She corrects her footing. "Your girls. I've come for your girls. You said you'd let your girls come with me in exchange for the money."

"You're not taking my girls anywhere."

"But you said you wanted to do right by them."

"Yeah, and I could have if Isobel hadn't run off. Had it all planned out." He gestures to the suitcases piled behind him on the rear seats. "I was finally gonna get out of this shithole once and for all."

"What will you do now?"

"Ain't got no idea. No idea at all."

"I have the money with me. It's in my truck. If you give me the girls, I'll go get it."

"Why do you care so much about my daughters?"

"I just don't want to see them get hurt."

For a while Brian doesn't say anything Grace can hear. He mumbles words to himself before drifting back to silence. Twice his chin drops to his chest. The second time she gestures to the girls and speaks softly. "You two come along with me. I'll take you back to town."

Brian brings his fist crashing down on the steering wheel and his daughters scream. Grace grabs at the gun in her pocket but it's tangled in the silk lining. She almost falls backward out of the truck, barely managing to hold on to the back of the seat.

Brian rubs his face with the palms of his hands, pulling his lower lids downward and exposing the soft pink flesh of the inner eye. For a few seconds he looks like a bloodhound. His voice is rabid when he speaks. "Get out of here," he says, directly addressing his daughters for the first time. "All your whining is pissing me off. You sound just like your mother."

Like a lynx, the older of the two girls slides off the seat and slips straight past Grace. She's running toward the main road before Grace has a chance to tell her where to go. The youngest sister, a blond-haired, blue-eyed girl, who Grace guesses to be four or five years old, is wearing not much more than a T-shirt and dungarees. She scoots back against her father's side and tucks into the protective folds of his body.

Her father smiles and puts his arm around his remaining daughter. "I guess this one wants to stay with me."

Grace glances back toward her pickup truck. She knows she's lucky to have found two of Toby Larson's granddaughters, but she wants all three. "What's her name?"

"Cybil. Same as my mom."

Grace tries it out on her tongue. "Cybil. That's a nice name." She gazes at the girl and smiles, hoping she'll get something in return. "Your mom must love her to bits."

"My mom spoils her rotten."

"Must be nice."

Brian picks up Cybil and pulls her close, kissing her on the cheek and burying his head in the crook of her shoulder. Then he yells, "I told you to get out of here," hurling the child toward Grace.

Cybil's dimpled arms spin out into the air. She slips off the seat and curls into a ball under the dashboard. Grace leans over her, grabbing her beneath the shoulders, but the child wedges herself into the small space and refuses to move.

Grace struggles to keep her balance. "Come on, sweetheart. I'm taking you home."

Brian Camberwell's voice sounds off like cannon fire. "You best get hold of her before I change my mind."

Teetering on the running board, Grace falls forward and her legs bicycle kick the empty air behind her. Cybil is as tangled as a ball of twine. Grace begs her. "Please. I won't hurt you." And then more quietly, "I'll take you to your mom."

"I'm going to count to five," he says, pushing his gun against Grace's head so hard it feels like the barrel might bore right through flesh and bone.

"Please, I'm trying my hardest."

"One."

Grace cowers under the gun's weight. "Please."

"Two."

Grace crouches on her knees and bends low until her upper body is almost buried under the dashboard. She begs Cybil. "Come with me, sweetheart. Come with me now."

"Three."

"Please," screams Grace as she strains against all that resistance.

Cybil's shoulder bones shift in Grace's hands—a painful pop and the child's face is next to hers, red, raw, and screaming. They fly out of the truck backward in a faltering arc. The icy ground cracks beneath them. Their bodies buck upward from the road in a kickback that leaves Grace breathless. Her ears ring in a single high-pitched note and her mouth hangs open, wide and begging. Winded by the fall, she only sees the frosty trace left by her screams. She tries to break free of the child's weight but Cybil sticks to Grace's chest. Her young face is buried in the red wool of Grace's coat and her cries vibrate through the layers of fabric, making a determined line toward Grace's already panicked heart. Grace begs Cybil to be still, yelling at her with a voice barely registering above a whisper. Seconds later they are both silent.

Brian Camberwell has at last reached the number *five*.

Grace swallows back every word she's ever known. She rocks her head upward and expects to see him looming above them, gun in hand, but there's no one in the empty spill of light. Nothing moves except for the round flakes of snow that drift down, lazy and slow. They melt against the bare skin of their faces but all around them the landscape is covered in another layer of white. Her leg is twisted at an odd angle beneath her body. The pain in her knee is so intense that Grace can barely breathe. She counts in her head down from ten again and again. All the while she cradles the girl protectively, but her arms are numb and her fingers paw ineffectually at the exposed skin of Cybil's back. Cybil's breaths are shallow and her eyes droop like snowbound tree limbs.

"He's coming," she whispers warm into Grace's neck.

Somewhere close by Grace can hear muffled footfalls as Brian makes his way through the freshly fallen snow. Grace slows her breathing and waits for the final blow.

Brian nudges Grace's leg with his boot and she cries out. He mutters under his breath. "And I thought I was the stupid one."

His jacket is open. His big head is bare. Grace gazes up into his face and whispers *please* once more, but he only lifts his chin a fraction and clenches his jaw. He's crying when he removes his jacket and tightly cocoons his daughter. When he bends low and whispers in Cybil's ear, Grace can hear his muffled sobs. He buries his head in the nape of his youngest daughter's neck and strokes her blond head with hands that look powerful enough to crush her skull.

"I'm so sorry" is all he says.

Brian's legs buckle when he tries to stand. He catches himself with an outstretched arm and staggers to his feet. He looks toward the main road one last time and turns away. Without ceremony, he lumbers past his truck, heading into a wilderness that stretches for miles.

Grace is the only witness. She strains her eyes, but it's not long before he's swallowed up in a shroud of white.

She doesn't shiver. Her tired eyes gaze down the length of their bodies, past Cybil's tightly bound back and damp blond curls. Finding solace in the warmth of Cybil's breath against her neck, Grace puts her head down and stays perfectly still. She listens for Jared. He's a belief that's settled in like winter. She knows he's out there somewhere, smoking his cigarettes and driving up Route 93, shoulders hunched, he's hatless. With hooded eyes, he concentrates on the road ahead of him, cutting through the snowbound lanes like a determined knife. She gazes up into the falling skies and strains her ears for sirens. When she finally hears them she cries and cries and cries.

28

Dark clouds cover the sky and rain strikes like buckshot against the windshield. Below the road, the Flathead River tosses and turns in the early morning light. Chunks of ice the size of cars ride the swollen currents, and all along the eastern shore stands of pine trees wade knee-deep in floodwater. Spring has finally come to Collier.

Macy gazes past the flicking windshield wipers and yawns. The oncoming headlights reflect in the rivulets of rainwater that wriggle on the glass like worms. The roads are coated in slush and a gusting wind rocks her vehicle. She passes over the Flathead River on Collier's southernmost bridge and enters the industrial section of town. There's a single sheriff's patrol car guarding the entrance to an abandoned mill. She stops briefly to say hello and the officer waves her through. Her 4x4 rattles along the heavily rutted access road. The mill and a set of lowlying outbuildings are situated near the river. Black snow stubbornly clings to the shadows on the north end of the building. The rain has washed away the rest. She pulls up behind Warren's vehicle and looks around. Everything is boarded up, chained, and tagged with odd scrawls of graffiti. Until now she's only seen this place in photographs.

She puts her car in park and steps out into the rain. She is unprepared for the loud roar of the river. Just beyond the line of trees, its milky glacier water is spilling over its banks. A gust of wind blows up from behind and her hair flies around her face, slapping her in the cheeks. She secures it behind her ears and walks over to meet Warren. She's not seen him since she left Collier four and a half months earlier.

Warren smiles and asks after her son Luke. He and his wife sent her flowers and a baby blanket. It is pale blue and has baby elephants embroidered along the border. It's one of Macy's favorites.

Macy is still shy about motherhood. Her face reddens when anyone brings it up. She also tires of explaining her choices—that it is her mother, Ellen, who cares for Luke while Macy is at work; that there is no father named on the birth certificate. She often imagines what some people must think once they're fully aware of her situation.

Warren asks how she's settling back into work and Macy tries to sound more confident than she actually is.

"My mother is around to help while I'm at work, otherwise I'd be lost."

"That's the best way to raise children."

Macy thinks about the amount of overtime she's put in since Luke was born. "At a distance?"

"With family. I don't tend to trust anyone else."

Macy doesn't disagree. She looks around. In the crime-scene photos, layers of snow whitewash over decades of decay. The images are silent. You can't hear the wind whining in the rafters of the empty mill, the rush of the Flathead, or the creaking of the ice floes. She can only imagine how frightened Grace was when she came here on her own to negotiate with Brian Camberwell.

Macy stands in front of the old mill doors and looks up at a faded sign reading HARRIS AND SONS. Macy had gone into labor at about the same time Isobel Camberwell managed to flag down a passing car and call for help. Warren finished the case for her. She has read the report. She knows what happened, but it had been her case for more than eleven years. She asks him to tell her again.

Warren points to where Macy is standing. "While Grace was stand-ing right about here, Isobel Camberwell approached her from around the side of the building. They spoke and Isobel told Grace she was here with her father. At some point they drove around to the back of the building and Grace decided she would try speaking to him. She took her uncle's gun, the one Elizabeth couldn't find, from her bag and told Isobel to go to the main road to get help."

Macy looks over her shoulder. For a child it would be about a ten-minute walk. "Was it snowing heavily at that point?"

"No, but it really started coming down soon after. Isobel said she didn't think anyone would stop to pick her up because visibility was so poor. She's not sure how much time passed between leaving Grace and flagging down a driver."

Macy turns toward the far end of the main building. "Grace would have taken this route?"

"Yes, ma'am. She said she had the money and was going to meet a man who'd called her in the middle of the night. He had the photos of her and was willing to give them to her in exchange for the fifty thou-sand dollars she found in her mother's trailer. Until she met Isobel she had no idea that the man was Brian Camberwell."

They round a corner and step into the shade. A stand of overgrown trees and the north-facing walls of the mill throw the entire area into dark-ness. The temperature drops along with the light. The wind is stronger here. It rushes through the narrow corridor, spreading ripples across the deepening pools of rainwater. In front of them an abandoned railway bridge spans the Flathead River.

"We found Brian Camberwell's vehicle parked here. The lights were on and the engine was running."

Macy looks down at the spot where Grace and Cybil were discov-ered. Grace had broken her leg, and both of Cybil's shoulders were dis-located. Cybil told her mother that Grace had pulled her from the truck when her daddy had threatened to shoot Grace in the head.

Macy looks around. "By the way, where is everyone?"

"Forensics decided to park in a turnout off of Route 93. It's less of a hike from there to where the boys found the body." He points to the railway bridge. "I thought you'd prefer to retrace Brian's last steps. He would have crossed the Flathead here."

"Is it safe?"

"Safe as any of the bridges around here. It was built to last. They used it for transporting timber from the mill up to the main railway line. Brian would have known that he could follow it all the way there."

"But that's not what he did."

"About a mile along, he headed north and walked until he came to a tributary."

"And then he just sat down in the snow and died?"

"Seems to be the case, but they're still digging him out so we'll know better once they've had a look at him."

"His gun was found in his truck so we know he didn't shoot himself. It seems more likely that he died of exposure."

"It's suicide all the same." Warren starts walking toward the bridge. "Shall we?"

Everything Warren says during the crossing is lost on the wind, the river's constant roar, and the sound of ice floes scraping against each other. The iron bridge is solid but the surfaces are slippery. There are gaps in the metal walkway. Macy can see straight through to the white-capped water churning below them. She grips on tighter to the railing. She's seen firsthand what the Flathead can do to a man. A week after he disappeared off Olsen's Landing, they found Dustin's body downstream near Walleye Junction in full view of Route 93. He'd become entangled in some tree branches that hung far out in the middle of the river. He was suspended there like a scarecrow. He'd already gone over the rapids south of Collier, and during his time dangling from the tree branches he was regularly buffeted by fallen trees and chunks of ice that had escaped from upstream. The medical examiner counted thirty-five separate fractures. Both his legs were broken and his pelvis was crushed.

Warren holds out his hand for Macy so she doesn't fall negotiating the steep steps, which drop down onto the opposite shoreline. The earth is sodden. It squelches under her boots. The railroad tracks stretch out in front of them as straight as a plumb line. Branches arch overhead, dripping water on Warren and Macy.

There are signs of foot traffic everywhere.

"Have you had a lot of people come through here?"

"I'd say this stretch of land is the most visited place in the whole of the Flathead Valley. People have been out here looking for Brian since the day he vanished."

"That's a pretty morbid day out."

"Fifty thousand dollars is a lot of money around here. There were also rumors going around that he had drugs on him."

"Not to mention pictures of Grace Adams."

"That too. Given the public interest in the case, I suspect they'd fetch a fair amount."

"So far nothing has shown up on the Internet. I check once a day. Makes me feel queasy every time I type her name into the search engine."

"Maybe we'll get lucky and find them today."

"Did you hear about the latest indictment? A district court judge. Those files you found in Brian Camberwell's garage are a gold mine."

"There were far more people caught up in Arnold's side business than we initially thought."

"It was still a bit of a risk keeping those incriminating files in his office."

"Given he had a few judges and a sheriff under his control, I'd say he wasn't too worried about his home being searched."

"It does surprise me that Arnold let Dustin go after getting hold of those photographs of Grace."

"It's hard to say. Dustin might have had something on Arnold. They knew each other for years."

"Scott Pearce finally agreed to cooperate, so we're getting more of a sense of how the trafficking operation was organized. The exchanges usually took place at the truck stop. Brian drove the girls over and left his rig overnight. After Leanne took payment, the girls were taken by a third party."

"Did Leanne know what was going on?"

"He says she knew everything, but he's the only one left and he's giving evidence in return for a lighter sentence so I don't trust him."

They walk in silence for a few minutes. The rain has stopped and sun breaks through the cloud cover. The damp foliage glistens in the slanting light, blinding Macy.

Macy falls in next to Warren. "Did you go to Elizabeth's funeral?"

"I couldn't stay away. It's easy to forget how much good she did in the community."

"I suspect she was overcompensating."

"I also think she loved Arnold Lamm a bit too much to see him for who he really was."

Macy looks away. "Who we love is one of those things we really can't control."

"You're right about that." Warren stops in front of a well-defined break between the trees. The ground to the north of the tracks is heavily trampled. He warns Macy that from here on out the path is very muddy.

"Do you know the boys who found the body?"

"I've not come across them before. They're a bit too young to be in any real trouble yet. They're only in the fifth grade."

"That makes them between ten and eleven years old."

"The parents didn't know they were coming out here after school."

"Any chance someone beat them to it?"

Warren holds back some tree branches for Macy. "Brian's body was found on the north-facing bank of a small tributary that joins with the Flathead a mile further on. The area is sheltered from the sun and rain so the snow hasn't melted. The medical examiner thinks the body was completely encased in ice and snow for most of the winter. When they spotted it all the boys could see was the top of his head."

"What about animals?"

"Believe me when I say no one has touched it. Brian looks like he's been kept in a freezer for a few months."

They come to a clearing in the trees. The forensic team has erected a tent along the banks of the narrow tributary. They wade through water and mud in their protective suits.

Ryan Marshall, the medical examiner on site, is familiar to Macy. He once worked in Helena. He has a slight build and wears the thinnest wire-framed glasses Macy has ever seen. His white protective suit is covered in mud all the way up to the armpits. He doesn't offer to shake her hand.

"This is one of the messiest sites I've ever had to work in," he says, after they say a quick hello. "It's just like I thought, Brian Camberwell died of exposure. I'll have to examine him more thoroughly but I doubt my findings will change. There are no signs of injury."

He leads them over to the tent and pulls back the flap. Brian Camberwell sits cross-armed with his back against the muddy bank. His big round head is blackened and his eyes are closed. As expected, he wears only a T-shirt and jeans. Robert picks up a clear plastic evidence bag. A soggy envelope is inside.

"I didn't find the money everyone is looking for, but I did find this."

Macy stares. "The photos?"

"They were stuffed into the back pocket of his jeans. They're a bit fragile so you'll have to handle them with care."

Downtown Bozeman is bathed in the spring sunshine. Macy parks her car and gazes out the window at the recently renovated apartment building before once again checking the address in her file. Across the street, the park is full of people enjoying the afternoon. Macy spots

Grace coming toward her with a large black dog at her side and notes that she walks with a slight limp. Her hair is cut in a very short pixie and her complexion is so pale she glows in the hard, angled light. Macy gets out and waits for her on the steps leading up to the front door of the building.

As they approach, the dog strains against the leash and barks just as Grace looks up and smiles. The last time they saw each other was in the hospital. Grace's leg was in a cast and Macy was recuperating after giving birth. When Luke curled his little hands around Grace's pale fingers, they both cried.

Macy hangs back while Grace reassures her dog. "This is Macy. Don't worry, she's one of the good guys."

Macy offers the dog a hand to sniff. "What's his name?"

"I call him Jack, but he seems to answer to most anything. I picked him up at the pound a month ago."

Macy looks up at the building. "I'm surprised your landlord allows dogs."

"I guess I'm my own landlord so it's okay."

"You bought a place?"

"I had a little help."

Her apartment is a small one-bedroom with windows overlooking the park. Macy thinks she recognizes several pieces of furniture from the house on Summit Road. Otherwise it's filled with finds from junk shops.

Jack pads across the room and immediately stretches out in a sunny position by the window, while Grace goes into the kitchen to make coffee. "We're alike, me and Jack. A couple of strays."

"You seem to have settled in quickly."

"I have. At least I think I have. Anyway, I'm getting there. I've signed up for courses at the community college in the fall."

"That sounds promising."

Grace's hands shake and the cups rattle against each other as she places them on the counter. She steps away and crosses her arms tightly to her body. For a second she looks like she's forgotten what she's doing.

"Grace, are you okay?"

Grace won't look at her. "Why are you here?"

"I didn't want you to find out from anyone else so I came in person. We found Brian Camberwell's body."

Grace stands quietly and waits for Macy to say more.

"We found the photos."

"Did you look at them?"

Macy spreads her hands out in front of her. "I'm sorry, Grace, it's my job. I had to."

"Who else saw them?"

"The medical examiner and the state attorney. That's all."

"Where are they? Do you have them here with you?"

"They're in a sealed evidence box. The state attorney has assured me they'll be destroyed as soon as possible." Macy walks to the other side of the counter and takes the kettle off the stove. "I'll make coffee. You go sit."

Grace slumps down on the edge of the sofa and Jack comes over and puts his head on her lap.

Macy slides open a drawer, searching for spoons, and finds a small handgun instead. She looks up and Grace is gazing back at her with a tissue wadded up in her fist. Macy pushes the drawer shut and finishes making the coffee.

"Do you want to talk about what happened?"

"Not really."

"We didn't find the money, but I don't think that should surprise you."

Grace continues to stare straight ahead.

"I'm right, aren't I? You've had it all along. Brian kept the photos and you kept the money."

"Does it matter? I got the girls back."

"No, not really. I just want to know if I should waste any more time looking for it."

"I think we should all move on."

Macy puts two cups of coffee on the table between them and they sit quietly for a few minutes. According to Warren, the doctors offered Toby a paternity test, but he declined. Once he saw Grace and Isobel in the same room it didn't seem necessary. It wasn't long after that Toby was filing for divorce.

"How are you getting on with Toby and his family?"

"Okay, I guess. It's not been easy with Pamela's court date coming up."

"I imagine it makes things a little awkward."

"Hayley has been okay but I think that's due to Jared. It's been more difficult for Hayley's daughters and her sister Janice."

"She and Jared are definitely together then?"

Grace purses her lips. "He doesn't seem happy though."

"I doubt he knows what to do now that he has everything he wants. He's grown too used to being miserable. What about Toby? How's he been with you?"

She smiles but there are tears in her eyes. "He calls me every day to check on me."

"You should know that Pamela has been talking."

"Oh yeah, what's she been saying?"

"She's saying she made a deal with Brian because she wanted to protect Hayley and her granddaughters. She would deliver Leanne in exchange for Brian leaving town. Apparently, pointing us toward Toby was an afterthought."

"I'll never forgive Pamela, but I understand why she did it. When I couldn't deny that Isobel was part of my family things changed. I would have sold my soul."

"You are aware that this could have ended very differently."

"I know, but this ending feels right for some reason. Somehow, I think we all got what we deserved."

Macy holds up her cup but doesn't drink. Even with the gun, the dog, and Toby's daily phone calls, Grace seems as fragile as the day Macy met her. Macy puts her coffee down and brushes off her jeans.

"I need to get going," she says, easing out of her chair.

Grace glances around like she's looking for something. "I almost forgot. I have a present for you."

"Grace, you didn't need to do that."

Grace hands her a gift wrapped in pale blue paper. "Please, put it in your bag and open it after you've gone."

Macy feels the raised edge and knows it's a frame. "I want you to call me if you need anything."

"You have a child to look after, you can't be worrying about me anymore. Besides, I'm fine here with Jack."

Macy gazes out the window. The sun is just about to disappear behind the trees in the park. "You know, sometimes I forget I'm a mother."

"It probably makes it easier to be away from your son."

"Maybe you're right," she says, letting herself out. "It is better if I don't think about it too much."

Macy stands at the threshold and holds out a hand but Grace hugs her instead.

"Good-bye," says Grace, finally letting go. "Try to be happy now."

"Only if you promise to do the same."

Behind her Grace's door shuts with the softest of clicks.

Macy is waiting in her car at a red light when she pulls the gift from her bag. She turns it over in her hands before peeling back the paper. The pencil sketch is simple but beautifully rendered. Using the barest number of lines, Grace has captured a tender moment between Macy and her son. Macy remembers the evening Grace sat at the end of the hospital bed with a sketchpad in her lap. Macy had only given birth one day earlier and had felt irritated at the intrusion, but in the portrait she looks so serene. Macy continues to stare. The traffic light changes to green and car horns sound from behind. She places her fingertips on her son's face. Nobody warned her what it would be like. She switches on the sirens and drives. It's been a long day and she's finally heading home.